"WONDERFUL"
Chicago Tribune

"IRRESISTIBLE"
Washington Times

"PERFECT"
Detroit Free Press

"UNFORGETTABLE"
New Orleans Times-Picayune

"LEONARD STILL SETS THE GOLD STANDARD."
New York Times

"GRIPPING . . . ELMORE LEONARD,
MASTER OF THE GENRE, KEEPS GETTING IT RIGHT."

ELMORE LEONARD
MR. PARADISE

Books by Elmore Leonard

New in Hardcover

The Hot Kid

ELMORE LEONARD

MR. PARADISE

HarperTorch
An Imprint of HarperCollinsPublishers

❦

HARPERTORCH
An Imprint of HarperCollins*Publishers*
10 East 53rd Street
New York, New York 10022-5299

Copyright © 2004 by Elmore Leonard
ISBN: 0-06-008396-4

First HarperTorch paperback printing: June 2005
First William Morrow hardcover printing: January 2004

HarperCollins®, HarperTorch™, and ❦™ are trademarks of HarperCollins Publishers Inc.

Printed in the United States of America

Visit HarperTorch on the World Wide Web at www.harpercollins.com

10 9 8 7 6 5 4 3 2 1

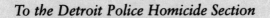

To the Detroit Police Homicide Section

MR.
PARADISE

LATE AFTERNOON CHLOE AND KELLY WERE HAVING
cocktails at the Rattlesnake Club, the two seated
on the far side of the dining room by themselves:
Chloe talking, Kelly listening, Chloe trying to get
Kelly to help her entertain Anthony Paradiso, an
eighty-four-year-old guy who was paying her five
thousand a week to be his girlfriend.

Now Chloe was offering Kelly a cigarette from
a pack of Virginia Slims, the long ones, the 120's.

They'd made their entrance, the early after-
work crowd still looking, speculating, something
they did each time the two came in. Not show-
girls. More like fashion models: designer casual
wool coats, oddball pins, scarves, big leather
belts, definitely not bimbos. They could be sisters,
tall, the same type, the same nose jobs, both
remembered as blonds, their hair cropped short.

Today they wore hats, each a knit cloche down on her eyes, and sunglasses. It was April in Detroit, snow predicted.

Now they were lighting the cigarettes.

The waitress, a young blond named Emily, came through the room of white tablecloths and place settings with their drinks, alexanders straight up, with gin. She said as she always did, "I'm sorry, but you're not supposed to smoke in here. It's okay in the bar."

Kelly looked at Emily in her black pants and starched white shirt. "Has your boss said anything?"

"He hasn't yet."

"So forget about it," Chloe said. "He likes us." She brought a Ritz-Carlton ashtray from her coat pocket and placed it on the table, Emily watching.

She said, "They're always from a different hotel. I like the one, I think it's from the Sunset Marquis?"

"It's one of my favorites," Chloe said. "Next time I'm in L.A. I'll pick up a few more."

Emily said, "Cool hats," and left.

Kelly watched her moving through the empty tables.

"Emily's a little weird."

"She's a fan," Chloe said. "Fans are weird."

"I'll bet anything she comes back with a catalog."

"What're you in this month?"

"Saks, Neiman Marcus—she'll have Victoria's Secret."

"Remember she asked if I modeled," Chloe said, "and I told her now and then but mostly I did hands? She said, Oh."

"You called it hand jobs. Show her your *Playboy* spread, she'll freak," Kelly said, and saw Emily coming back through the tables with a catalog, holding it to her breast with two hands, Victoria's Secret, a look of pain on Emily the waitress's face, hesitant now as she stood before Kelly.

"I hope you guys don't think I'm a pest."

"I don't mind," Kelly said. "What page?"

Emily gave her the catalog and a Sharpie. "Sixteen, the Second Skin Collection. Could you sign it like right above your navel?"

"I'm in the Seamless Collection," Kelly said, "Second Skin's the next page," and wrote *Kelly* in black over bare flesh. "I'm in another one somewhere."

"Page forty-two," Emily said, "the new low-rise bikini. And on the next page, the low-rise v-string and low-rise thong?"

Kelly turned pages until she was looking at herself in white panties. "You want each one signed?"

"If you wouldn't mind. I really appreciate it."

Chloe said to her, "Which one do you have on?"

Emily made a face, clenching her teeth. "I'm trying the v-string."

"Feels good?"

Emily squirmed a little. "It's okay."

"I can't wait to get them off," Kelly said. She handed Emily the catalog.

"I kinda like the way a thong grabs you," Chloe said, "but haven't worn one lately, and if you want to know why, ask the old man."

Emily left.

And Chloe said, "Aren't you glad you're not a waitress?"

"Yeah, but I think I'd be good at it," Kelly said. "I'd take orders for a table without writing anything down. The woman with blue hair, the whitefish, the scotch drinker, pickerel. And I wouldn't call them 'you guys.' "

"Your style," Chloe said, "make it look easy. But you fly to New York to work instead of living there."

"The traffic," Kelly said. "You spend most of your time waiting for it to move."

"So what? You're sitting in a limo."

"I like to drive."

"You could work for Vicki's full-time, make a lot more money."

"I do okay."

"Go to parties with movie stars—"

"Who want to jump you."

"What's wrong with that?"

"I have to be in love. Or think I am."

They sipped their alexanders and smoked their cigarettes and Chloe said, "Hon . . . I desperately need you."

"I can't, I have to take my dad to the airport."

"He's still here?"

"Playing the slots all day and giving me advice at dinner. He thinks I should get a new agent."

"Isn't he a barber?"

"He has time to think about things."

"Get him a taxi."

"I want to be sure he makes the flight. My dad drinks."

"Can't we work around it? I'm talking about three hours, max. By midnight the old guy's asleep in his chair. He even nods off while we're talking, drops his cigar. I have to watch he doesn't set himself on fire."

"Not tonight," Kelly said, but then began to let herself give in a little because they were good

friends and had been sharing a loft the past couple of years, Kelly saying, "If I did go with you
sometime, would I have to do anything?"

She wouldn't mind getting a look at Mr. Paradiso.

The way Kelly understood the arrangement,
the old man was laying out five thousand a week
to have Chloe available, all to himself. It was a lot
for not having to do much, almost twice what
Kelly made in her underwear. What didn't make
sense, Chloe kept saying she was tired of thinking
up ways to entertain the old guy, but wouldn't
quit, and the five grand a week had nothing to do
with it. Chloe had money. She'd paid cash for the
downtown loft with a view of the river.

Kelly didn't ask, but had to assume the reason
Chloe didn't walk out, she was looking for a big
payday when the old man died.

"His favorite entertainment," Chloe said, "he
loves cheerleaders, live ones, with all the cute
moves? I've got routines worked out."

"We stand in front of him," Kelly said, "and
do cheers?"

"We stand in front of the TV set, on each side
of the screen while he's watching a University of
Michigan football game, a video. He must have a
hundred of them, but only games U of M won.
Tonight he wants to watch the '98 Rose Bowl,

Michigan and Washington State. He pauses the game while we cheer. I've got little pleated skirts we wear. Tony's idea was to get real Michigan cheerleaders, so he sent Montez to Ann Arbor, see if he could talk a couple of girls into doing it and get paid, like once a week."

"Who's Montez?"

"I told you about him—"

"The houseman?"

"That's Lloyd. They're both black. Montez is Tony's number one, he takes him places, gets things for him."

"Like what?"

"Like me, off my Web page. So Montez tried to get a couple of real cheerleaders to come to the house. He's a cool guy, but could be a pimp in a business suit and the cheerleaders turned him down. He offered to buy their skirts, got turned down again and had a couple made to my size. With pleats, maize and blue. In fact one of the cheers I made up is, 'Go maize, go blue, we're the chicks who'll go down on you.' Tony likes the cheers spiced up. 'We're Big Ten and we are flirty.' Do a double clap, twice. 'When we go down, we go down and dirty.' "

"Yea, team," Kelly said. "You have sweaters with little megaphones on them?"

"It works better topless."

"Uh-unh, not me. Get somebody else."

"I've tried. The one girl I know who loves to do it's out of town this week. I'm hoping," Chloe said, "Tony gets tired of cheerleaders, or one of these nights he gets excited—you know, his old ticker finally quits and he goes out with a big grin."

"I thought you liked him."

"I'm not hoping he'll die. It's just that I can't help having mixed feelings about it."

"You're in his will," Kelly said.

"Not even if I were a nun. Tony's a widower with three married daughters, grandchildren, and a son who's a prick. The guy scares me to death. Tony wanted to put me in his will and I said, 'You know your son'll take me to court after you're gone.' I didn't say, 'Or have me fucking killed if he has to.' Tony Jr. runs the old man's law firm, all criminal and personal injury."

"But he's leaving you something," Kelly said, "and that's why you don't walk out."

Chloe, smoking, nodding, said, "He won't tell me what it is, but I think it's a life insurance policy, like one that he's had for years and recently made me the beneficiary? Otherwise, if he just took it out at his age, they'd turn him down."

"You think it's a lot of money."

"Well sure. He said get a good financial adviser

and I could be set for life. I'm thinking it's for around five mil, if it's like enough to retire on."

"He has the policy?"

"He doesn't want Tony Jr. to know about it. He might've been the beneficiary originally—if that's what it is, insurance. But what else could it be?"

"Where's the policy?"

"In a bank deposit box."

"You have the key?"

"The box is in Montez Taylor's name."

"The guy," Kelly said, "who looks like a pimp in a business suit? You trust him?"

"What's in the box is mine, not his. Tony dies, Montez will see that I get whatever it is. Why're you making a face? Tony trusts him. He says Montez is like a son to him, even if he is colored. Tony hasn't caught up yet with being politically correct. Montez is a cool guy, mid-thirties, nice-looking. He takes Tony everywhere, all the U of M games, ten years he's been doing it. Tony says he's leaving Montez the house, since none of his kids want to live in Detroit. It's in Indian Village off Jefferson, not far from here."

"Is it worth much?"

"I'm not sure. If it was in Bloomfield Hills it would go for a couple of million, easy."

"He has servants?"

"Maids come in but they don't stay. I mentioned the houseman, Lloyd? He's not as old as Tony but he's up there. Lloyd looks like a cross between Uncle Ben on the rice box and Redd Foxx. He'll say goodnight and Tony'll call to him as he's leaving the room, 'I'm gonna get laid tonight, Lloyd.' And Lloyd goes, 'Be careful you don't hurt yourself, Mr. Paradise.' "

"Do you call him that, Mr. Paradise?"

"When I'm sucking up. Montez and Lloyd've been calling him Mr. Paradise forever. The old guy loves it."

"Can he . . . you know, perform?"

"Once in a while he seems to get off. His specialty is muff diving." Chloe slipped off her sunglasses as she looked at her friend the catalog model, hope in Chloe's blue eyes. "I've mentioned you to Tony. I mean that you're fun, you're smart, you're interesting—"

"Trustworthy, loyal."

"Good to your dad."

"I'll tell you what," Kelly said. "If you can put off the cheerleading till tomorrow night, and if I don't have to do it topless . . ."

They drove out 94 toward Detroit Metro, snow swirling in the Jetta's headlights, Kelly keeping it close to sixty, anxious to get her dad on his flight;

her dad enjoying the ride, talkative, a fifth of vodka in his carry-on; her dad wearing a nylon jacket, a straw hat and sunglasses, nine o'clock at night, snowing in April, the dude barber from West Palm who drank and chased women, now wanting to know why he wasn't introduced to Chloe, and Kelly saying she wasn't around.

"What's she do?"

"Takes care of an old man."

"That don't pay. How's she afford to live with you, even going halves?"

Kelly was tired of being the nice daughter who lived with her nice friend.

"It's hers. She paid four hundred thousand for it, cash."

"Jesus, her daddy leave her money?"

"She earned it. She was an escort."

"A what?"

"A call girl. She started at four-fifty an hour, was featured in *Playboy* and her rate jumped to nine hundred."

"For one hour?"

"Plus tip. Three grand for all night, and she gave it up to entertain the old man."

"Jesus Christ," her dad said, with maybe ten bucks in his jeans from the six hundred she'd given him, "and you didn't introduce me?"

DELSA GOT THE CALL FROM RICHARD HARRIS AT
home, six in the morning, barely light out, Delsa
in his skivvies and a wool sweater, cold in the
house, waiting for the coffee to perk. Harris said
the firemen had to secure the place before anybody could go inside. Mostly smoke and water
damage, windows broken.

Delsa said, "Who's dead?"

"Three guys in the basement we saw through
the window. You go in this pen around back, all
mud and dog shit. A pit bull in there's shaking
he's so scared. A pit bull. There's a dog treadmill
in the living room, a big-screen TV, PlayStation,
X-Box, coloring book and crayons, and this rig
called a Love Swing, still in the box. You know
what I'm talking about?"

"I've heard of it," Delsa said.

"I'll bring the instructions, show how it works."

"Just the three guys in the house?"

"Yeah, but they don't live here. It's an old duplex two blocks west of Tiger Stadium, an empty building on the corner and then this house. The woman in the other half is Rosella Munson, thirty-four, medium dark, chunky. She says the guy rents the burnt-out flat goes by the name Orlando. Mid-twenties, slim, light shade, wears his hair in rows. Lives here with his girlfriend Tenisha."

"Kids?"

"No, but Rosella's got three, none over seven years old. She called the fire department around four A.M. and got her kids out. Now she's back in there packing to move."

"The guys in the basement," Delsa said, "what are they?"

"I thought at first they brothers. See, the fire was started down there, so parts of 'em are burnt good, other parts just blistered. You know, like the skin's peeling? But they got tats on 'em make 'em Mexican, some southwest gang. I asked Rosella did she see them. No, she minds her business, but let me know this Orlando sells weed. Meaning what we could have here's a busted deal."

It didn't sound right. Delsa took time to pour a cup of coffee. "They were shot?"

"Stripped and popped in the back of the head, all three. But one of 'em had a chain saw taken to him, the chain saw still in the basement, scorched but brand-new, the box sitting there. The tech says there's human tissue in the teeth of the saw. No shit. Cut a man into five pieces, I imagine so. But why didn't they finish the job, do the other two?"

Delsa said, "Would you want to? You're covered with the guy's blood? I think after doing the one somebody said fuck it. But was it Orlando? He's selling weed, or he's buying from his source. There's a disagreement. He takes the three guys down to the basement—by himself? Makes them strip, shoots them and then sets his own house on fire. What's wrong with that?"

"I see what you mean," Harris said.

"Get next to the neighbor," Delsa said, "Rosella Munson. Get her to tell you about the girlfriend, Tenisha. Maybe they like to have coffee. Maybe Tenisha had the kids over to play video games and color—you say there's a coloring book. Richard, get us Tenisha quick as you can."

"Hold on," Harris said. He was back in less than a minute saying, "Two guys from Six just arrived and Manny Reyes from Violent Crimes."

"Manny might be able to I.D. the three guys," Delsa said. "What've you got for time of death?"

Harris said, "The three panchos, late last night, they're in and out of rigor, removal service is on the way. Frank, the M.E. death investigator —was Val Trabucci—took his pictures and then laid the dismembered guy back together. I said, 'What you doing that for?' Val goes, 'Make sure the parts match.' Hey shit, huh?"

Frank Delsa, thirty-eight, acting lieutenant of Squad Seven, Homicide Section, Detroit Police Department, had been living by himself in this house on the far east side since his wife's death: now almost a year alone after nine years with Maureen, no children, Maureen herself with the Detroit Police, lieutenant in charge of the Sex Crimes unit. Married nine years when they decided they'd better start a family if they were going to have one, Maureen, already forty, three years older than Frank, went to see her doctor and was told she had cancer of the uterus. The hardest time for Frank was coming home, walking into the silence of the house.

Last night he'd made a run with Sergeant Jackie Michaels, forty-three, to the Prentiss Hotel on Cass. "Home to hookers, winos and crackheads," Jackie said. "My neighborhood, Frank, when I was growing up. I might even know the complainant." In some ways Jackie reminded him of Maureen. They'd been rookies together working out of the Tenth, the black girl and the white girl close friends, both from the street; nothing surprised either one.

The complainant at the Prentiss Hotel was Tammi Marie Mello, W/F/49, lying on the stairway landing between the fifth and sixth floors. Apparent cause of death, the evidence tech said, a single gunshot wound to the back. "Yeah, I remember her from when I was a little girl," Jackie said. "Tammi Mello, been selling that big ass of hers all her life." They followed a trail of blood up the stairs and along the hall to 607 where a uniform stood by the open door, Jackie Michaels saying to Delsa, "Do you thank God like I do they're stupid? Or stoned or lazy or generally fucked up?" The occupant of 607, Leroy Marvin Woody, B/M/63, unemployed bus driver, sitting by himself hunched over, a nearly full half-gallon of Five O'Clock gin next to him, ashtray full of cigarette butts, blood on the front of his white T-shirt, seemed in a nod. He didn't respond to Jackie saying, "What'd you kill that woman for, Uncle? She make you mad? Say something mean and you lost your temper? Look at me, Mr. Woody. Tell me what you did with the gun."

*   *   *

In the morning, after the call from Harris at the scene of the triple, Delsa had his coffee and got ready for work.

The car they gave him to use was a dark blue Chevy Lumina with 115,000 miles on it and a *Service Engine Soon* light that was always on. He parked on Gratiot, a block from 1300 Beaubien, Detroit Police Headquarters for the past eighty years, the worn-out nine-story building hemmed in by high-rise wings of the Wayne County jail, the Frank Murphy Hall of Justice and, a few blocks south against the sky, the Greektown Casino.

Most of Homicide was on five.

Delsa walked past Seven's squad room to the end of the hall and the office of his boss, Homicide Inspector Wendell Robinson, a cool guy, twenty-eight years with the Detroit Police. Wendell was up on the triple, he'd stopped by the scene on his way in.

"Frank, it's over by Tiger Stadium, that famous old ballpark of no use to anybody." Wendell had hung up his trench coat and now stood by his desk, still wearing his Kangol cap, this one beige. Wendell had been wearing those soft Kangols as long as he'd been here, longer than Samuel L. Jackson had been wearing his backwards. He said, "Right across a parking lot's a White Castle. You can smell those beautiful sliders with the onions fried on 'em, seven in the morning. How we doing?"

Delsa wanted to remind Wendell that he needed people. With Seven's regular lieutenant in Iraq working for army intelligence, two on furlough, one home with her new baby, his executive sergeant, Vinnie, gone to Memphis to question a witness, Squad Seven was down to three: Delsa, Richard Harris and Jackie Michaels.

But Wendell wanted to hear about the shooting out on East Eight Mile at Yakity Yak's two nights ago.

"Where are we, Frank?"

"I've got a guy housed at the Seventh," Delsa said, "Jerome Juwan Jackson, also known as Three-J. He's twenty, a weedman on and off, went down a few times in his youth, wears Tommy Hilfiger colors with his cargo pants hanging off his ass."

"I know him," Wendell said, "without ever having seen him."

"Yeah, but Jerome aspires to be ghetto fabulous and I'm helping him make it."

"He give up anybody?"

"Let me tell it," Delsa said. "Jerome and his half-brother Curtis they call Squeak? They're at

Yakity's to see the bouncer. They want to hire a couple of strippers for a party they're having and the bouncer can arrange it."

"Get 'em some white chicks," Wendell said. He took off his Kangol, sailed it like a Frisbee at the coat tree and missed.

"Jerome calls them titty bitches. He said he had to be honest with me, he was smoking blunts and sipping Rémy all day, so that evening wasn't clear in his mind what happened."

"You ask him did he want to be a witness to this gig or a defendant?"

"I did," Delsa said. "See, Harris'd already had Squeak in the pink room. Squeak claims he didn't know the shooter, but Jerome did, and now Jerome's looking over his shoulder."

Wendell said, "Tell me who he gave up."

"Tyrell Lewis, T-Dogg. Deals weed and blow, set up his girlfriend in a hair salon with crack money. That night at Yakity Yak's he's giving her a hard time about something. They're in the parking lot and he's got her against a blue Neon, yelling at her, getting rough. A guy comes out of the bar, five-five, one-fifty, has his dreads in a ponytail. The guy's all hair and he's stoned. Comes to the lot and says to Tyrell, 'Get your bitch off the car.' "

"It's his car," Wendell said.

"No, we had that wrong. Tyrell stops abusing his girlfriend and pulls a nine out of his jacket. The little guy with the dreads pulls his nine, levels down on Tyrell and says, 'I got one too, motherfucker.' "

Wendell said, "And got killed for showing off."

"You want to let me tell it?" Delsa said. "Another guy comes out of the club and starts yelling at the two gunfighters, calling 'em punks. 'You nothing but punks playing with guns.' Tyrell says, 'You think this is a game, huh,' and shoots the guy five times. Jerome says, 'Yeah, 'cause he punked him out in front of his baby's mama.' "

"Another one popped for nothing," Wendell said. "You pick up the little fella with the hair?"

"Nobody knows him or ever saw him before."

"Gets a man killed and takes off. You say it wasn't even his car, this blue Neon."

Delsa said, "You know whose it is?"

"You may as well tell me."

"My witness, Jerome."

Wendell sat down at his desk without taking his eyes from Delsa. "You're looking at a way to use it."

"I wrote up two witness statements. In one of 'em it's Jerome who says to Tyrell, 'Get your bitch off my car, motherfucker.' "

"What about the little fella with the hair?"

"He's gone. I don't mention him in this version. Then I have Jerome say in the statement, 'He pulled a nine and I pulled mine.' When I read the page back to Jerome I stopped there and said, 'Man, that sounds like rap, "He pulled a nine and I pulled mine." Who'd you get that from, Ja Rule, Dr. Dre?' Jerome says no, he must've thought it up as he told what happened."

"He knows he didn't say it," Wendell said. "Does he know you know he didn't?"

"He doesn't care," Delsa said, "he sees himself with a new image. In the statement he names Tyrell as the shooter and tells what he did after that. Got in his car, went home and smoked a blunt. I asked him to read the statement and if the information's correct sign each page."

"Looking him in the eye," Wendell said.

"He signed them."

"I bet he did, and pretty soon he'll believe it. Tells everybody on the block what he did and becomes a street legend. Stood up to a gangbanger and pulled on him. You pick up Tyrell?"

"Jerome says he works half days at the Mack Avenue Diner in Grosse Pointe Woods. We'll pay a courtesy call to the police, stop in the diner for breakfast, Violent Crimes outside and scoop him up."

"Jerome'll testify in court?"

"I don't want him to. The prosecutor can use Jerome to offer Tyrell second degree, the best he can do. Tyrell will get something like six to fifteen and do the whole bit, 'cause he'll fuck up inside. I want the word to get around Jerome refused to testify. Stood up to Tyrell, dissed him to his face, but will not disrespect him in the man's court. Be a traitor to his kind by helping to send Tyrell down."

"You sound like an old-time Black Panther," Wendell said. "What's this 'his kind'?"

"Assholes," Delsa said, "the kind we bring in here every day and lie to each other, asking questions and taking statements."

"What you're doing with Jerome," Wendell said. "Setting him up to be an informant, huh? Does he know it?"

"Not yet. I'll pick him up later on, bring him here for another talk. See where he stands on ratting out people he knows."

"What's his incentive?"

"Tell him there's money in it."

"It could work once or twice," Wendell said.

"The one last night," Delsa said, "the hotel on Cass, the guy couldn't explain the blood on the carpeting. Jackie asked him how he got blood on his shirt and he said, 'Oh, Tammi hugged me and she has a tendency to bleed.' Tammi's the complainant. He shot her for taking twenty-eight bucks off the dresser. The man's son, and a guy he sells crack with in the lobby, came up to get rid of the body. They got partway down the stairs and left her."

"Too much like work," Wendell said.

"I guess."

"What else? The guy sitting in his car on St. Antoine."

"Talking to his wife on the phone," Delsa said. "She hears three shots. We've got no witnesses, nobody to focus on. And we're still looking for two white guys going around shooting black drug dealers. They should stick out like they're wearing signs, but we're not getting anywhere."

"The guy out by Woodmere," Wendell said, "back of the cemetery. What's a man thinking, he shoots another man thirteen times?"

Delsa said, "What're any of them thinking."

EARLY EVENING MONTEZ TAYLOR WAS IN THE MAN'S brown Lexus leaving downtown Detroit by way of East Jefferson. His phone rang. Montez brought it out of his tan cashmere topcoat, muted gold tie against dark gray underneath, and said, "Montez." Always Montez, because it always could be Mr. Paradise.

It was Lloyd.

Meaning the man had told Lloyd to call and have him pick up something like booze, cigars, porno movies. Montez didn't wait to hear what it was, he wanted to talk and said, "I'm at the office checking on that little girl's new there, Kim? Tony Jr. comes along with his big ass, wants to know what I'm doing. I said picking up his daddy's junk mail. He tells me soon as the old man's gone I am too. I said, 'What about my benefits, my bonus, my Blue Cross?' Junior says, 'You got to be kidding.' "

Lloyd said, "Like you didn't know they gonna throw your ass out in the street."

"Hey, I was fuckin with him. What's the man doing?"

"Watching his show, *Wheel of Fortune*. He wants you to pick up some of those Virginia Slim 120's, the real long ones. The girlfriend's coming this evening."

Montez said, "Wait now." Stared at taillights running away from him in the dark, realized he was slowing down, and punched the gas pedal to catch up. Lloyd was mistaken, getting old. "You're thinking of last night she was coming. I told you, I went to pick her up, she wasn't home."

"That's why she's on for tonight," Lloyd said.

"He never said a *word* to me she was coming."

"He told me and I'm telling you. So stop and get the fuckin cigarettes," Lloyd said, and was gone.

Montez replaced his personal flip phone and brought out a cheap cell from the inside pocket of his suit: this phone to use when he called the number he jabbed in now with his thumb. A woman's voice he recognized said hello. Montez said, "Lemme speak to Carl." The woman's voice said he wasn't there. Montez asked where he was and if he was coming back. The woman's voice said, "Who knows where that shithead is." Said, "Don't call here again," and hung up.

Montez said, "Fuck," out loud, turned left off Jefferson, oncoming cars blowing horns at him, screeching tires, cruised up Iroquois to the middle of the second block, turned into the circular drive and eased up to the front entrance.

He used his key to step from the eighty-year-old Georgian façade into the gloom of dark furniture, heavy chests and tables, chairs nobody ever sat on, old paintings of woods and the ocean, scenery, light coming through trees, the clouds, nothing going on in the pictures. All this old shit would be gone once the man was. He'd said, sounding pissed, none of his kids wanted to live in Detroit, happy to be out in West Bloomfield and Farmington Hills. So he was giving the house to someone who'd lived in the inner city all his life and would appreciate it. The man sincere, rewarding Montez for ten years so far of faithful, ass-kissing service.

But then just last month:

Montez explaining to the man how he could turn his study into an entertainment center with a big plasma TV screen on the wall, the latest kind of sound system, all hi-tech shit, and the man said, "I know your game, Montez," his mind working on and off, "you want me to pay for how you'd fix it up."

Then like getting punched in the stomach:

"Montez, I've changed my mind about giving you the house." Saying he was sorry but not sounding like it. "I know I promised it to you . . ." but now his granddaughter Allegra, Tony Jr.'s married daughter, thought bringing up her kids in the city would be a stimulating experience. The man saying, "And you know when it comes to family . . ."

Montez saw what he had to do. He shrugged, showed the man a sad kind of grin, said, "I can't compete with little Allegra"—being cute getting the bitch anything she wanted—"and can appreciate her wanting to live in the inner city, even with crime the way it is here, it's way more stimulating than Grosse Pointe."

"Ten to one," the old man said, "Allegra sells it before she ever moves in. I know her husband John wants to move to California, get in the wine business."

Fuck. Another punch in the gut. Montez made himself shrug and grin, knowing the man would have to offer him something else instead. And he did.

"You'll get a check in the form of a bonus from

the company," the man said, "so your name won't come up in the will and cause a commotion."

This time Montez could not shuck and jive the man with a shrug and grin. He stared at the man that time last month, stared and said, "Mr. Paradiso, do you believe your son would actually give me *any*thing?"

The man didn't care for that. It was like being talked back to. He said, "If I tell my son you have something coming, you're gonna get it, mister."

His serious tone and that "mister" shit meaning the conversation was over. Except Montez could not leave it there. He had to ask the man:

"When you're gone, how you gonna make Junior do what you want?" Paused and said, "When he don't give a fuck what you want anyway?"

Blew it. The man didn't say another word. Went over to his big double-size easy chair full of pillows and sat down in front of his old TV console, like a piece of furniture in the living room.

Where he was now.

Mr. Paradise shrinking and going frail with age, strands of white hair combed just right to cover his scalp, the man watching the end of *Wheel of Fortune*, Pat Sajak and Vanna White busting their ass to stretch the conversation through the closing seconds.

"Vanna doesn't give him much help," the man said. "She can't wait to say 'Bye' and wave to the audience. What she's good at."

He was wearing a warm-up suit, the dark blue with yellow piping. He had glanced at Montez coming in the room and gone back to Pat and Vanna.

Montez said, "Chloe's coming tonight, huh?"

"Yeah—you get the cigarettes?"

"Not yet. You want me to pick her up?"

"That's what you do, isn't it?"

Montez could say not always, but this was edgy enough. He said, "What time?"

"Nine-thirty."

Montez waited a moment. "You know I didn't have any idea she was coming?"

The man was watching a sappy ad now about Mr. Goodwrench. He said, "Don't forget the cigarettes."

"Come on, Mr. Paradise, do I ever forget anything?"

The man looked up at him and said, "You forget who you are sometimes."

Lloyd, in the white shirt and black vest he wore with a black bow tie, was in the dining room clearing the table. He said to Montez coming in,

"Put something in your hands." Montez picked up the bottle of red, down more than half, and followed Lloyd to the kitchen.

Montez saying, "He still got the bug up his ass."

"You're the one put it there," Lloyd said.

"How come I didn't know his girl's coming?"

"You still on that?"

"What if I'd gone someplace?"

"You'd have gotten permission, wouldn't you? Ask Mr. Paradise sir was it all right? He'd tell you no, you got to pick up his ho," Lloyd said. "Least he'll be in a good mood later on. You see what he's wearing? His ath-e-lete suit. Means we gonna have some cheerleading tonight." Lloyd said to Montez walking out, "The ho's gonna bring another ho to do it with her."

Montez went out the back door and cross the yard toward the garage thinking, Jesus Christ, two of 'em now. He brought out his special phone, the cheap one, and punched the number he'd tried in the car. When the woman's voice came on, the same woman saying hello like she hated answering phones, Montez said from a hard part of his throat, "Don't fuck with me, Mama." She hung up on him. He put in the number again, listened to it ring and ring until Carl Fontana's voice came on saying he was out and to leave a message. Montez said, "There's no game tonight. Understand? Call me by nine."

That was all. He knew better than to get his name and too much of his voice onto tape.

JEROME LOOKED AT HIS STREET-MARKET ROLEX.

It was 8:15 P.M., fluorescent lights on in the squad room: Jerome sipping on a can of Pepsi-Cola in a swivel chair Delsa had brought over to put next to his desk, Delsa reading what he said was Jerome's LEIN report. They were the only ones in the room. Jerome tried to figure out what LEIN meant and finally had to ask.

"Law Enforcement Information Network," Delsa said.

"I'm in there?"

"Anybody commits a crime."

"What they have me doing?"

"Possession with intent."

"Was only dank. I never had any intention to sell it. Was the judge wouldn't believe it was for my own smoking pleasure."

"How much did you have?"

"Four hundred pounds. Got me thirty months in Milan, man."

He thought the detective would start talking about prison now, asking did he want to go back, waste his life inside. Preach at him. No, that seemed to be it. Now he was looking for something on his desk. Having trouble finding it, all the shit piled there. One thing about him, he never yelled, never got in your face and screamed at you, like some of those old-time white dicks still around. Jerome swiveled in his chair away from Delsa and pushed up.

He said, "You got all white fellas in here?"

Delsa looked up at Jerome, standing now.

"We had eight in the squad, five black, three white. Three of the eight women, but now we're down, shorthanded."

"You the boss, you sit at the front desk?"

"Acting head. The lieutenant's in the army reserve. He's over in Iraq."

He had always a quiet tone of voice, answered your questions. It gave Jerome the feeling you could talk to him. Jerome believed he was Italian, dark eyes that were kinda sad, dark hair that looked like he combed with his fingers. What he should do, have it straightened some and slick it back with a dressing, give it a shine. The blue shirt and tie could pass, if it's what you had to wear working here. The man didn't have much size to him—was stringy, but could have been an athlete at one time. Or he ran and did that weight shit, like in the yard at Milan.

Jerome looked around the room, took a few shuffle steps and paused. When he wasn't told to sit down he began to stroll, checking out the shit on the desks:

Case files, witness statements, preliminary complaint reports—Jerome reading titles on the sheets—scene investigation and Medical Examiner reports, M.E. proof sheets of gunshot wounds—six in the back of the head, Jesus Christ, exit wounds in the man's cheek—Polaroids of a woman lying in the weeds, phones, computers, directories, mug shots and coffee mugs. Four desks on one side of the room, two pair butted together, three on the other side. The one Delsa sat at faced down the aisle between them to a door that was open and what looked like a walk-in closet inside, painted pink.

Why would they have a pink room in here?

Why would they have a fish with big ugly lips in a tank on top a file cabinet? The fish looking at him.

A printed sheet with a fancy border of flowers, taped to the side of the cabinet—you had to get close to read—said:

TOO OFTEN WE LOSE SIGHT OF LIFE'S SIMPLE
PLEASURES. REMEMBER, WHEN SOMEONE
ANNOYS YOU IT TAKES 42 MUSCLES IN YOUR
FACE TO FROWN. BUT IT ONLY TAKES 4 MUS-
CLES TO EXTEND YOUR ARM AND BITCH-SLAP
THE MOTHERFUCKER UPSIDE THE HEAD.

Delsa said, "Jerome? You have an idea what
happened to the gun?"

He watched Jerome in his green and red
Tommy jacket and black do-rag, blousy cargo
pants sweeping the floor, turn and come back to
the chair next to the desk.

Jerome said, "What gun you mean?" sitting
down again.

"Tyrell's, the murder weapon."

"How would I know?"

Jerome swiveling the chair back and forth now
in slow motion.

"You said he pulled a nine."

"I could be mistaken."

"Jerome, don't bail out on me. I swear you
won't have to testify. Nothing you tell me leaves
this room."

"Was a Beretta, the one holds fifteen loads."

Delsa said, "Your girlfriend's name is Nashelle
Pierson?"

"That's right."

"She has a half-brother named Reggie Banks?" Jerome hesitated. "Yeah . . . ?"

"And Reggie, who works at the Mack Avenue Diner with Tyrell, is a homey of yours?"

"How you know that?"

"I ride the block and talk to people. Who's this Jerome Juwan Jackson I hear about? Has style, tight rims on his car. A girl sitting on her front steps says, 'Oh, you mean Three-J? Yeah, lives in the house down the block, in the house has boards over the windows. Protect him from dudes shooting at him.' "

"Uh-unh, the windows already busted when I moved in."

"Rent free," Delsa said, "looking after the house for, I believe, your uncle doing time?"

"How you know that? Me and him have different names."

"I told you, I talk to people. Most of 'em want to help us, Jerome. I mean ordinary people, not just paid informants. Nobody wants a crack house on their block. Hear gunfire in the night. See innocent children, babies, killed in drive-bys. You know how many times in a drive-by they get the wrong house? You see a car cruise past a couple of times? Now here it comes back? What do you do?"

"Hit the floor, man." Jerome grinned. He said,

"Tell me something. How much these paid informants get paid?"

"Depends on how good the information is. We get tips all the time. A guy has a grudge, wants to pay somebody back and names him as a perp. Guy writes from jail. 'Get me out of here and I'll give you the guy did Bobo.' It's our junk mail. The pay for information we need comes out of what's called Crime Stoppers. It's a program."

"What I want to know," Jerome said, "is how much that comes to."

"A reward's offered, you're into big money. I know of a C.I. who identified the guy who raped and murdered a teenage girl, and collected ten thousand. Crime Stoppers pays a grand for information leading to an arrest."

"Is that right?" Jerome said. "What's this C.I.?"

"Confidential Informant—and when I say confidential, I mean we won't even reveal a C.I.'s name in a court of law."

"I'm getting paid for giving up Tyrell?"

"That one's different, since we have a few more eyeball witnesses and you're not gonna testify. But we have other cases, Jerome, you might be of help with. We've got one, three Mexicanos shot in the back of the head, one of 'em dismembered with a chain saw."

"Cool," Jerome said.

"You don't care for Mexicans?"

"Motherfuckers say they gonna deliver? They gonna rip you off and shoot you they get the chance."

"We're looking for a guy named Orlando," Delsa said, "we think could give us some information."

"I mighta heard the name's all."

"Had a place off Michigan Avenue, behind the old ballpark."

Jerome said, "Yeah, Orlando," nodding his head.

"Also, I mentioned Nashelle's half-brother Reggie Banks? We got a tip he dumped Tyrell's gun for him."

Delsa waited.

"Yeah . . . ?"

"And you might know something about it."

"You didn't get that from Nashelle."

"It was another detective talked to some girl who knows Reggie. I don't have her statement in front of me, but it's in the case file."

"She say I was with him?"

"I don't know, but if you have something to tell me, it comes under what we've been talking about, confidential information."

Jerome said, "Lemme think on it."

Delsa said, "You got ten minutes." He brought

a pack of Newports from his desk drawer and offered one to his C.I.

Jerome said, "I thought this was a no-smoking building."

Delsa said, "Only if you get caught."

AS SOON AS THEY WERE IN THE CAR, STILL IN FRONT
of the loft, the guy turned to them in the backseat. He gave her kind of an impatient look, mad,
and said to Chloe, "How come nobody let me
know?"

Sounding like it was her fault.

Chloe said, "What're you talking about?"

Montez didn't answer. He was a terrible driver,
changing lanes in the East Jefferson traffic as he
made a call on his cell, Chloe telling him, "Will
you watch the fucking road? Jesus." When he
didn't get an answer to his call he said, "Fuck,"
and dropped the phone on the seat next to him.

Behind him in the dark Kelly leaned close to
Chloe and said, "You think he's cool, huh?"

Chloe raised her voice saying, "Montez?
What's wrong?"

Kelly saw him look at the rearview mirror. He said, "Don't bother your head," and was quiet after that, but kept glancing at them in the mirror.

They arrived at the house, lights shining on its gray stone from the shrubs. Montez stopped in the circular drive and asked Chloe how long she thought they'd be.

"It's up to Tony," Chloe said. "You know that."

Montez said, "See if you can cut your bullshit cheerleading short this evening."

As soon as they were inside Chloe brought Kelly through a hallway to the living room and introduced her to Mr. Paradiso, the old man seated in his chair that was like a cushy love seat facing a TV console. He said, "So you're Kelly," smiling at her but didn't get up. Kelly had to lean in to kiss his cheek and felt his liver-spotted hand slip into her coat to close on her breast, the left one, inside a cotton sweatshirt. As she straightened he said, "What're you wearing that sweater for?"

"I have a cold," Kelly said. "But, hey, it's from the University of Michigan," gave him a darling smile and said, "go blue."

Chloe sat on his rickety lap to kiss him on the mouth and he slipped both hands into her coat saying, "Here my little cheerleaders."

"If you're a good boy," Chloe said to him, "I'll let you paint my *M* on." She brought a blue Magic Marker out of her coat and put it in his hand. "Want to?"

Kelly thinking, I'm gonna be sick.

She was aware of Montez hanging back, not saying anything to the old man. Lloyd the houseman appeared, took their drink order and Montez followed him out of the room. He was back in a few minutes opening a bottle of Christiania vodka; he freshened the old man's drink and left the bottle in the ice bucket, on a table close by. Now he seemed to wander around, antsy. Kelly watched him go through the hallway to the foyer and stand by the front double doors with their etched-glass panels, pale rose in the dark wood.

Mr. Paradise said, "There," as he finished applying Chloe's *M*, a crude letter below her perfect breasts. He turned his head and Kelly saw he was looking toward Montez in the foyer, Montez returning now to the living room.

The old man said, "The hell you doing skulking around?"

Montez gave him a dumb look, surprised, said, "Nothing," and held up empty hands.

Chloe said, "He's pissed he had to pick us up."

The old man said, "No, no, it takes more than that to get under Mr. Montez Taylor's skin. He has a great capacity for taking shit, knows how to accept it and grin. But I did find his pissed-off threshold. I was gonna give him this house, help him with his social acceptability. I don't mean it as a racial thing, Indian Village is half colored anyway. No, what I'm saying is Mr. Taylor could put on the dog and be accepted as a colorful character —no pun intended. But, can he earn a living once I'm gone? Pay the taxes? Keep the place up? I realized the obligation would be too much for him. He'd sell the house and spend the money on having a good time. So my granddaughter Allegra will get it. Live here or sell the property and put her kids through college. I told Mr. Taylor I'd changed my mind, then watched his chagrin rise and boil over when I told him he'd be taken care of by my son Tony. Now Mr. Taylor was so pissed off he insults *me* by insulting my son."

Chloe said, "Oh, it can't be that bad. You know yourself Tony Jr.'s not"—she hesitated, the old guy staring at her—"well, not as congenial as you are."

He said, "You're close to getting in trouble yourself," and moved his gaze to Montez. "You deny it?"

Montez said, "Deny what?"

And Kelly had to look at him; he sounded different, at ease now, in no hurry.

"That you insulted my son."

"You insult me in your own way," Montez said, "and it's okay. Calling me Mr. Taylor. Meaning I'm uppity, have no business saying anything against your boy. Meaning I can't say anything to you one man to another."

Still with the quiet tone, in no hurry.

"Like you said to me this evening you're watching your show. You said I forget who I am. Meaning, my place. Like I had talked back to you."

Kelly watched, surprised he could be so calm giving it back to his boss. She heard the old man say, "Montez," and turned to see Mr. Paradiso raise his hand to wave Montez off, like telling him to forget it.

"Okay, let's say we were both pissed off—and I'm not supposed to let anything bother me, doctor's orders. I know who you are, you're my number one, Montez, my walking-around guy. Okay?"

He let it hang there until Chloe said, "And you're our Mr. Paradise."

Lloyd brought them alexanders in crystal lowball glasses they took upstairs with their coats and handbags. They'd have a cigarette and a drink while they fooled with their makeup, did something with their eyes. Chloe led the way to a bed-room. They put their coats on the bed and went in the bathroom and looked at themselves in the mirror, Kelly saying, " 'And you're our Mr. Par-adise.' " She leaned over the sink and poked a fin-ger into her open mouth a few times.

"It's what you do," Chloe said, "you're a mis-tress."

"What do you think Montez said to him?"

"He probably called Tony Jr. an asshole. You're keeping the sweatshirt on?"

An extra-large that Chloe loaned her and hung below her cute skirt.

"If it was just the old guy I might take it off. I'm not showing my tits to the help."

"Because they're colored guys?"

"I went with a black guy once, a professor at Wayne, an intellectual type. He really was, but he said 'You understand what I'm saying?' about every other sentence. I think to let me know he was street before he got educated, knows waz-zup."

Chloe said, "I've usually had a good time with colored guys. When they're cool they're really cool. Like Montez, the way he gave it back. That was cool."

"Yeah, well, I broke up with my black guy, he was so fucking boring. I said, 'Look, just assume

I understand what you're saying. If I don't, I'll tell you.' And, yes, I'm wearing the sweatshirt."

"It's way too big for you."

"So?"

The old man didn't seem to mind the sweatshirt, since it was from U of M. He said he liked it when they jumped up in the air. They did the stupid cheers, "We're the girls from Mich-i-gan . . ." and acted nasty in cute ways.

Montez wasn't around for the show. He said he'd be in the kitchen, said he hadn't eaten and was hungry. That was all he did say after the row with the old man. "I'll be in the kitchen, Mr. Paradiso."

Kelly caught it but didn't think it registered on the old man. Montez was Montez and Mr. Paradiso was not Mr. Paradise. They had left their unfinished alexanders upstairs. Lloyd brought them each another and the old man said, "Tell Montez to get out here."

Kelly watched him come through the dining room still wearing his gray suit, his eyebrows raised to the boss, not speaking, but this way asking what the man wanted, sitting there on his throne with a vodka on the rocks.

Kelly imagining the way Montez saw him.

Mr. Paradiso said, "You don't think I treat you fairly. All right, give me a coin, a quarter."

Montez brought change out of his pants pocket, found a quarter and gave it to the man.

"What I'm gonna do, Montez, my number one, I'm gonna share my ladies with you. I don't want to show favoritism, so I'm flipping the coin. Heads, Chloe goes upstairs and you have a party on me. Tails, and I mean a nine-hundred-dollar piece of tail, Montez, you get Kelly here. How's that sound to everybody?"

TEN TO ELEVEN DELSA WALKED IN THE SQUAD room taking off his duffle coat, the kind with the hood and wooden toggles, the coat, the turtleneck and blazer a deep navy blue.

Harris said, "You're back?"

"You see me," Delsa said.

Jackie Michaels was playing slot machines on her computer, the calliope *ding-dong* sound turned low. Jackie had the 8:00 P.M. to 4:00 A.M. She looked at Delsa taking off his blazer with the duffle and hanging them on the rack.

"Richard said you went home."

"I did, I had something to eat."

Richard Harris, forty-four, cool mustache, gold cuff links, a white girlfriend named Dawn who hustled drinks at the Greektown Casino; Harris a year with Squad Seven after a few years of patrol and a few more on the Violent Crimes Task Force, was looking at the Love Swing instructions book. He said to Delsa, "Can't stay away, huh?"

Jackie knew better. Frank's problem was staying home. Walk in the house and get the TV on fast. Until a couple of months ago Maureen's clothes were still in her closet and chifforobe. He mentioned it at the Christmas party, Frank half in the bag but still quiet telling her. Jackie's advice, get rid of the clothes, everything; she'd help him if he wanted. St. Vincent de Paul shoppers were wearing Maureen's clothes now, and Delsa was practically living in the squad room: the man sounding the same as always but buried in police work from morning into the night, glad to have the paperwork.

At his desk now he said, "You want to know what happened to Tyrell's gun?"

"It's in the river," Harris said, "or it's in pieces all over the city of Detroit."

"My man Jerome," Delsa said, "*drove* the guy who got rid of it for Tyrell. Reggie Banks, they call T-Bone, half-brother of Jerome's girlfriend, Nashelle. Sunday, the night after Yakity's, Reggie wants to cruise Belle Isle. Jerome says, 'Man, it's freezing cold,' but lets Reggie talk him into it,

Jerome suspecting what the trip's for. So they go over and cruise Belle Isle, Jerome with his sounds turned up, all that heavy bass chugging out of the car—"

"Bouncing his shit," Harris said.

"On the way back they stop on the bridge and Reggie chucks the piece over the side. Jerome says he knows the exact spot where Reggie was standing."

Jackie said, "How you get him to tell you all that?"

"We let him deal some weed, keep him out of court," Delsa said, "and he tells us things." Delsa turned from Jackie, at her desk, to Harris across the aisle. "I asked him if he knew Orlando, both of them dealing weed. He says he's heard the name."

"He'll see the man's burnt-up house," Harris said, "he watches any TV."

"What about Orlando's girlfriend?"

"I did what you said, got next to the neighbor lady, Rosella Munson. She told me Tenisha and her mother were close, she'd probably run to her mama's house, and that's where I found her. The mother doesn't care for Orlando. She told Tenisha, answer my questions or she'd take a stick to her."

Jackie asked how old Tenisha was.

"Twenty," Harris said. "She and her mother are at Northland all day yesterday, shopping. The mother says she took her home around five. Tenisha goes in the house, Orlando's mopping the floor in the dining room with Pine Sol and bleach, using so much, Tenisha said, it burned her eyes."

"She didn't ask," Jackie said, "what he was cleaning up, did she?"

"Said she couldn't remember if she did or not."

Jackie said, "You *know* this Orlando's never touched a mop before in his life."

"She goes next door," Harris said, "to get away from the fumes, the smell, and sits down with Rosella to watch a movie on TV. After while she hears a car, looks out the window and sees two friends of Orlando's standing by a black SUV. Orlando comes out with some trash bags—they're full of something but she doesn't know what—and puts them in the back end. Now Orlando drives off in the SUV, by himself. The two guys—one of 'em she remembers as Jo-Jo—tell her to go on back next door. Stay there till they come get her. Tenisha says this is her house, she can do what she wants. She goes upstairs and comes back down with her coloring book and crayons. Frank, they were hers."

Delsa said, "You never know."

"There's a part here," Harris said, "we didn't learn about till a few hours ago. Orlando and Jo-Jo, that afternoon, went to Sterling Auto Sales and took the SUV out for a test drive—be right back. Okay, later on Orlando drives off with the trash bags. He's on Michigan Avenue westbound, a radio car from the Fourth flashes him to pull over. Orlando takes off, runs a red light, turns a corner, sideswipes a couple of cars and jumps out, abandons ship. They look for him but it's dark now and he gets away. They look in the SUV, Ford Explorer, find like a hundred pounds of grass in three of the bags, bloody clothes in another, and a Chinese AK-47. Sterling Auto Sales had reported the SUV stolen."

"If he used the AK on the Mexicans," Delsa said. "Now he has to dump it."

"That's how it looks," Harris said. "And stash the weed at his mother's, like they do. Hundred pounds, Jackie. How long would that last you?"

"That was white-boy Glenn's habit, not mine. I'm done with him. My evenings off, I'm out at Sportree's sipping Bombay, looking to bring a tall black dude into my life. Little Glenn was fun, but he made me nervous."

"I'm not done," Harris said. "Orlando comes home in a taxi and now he's tripped out, can't sit still. He says, 'My prints are all over that shit. My fuckin life is done.' This is good. Jo-Jo says to him, 'So you didn't get the gasoline and the fuckin chain saw like you suppose to.' They get in an argument, Orlando wanting to know how he's gonna get the gasoline and the fuckin chain saw with cops on his ass. The taxi's still there, the driver a friend of theirs, so Jo-Jo takes it and comes back with, Tenisha says, 'the things they needed.' "

Delsa said, "They talk about the guys in the basement? Who they are? What happened?"

"No mention of 'em. Orlando puts Tenisha in the cab and tells the driver, take her to the Parkside Motel on West Warren. They called and reserved two rooms."

Jackie said, "Did she put up any kind of fuss? Or just went along with whatever?"

"Says she was too scared to say anything."

Delsa said, "She bring her coloring book?"

Harris was shaking his head. "What the girl did was fall asleep. Laid down on the bed and woke up to Orlando pounding on the door. His homies had the other room but came in to sit around and smoke dope. Here's the good part. Orlando makes a phone call. Tenisha hears him say, 'The three dudes are in the basement.' Then he says something like, 'All the stuff's there.' I think meaning the gasoline and the fuckin chain saw. She falls asleep again while Orlando's watching TV. She wakes up, asks him why he doesn't turn it off so they can get some sleep. He says, 'I'm waiting to see if I'm on the news.' I asked her what he meant by that. She says, 'I guess about the dead guys, if they were found.' I asked did she see them at any time. No." Harris paused and said, "You like it so far? Wait. There's one more part you gonna love."

Jackie's phone rang.

Delsa turned to her as she was saying, "Squad Seven, Sergeant Michaels."

Then back to Harris.

Harris saying, "Four o'clock in the morning somebody's knocking on the motel door. It wakes up Tenisha. She sees Orlando go over to the door, open it partway and now he's talking to a guy she thought was a light-skin brother. She couldn't see him good."

Delsa looked at Jackie, busy now making notes.

Harris saying, "She can feel the cold, the door open. So she calls to Orlando, 'Honey, I'm freezing to death.' The guy Orlando's talking to raises his head and says to her, 'You cold? You look hot to me.' "

Harris waited for Delsa still looking at Jackie.

Jackie saying into the phone, "How many?"

Harris said, "Frank, you hear what I said?"

"The guy told her she looked hot."

Harris said, "Yeah, but from his voice she could tell the guy was Mexican."

Delsa eased into saying, "Is that right?" in his quiet way.

Harris said, "What do you think?"

But now Jackie was off the phone. She said, "We just got a big-time double."

"How big?" Delsa said, the Mexican in the motel doorway gone.

"Anthony Paradiso, at his home on Iroquois, Indian Village, and a young woman."

Harris said, "Which Paradiso?"

"The old man."

Harris said, "*Damn*. I was hoping it was his kid." He looked at Delsa. "I bet you were too. You know who fat-ass Tony's gonna say did it, some quick-draw cop. Some cowboy they sued on a wrongful death and it cost the city money."

Delsa was looking at Jackie. "Who's the woman?"

"They don't have a name yet. Blond, mid-twenties, wearing a little pleated skirt. Response was from the Seventh, the OIC's your old buddy Dermot Cleary."

"Where were they found?"

"Didn't say. Three others in the house when the shots were fired."

"They still there?"

"Waiting for us," Jackie said.

THEY PARKED ON THE STREET, THREE FIGURES
now in dark coats leaving the car, Harris wearing
a brown Borsalino, saying, "The advantage of
the swing, Frank, you don't get a backache, or
rug burns when you have to do it on the floor."

They walked toward the house all lit up, the
driveway full of cars, Jackie Michaels saying,
"White-boy Glenn brought one of those home—
you have to be a trapeze artist to get laid in it, believe me. Glenn fell out on his head and that was
the end of the Love Swing."

They ducked under police tape and the dark
sedans in the drive became radio cars and it was
a crime scene.

The sergeant from the Seventh Precinct, Dermot Cleary, Delsa's partner his rookie year, was
waiting near the entrance. He said, "Two of 'em

for you, Frank. Anthony Paradiso—a shame it
isn't Tony Jr., the fuck, and a Kelly Barr, white
female twenty-seven, resides on River Place off
Franklin. They're in the living room."

Delsa said, "And three witnesses?"

Cleary, flipping open his notebook, stepped
into the light above the double doors. Delsa saw
one of the rose-colored panes of glass had been
shattered.

"Montez Taylor, black male thirty-three, lives
on the premises." Cleary looked up from his
notes. "Dresses like a fuckin lawyer, pinstripe suit
and tie. Says he's Mr. Paradiso's personal man. I
said, 'What's that mean, you shine his shoes?'
Montez refers to the old man as Mr. Paradise.
Been with him ten years. Also on the scene, a
Lloyd Williams, black male seventy-one. Lloyd
admits he's a servant, the houseman, also lives on
the premises. Says he was sound asleep, didn't
hear any gunshots."

"How many?"

"Four. The old man and girl two each."

"The third witness?"

"If you want to call her that, Chloe Robinette,
white female twenty-seven. Same age, same address as Kelly Barr. They live together. This is according to Montez. I only saw Chloe for a minute.
She's in a bedroom upstairs, an officer with her."

"She tell you anything?"

"Like pulling teeth. Montez says she's in shock."

"Montez a doctor?"

"He's a talker, Frank. Montez sees it as a fucked-up home invasion. Says he scared the guy off before he could take anything."

"Where was he when the shots were fired?"

"Upstairs with Chloe. Montez says they're hookers, very high class. Nine bills an hour, if you can believe it."

Delsa looked at Jackie, at one time in Vice. "Kelly Barr and Chloe Robinette?"

Jackie shook her head. "Too high class to be in the files."

"He hears the shots," Delsa said, "runs out of the bedroom and sees this one-man home invader?"

"Going out the door, a black guy," Cleary said. "Frank, you can tell this Montez struts his shit. Only in this situation he has to act like he wants to help."

"He sound educated?"

"Take off the pinstripe suit," Cleary said, "he hangs on a corner. Not a big guy, middleweight, about your size."

"I thought the Village had a security patrol."

"They stopped by, see what was going on."

"Why this house?"

"It was a hit," Cleary said. "I don't buy that one-man home invasion shit either. Not a house this big."

"We don't know anything yet," Delsa said. "We don't know if the guy came in this way or smashed the glass on the way out. We don't even know for sure the girls are hookers. Montez could have his own reason for saying it."

"Take a look at the broad in the chair," Cleary said, "you'll know."

Delsa, buttoned up in dark navy, crossed the living room to view the dead, Jackie and Harris coming behind him. He motioned to a uniform in the arched entrance to the dining room. The officer came over. Delsa said to him, "That's Montez?"

"Yes sir, Montez Taylor."

A good-looking black guy sitting at the head of the dining room table smoking a cigarette, gray suit and gold tie on a dark shirt, legs crossed, his chair turned to watch the evidence techs working the living room. A woman's handbag was on the table, away from him.

Delsa asked the uniform if he knew what Montez was smoking. The uniform said no, he didn't. Delsa said he'd lay five bucks it was a

Newport. Harris said he'd take it. Delsa said to him, "Get a tech to bag the cigarette butt," and now approached the chair facing the television set. A tech by the name of Alex was photographing the bodies. He stepped aside to give Homicide a close look at the old man and the girl:

Their faces masked with dried blood from gunshot wounds centered on their foreheads, mouths slack, eyes closed. The wound in the girl's chest had brought an eruption of blood over her bare breasts, her stomach, and stained the waist of her maize and blue pleated skirt, the hem folded up to show her sex, a dense patch of dark hair. The front of the old man's warm-up jacket was stained black.

Delsa said, "Their eyes were closed?"

"Haven't touched 'em," Alex said. "Had their heads back like that, not slumped over. I checked with Sergeant Cleary. They were looking right at it when they got popped."

"What's that on her chest, a tattoo?"

"Magic Marker. It looks like somebody drew a big *M* on her."

"The TV set was off?"

"Yeah, I checked that, too. We'll dust it good, the glasses, get elimination prints off the witnesses and test 'em for gunshot residue."

"What about the wounds?"

"The ones in the head are through and through, but I haven't dug 'em out of the chair yet. No casings on the floor."

"What about her skirt?"

"That's how it was. Like somebody folded up the hem to check out her pussy. The guys from the Seventh were commenting on it. You hardly ever see a mop like that on a young girl. They get their cooze waxed and it reminds you of Hitler."

Harris said, "I heard that kind referred to as a Charlie Chaplin."

"That'll work," Alex said. "I've seen all kinds, even heart-shaped ones."

Jackie said, "I'm gonna leave this one alone."

Delsa turned to her. "Why don't you check on Chloe? Find out if she's a prostitute. Hey, first call the M.E.'s office, ask if they want to send a pathologist, we know the time and manner. They'll send their death investigator and he can call the removal service. Okay?" He said to Harris, "Talk to the houseman, Lloyd Williams, and send Montez over."

Delsa looked at the girl again, Kelly, at her spiked blond hair, concentrating then to see her face beneath the blood and the makeup masking her eyes, trying to see her alive. He heard, "Detective," and turned to see Montez Taylor coming in his gray pinstripes, a man who wanted you to notice him.

"I been waiting for somebody to cover her up," Montez said, "once they checked out her bush. Be the decent thing to do. Never mind how the girl made her living."

"You knew her pretty well?"

"I think she only been here a few times."

"What about Chloe?"

"Either one, they come by this evening to entertain Mr. Paradise, do their cheerleading routines. The man's favorite thing, cute girls doing cheers?"

"They're cheerleaders?"

"Only for the man. They do ones they make up like, 'We the chicks from Mich-i-gan, nobody can fuck you like we can.' I don't know if that means doing it, or what they charge for doing it. Know what I'm saying? They high class, Mr. Paradise don't invite skanky bitches to his home."

Montez stood with his hands hanging folded in front of him, a pose of respect.

"You were upstairs with Chloe," Delsa said.

"That's right, while the man watched a football game with Kelly. A video, some Michigan game. The man has all the ones they won. Or it could've been Chloe. As I say, either one. They like his girlfriends."

"Interchangeable," Delsa said. "And he lets them fuck the help?"

It got Montez to stare at him straight on, dead-pan, before managing kind of a smile.

"Would I be up there 'less it was his idea?"

"You ever mix it up, you and the boss and a girl or two?"

"I ain't even gonna answer that."

"What were you doing tonight, trading off?"

Eye to eye Montez said, "The girls did their cheerleading number and Mr. Paradise sent me upstairs with Chloe. Said have a party on him."

"You ever take Kelly upstairs?"

"I oblige the man whatever he wants."

"You ever had Kelly?"

"No, I haven't."

"Are you in his will?"

"That's all, no more questions."

"Are you?"

"That's the man's private business."

"It sounds to me," Delsa said, "if he lets you fuck his girlfriends, you have a pretty good deal here. How much is he leaving you?"

"I don't know he's leaving me anything."

"He ever talk about dying?"

"His health? He'd kid about his old ticker with these young girls."

"He's with Kelly and you're with Chloe."

Montez hesitated. "That's right."

"They're watching TV together in the chair."

"How I last saw them."

"You're upstairs with Chloe. Then what?"

"Was what happened, this nigga busts in and shoots 'em."

"This home invader."

"What else could he be?"

"You heard the shots."

"Was four. Pow, pow, then quiet, then pow pow."

"What did you do?"

"Ran out to the hall. I look over the rail to downstairs, he's in the foyer. I yelled at him and he ran."

"What'd you yell?"

"I said I had a gun and he went out the front."

"Did you?"

"What, have a gun? No."

"Couldn't he see you weren't armed?"

"He hardly looked. Glanced up at me and split."

"You have a gun?"

"No."

"Is there one in the house?"

"In the man's room."

"Why didn't you get it?"

"I run out to the hall—I don't know what's going on. Did the shots come from outside? See,

I'm thinking of Mr. Paradise downstairs with the girl, with Kelly. Is he all right? It couldn't be her shooting, could it? She brought a gun?"

"In her little cheerleader skirt," Delsa said.

"In her coat, her bag—I'm not thinking where she kept it, I want to know is Mr. Paradise all right."

"You went from the bedroom to the top of the stairs," Delsa said. "Then what?"

"I yelled at him I had a gun."

"And you say he split. How'd he get in?"

"You come in the front, you musta seen the door."

"You hear the glass break?"

"I was upstairs."

"There's no alarm system?"

"I'm here, I don't put it on till I go to my rooms, my suite over the garage. I'm not here, Lloyd puts it on when he retires."

"What'd the guy look like?"

"Big full-grown nigga."

"You ever see him before?"

"No."

"What'd you yell at him?"

"I told you."

"Tell me again, the exact words."

"I said—I yelled at him, 'I gotta gun, nigga!' And he took off."

"You see his gun?"

"Look like a nine."

"Was he wearing gloves?"

Montez thought a moment. "I don't know."

"Did he take anything?"

"Bottle of vodka."

"Have you ever been convicted of a felony?"

"What? What you ask me that for?"

"I want to know."

"Was something I got into a long time ago. Mr. Paradise represented me."

"What was it?"

"Assault with intent—you gonna look me up anyway. It wasn't any big deal."

"What did you do for Mr. Paradise?"

"Look out for him."

"Why would anybody want to do him?"

"It turns out," Montez said, "if it wasn't a dirty cop out to pay him back—know what I'm saying?—there ain't any reason. It's why I told the police that come answer the nine-eleven, it was somebody broke in to rob the place."

"Why'd he shoot Mr. Paradise and Kelly?"

"Why's some guy stick up a Seven-Eleven and whack the clerk? Answer that, it's the same thing."

"After he went out the front door," Delsa said, "what'd you do?"

"I ran downstairs and see them in the chair, blood all over, man."

"You turn off the TV?"

Montez had to pause to remember. "It wasn't on."

"Did you touch the bodies?"

"I'll tell you something," Montez said, "I almost did. Not the bodies, I almost pulled the little girl's skirt down, but caught myself in time, or I'd be tampering, wouldn't I?"

"You didn't check to see if they're alive?"

"Man, look at them. That's how they been, like they'd bled out. I made the call." He stopped. "No, I'm about to, I see Chloe's come downstairs. She looks at these two and I see she's about to freak on me. She start screaming—I told her go on back upstairs."

"Why?"

"So I could think straight to make the call. I took her back upstairs first and then called."

"She quiet down?"

"I gave her something."

Delsa said, "Yeah . . . ?"

"One of my duties," Montez said, "I change the water in Mr. Paradise's bong, check to see there's dank, just street stuff, no crypto or wacky shit, you know, that might hurt him. For when the man wants to relax. I get the bong and give it to the girl, Chloe. I tell her, 'Put your mouth on this, it'll ease you down.' "

Delsa said, "I was talking to a guy today they call Three-J, lives out in the Ninth. Three-J witnessed a shooting, a fatal he didn't want to tell me about. He sees I know he was there, so he goes, 'Okay, I'm gonna be honest with you. I was smoking blunts all day and wasn't paying attention to anything.' You see what he's doing? Pleads to a misdemeanor he knows I don't give a shit about, to get out of telling me who the shooter was."

"You think it's why I mention the bong?"

"It's like that. You're telling me," Delsa said, "you have nothing to hide, I can believe anything you say. You ever been to Yakity Yak's?"

" 'Yakety Yak, don't talk back'—big hit by the Coasters. No, I never been there. He give up the shooter?"

"He felt better when he did," Delsa said. "Tell me about Kelly. Where she's from . . ."

"I don't know."

"If she has a family."

"I don't know as that kind of girl has a family. I mean one she keeps in touch with. You know what I'm saying? Like she calls up and talks to her mama, tells her she's turning tricks? Yeah, I suppose she could have a family. She does, they the ones'd make the funeral arrangements, huh?"

"Next of kin comes to the Medical Examiner's office," Delsa said, "to make a positive I.D."

"You want them identified?" Montez said. "That's Mr. Paradise and that's little Kelly, and I'm positive."

"And we'll need the M.E.," Delsa said, "to tell us the cause of death."

Montez said, "You're fuckin with me now, aren't you? Both of 'em showing serious bullet holes?"

"You worked for a trial lawyer, you know what I'm talking about," Delsa said, almost finished with him. "You said both girls are hookers?"

"Call girls, high class. They go nine bills an hour, man, each."

"You and Chloe in bed when you heard the shots?"

"Getting to it."

"These the clothes you had on?"

"All evening."

"You were 'getting to it,' " Delsa said. "What's that mean, you unzipped your fly?"

"Means I was about to disrobe but was interrupted. Pistol shots, man, can change your plans."

"How's Chloe? You think she's okay now?"

"You want, I can check."

"I'm going up anyway," Delsa said, "I'll save you a trip."

FIRST SHE HEARD A WOMAN'S VOICE COMING
from the hall.

"There's a girl in here."

The cop in uniform who came in moments
later asked if she was all right. She didn't answer.
He stood leaning over her in the chair she'd
turned to the window, his traffic-cop face close,
tobacco on his breath, his reflection above hers
on the glass. He asked if she had seen what happened. She understood what he meant but said
no. He said he didn't mean did she see it happen.
She said yes, she saw them in the chair. She put
her head down in the turned-up collar of her cinnamon coat. He asked if she had come with the
other girl. She didn't answer. He asked her name.
She didn't answer. He told her not to change her
clothes or wash her face and hands. He told her

to keep the light on and the door open. He left, but another uniformed cop, a black woman, remained in the hall.

She looked at her watch but couldn't read the time, the lamp behind her, on the other side of the bed.

If they got to the house a little before ten, came up here to fool with their makeup—her eyes still raccooned, her hair spiked—spent time talking, smoking a cigarette, neither of them in a hurry, it must've been close to eleven by the time they did the cheers, Lloyd served them another drink, and the old man tossed Montez' quarter in the air.

"Tails it is." He said to Montez, "You get Kelly for as long as you want. On me."

She told herself to take it easy, don't act stupid. Be cool, show some poise. Go up to the bedroom and get your coat. And as soon as he has his clothes off set him straight, you're not a hooker, and get out, leave the house. She finished her drink, started for the foyer and the old man's voice stopped her.

"Look how anxious she is. Go on, Montez, carry her upstairs and throw her on the bed." Kelly turned, a few strides from the hallway that led to the foyer, the old man laughing.

She saw Montez waiting to say something to

him, the old man sipping his drink now. Montez said, "Sir, you mind if I have Chloe instead?"

Mr. Paradiso stared at him.

"I mean you're giving me either one anyway, on the flip of a coin." Montez shrugged like it was no big deal, "Could you make it Chloe, Mr. Paradise?"

Chloe said, "Hey, now wait a minute."

Mr. Paradiso said, "Jesus Christ, I try to treat you with respect, offer you a nine-hundred-dollar piece of tail—no, she doesn't suit you, you want the other one. I give Lloyd expensive clothes I don't want, he couldn't be more appreciative. 'Thank you, Mr. Paradise, thank you, sir.' But you're never satisfied, are you? You prefer to insult me, throw my gesture back in my face."

Montez said, "All right, if this is how you want it."

He came to her, Kelly surprised to see his face bland, without expression, but then was rough taking her by the arm to the foyer and up the staircase to the second floor, Kelly hurrying with him in her sneakers to stay on her feet. They came to the bedroom where she and Chloe had left their coats and Montez shoved her inside, the light still on in the bathroom. She turned to him saying, "I'm not going to bed with you, so don't even think about it."

He stood in the doorway, his back to her, looking down the hall.

She said, "Listen, it's nothing personal, okay?"

He didn't turn or say anything. He didn't move.

Kelly went in the bathroom, lit a cigarette, and finished the alexander she'd left. Chloe's, barely touched, was on the counter. She picked it up and drank it down, all of it, and saw her face, the exaggerated eyes and weird hair, looking at her from the mirror. She stepped back into the bedroom, Montez still at the door, and sat down on the side of the king-size bed, smoked her cigarette and used the ashtray on the night table. She turned on the lamp. The ashtray was from the Pierre in New York.

Now she stared at Montez' back in pinstripes wondering what he was up to, what he was thinking . . .

Why he hadn't jumped her by now.

Why he wanted Chloe instead of her.

She wasn't actually offended . . .

Chloe had bigger boobs and that could be all there was to it, Montez eyeing her for months . . . If he made the move she'd explain to him, look, I'm not what you think, I'm not a pro, all right? I have to be in love and we hardly know each other. Like that, keep talking. Tell him you had an

African-American boyfriend once, a terrific guy, originally from the hood.

Montez hadn't moved from the door.

She said, "Tell me what you're doing."

He didn't answer.

She thought about washing her face, getting rid of the eye makeup, but didn't want to move. She said, "You're listening for something," and sat still, quiet, finished the cigarette, stubbed it out, lit another one . . .

And saw his shoulders jump at the hard, blunt sound of gunfire from downstairs—not like movie gunshots, but that's what the sound had to be, and heard it again, the sudden hard *pops,* and dropped her cigarette as she came off the bed and had to find the fucking Virginia Slim on the carpet and stub it out in the ashtray, and when she looked at the door again Montez was gone.

Kelly put on her coat. She picked up Chloe's from the bed and went out to the hall.

He was at the staircase railing where it came up and curved into the open area of the hall, looking down at the lighted foyer. Kelly brushed the wall as she moved toward him, Montez waiting . . . That's what it looked like, waiting for someone to appear. He called out, "Hey!" and it stopped her. He waited again.

Now he was running down the carpeted stairway.

Kelly moved along the wall to the stair rail, dropped to her hands and knees and looked down at the foyer, empty, through the marble balusters. She was directly over the short hallway to the living room. She could hear voices now but not what they were saying. Montez' voice and another one and another one, three different sounds in what could be an argument, two against one. She stood up to listen, draping Chloe's coat over the railing, and dropped down again pulling the coat with her.

Through the balusters now she watched two men in black raincoats and baseball caps cross the foyer to the front door. Now they turned to look back and stood there: both white, both about fifty—they looked short—nothing out of the ordinary about them, just guys, like workingmen. One held a gun, an automatic, the other a bottle of vodka by the neck, the one the old man had been drinking. The guy with the gun pointed it at the hallway and said, "Day after tomorrow, Smoke."

This one opened the door and Montez' voice came from somewhere below Kelly crouched behind the railing:

"Bust it!"

The two stepped outside, closed the door, and a shower of pink glass exploded into the foyer.

* * *

Her impulse was to run straight down the stairs and out the front door, gone, never here, right now, *do it*. But she hesitated. She'd forgotten her handbag, goddamn it, not thinking, in the bathroom and knew she couldn't leave it, her name on credit cards, her driver's license . . . She shouldn't be here. She didn't want to come in the first place. She was here but didn't want to see what was in the living room. If she didn't know what happened—what Montez *knew*, standing at the bedroom door, was about to happen . . .

He came out of the hallway to the foyer, turned and looked up, sensing her or seeing her through the balusters and it was too late to run. She got to her feet and waited as he came up the stairway.

Montez saying, "That nigga was an ugly motherfucker, huh? At first I thought he had on a ski mask. You saw him, didn't you?"

Kelly hesitated.

And Montez said, "Be careful what you say, girl. What happened, I was standing right where you are. Came out here when I heard the shots. Saw him down there, yelled at him I had a gun and he took off out the door. You didn't see the nigga, you still in the room. Understand? But that's what happened." He held out his hand to her saying, "Come on, I want to show you something," took Chloe's coat from her and draped it over the stair rail.

They went down to the living room, Montez talking, telling her, "I want you look at your friend, help you understand the kind of situation you're in. See what can happen you don't do what I tell you. You get sick, you clean it up, hear?" Crossing the living room he stopped halfway to the chair and turned her to face him.

"You know what you gonna see, Mr. Paradise and your friend Kelly sitting there dead."

She said, "I'm Kelly," reacting, not thinking.

And Montez said, "Uh-unh, you're Chloe."

He brought her upstairs again to the bedroom, the lamp still on. Kelly went in the bathroom to get her cigarettes and lighter, needing something to hold on to, Montez saying, "Come out here. Before I make the call, me and you gonna have an understanding."

"You knew," Kelly said, "standing by the door."

"I knew the old man's time had come—Jesus, finally. Your friend, y'all had come yesterday like you suppose to she'd still be alive. That nigga, the home invader, he sees her with the man, she's a witness. It's too bad but it's how it is. Wrong place at the wrong time."

"Chloe," Kelly said. "Why can't you say her name?"

"I told you, you're Chloe. It's your name till we finish some business. Go sit over there and don't think about nothing while I'm talking to you." His voice eased as he said, "You keep seeing her, huh? Knowing it could be you down there." He said, "Don't move, I'll be right back."

He had brought her across the living room to stand in front of the chair and the shock of what she saw turned her head. His hand clamped on the back of her neck, forcing her to look, and this time she gave herself up to the sight of Chloe's body. She didn't look at the old man. She stared at Chloe. With the blood, the eye makeup, it didn't look like Chloe, but it was and Kelly had to take a breath and another one, inhale and breathe slowly, compose herself and accept the sight of Chloe dead. Just that right now, nothing else. She reached for the hem of Chloe's skirt to pull it down. Montez said, "Uh-unh," caught her hand and told her to leave it be.

He came back in the bedroom with a bong, stopped to light it and suck up the smoke, the pipe bubbling in its quiet way. He loaded it again with a pinch of weed from a baggie, lit the pipe, covered the hole with his thumb and extended the bong. Kelly put her mouth over the top and inhaled the smoke swirling in the glass tube. Montez said, "One more," and lit it again. Kelly took another hit, not saying a word, and he placed the bong on the dresser.

He said, "You realize that coin flip saved your life? Man, I was thinking fast how to keep Chloe from being in the chair with him. He makes that remark, how he tries to treat me with respect but I'm never satisfied? Meaning I wasn't kissing his old wrinkled white ass no more? That's when I said to myself, let it play out. Let some ugly brother bust in and shoot the motherfucker."

She didn't argue with him, she was careful saying, "You wanted Chloe knowing the old man was leaving her something."

"That I'd help her get," Montez said. "She told you about that, huh? Good, it saves me some explaining."

"In a bank deposit box," Kelly said.

"She tell you what bank?"

"No, or what's in the box."

"We'll keep it that way till the time comes. Gonna have to work it out with you, give you a cut for being Chloe."

"What's it worth?"

"The man said a million six."

"That's all?"

"A long time ago a million six, the way I understand it. See, and the amount keeps going up."

"Chloe said it was life insurance."

"Chloe didn't know shit. See, the box is in my name and the old man's. He's gone, now it's just in mine. Day after tomorrow I get what's in there and bring it to you."

"It's stock," Kelly said.

"You want to believe that, go ahead."

The confidence in his voice made her want to hit him with something heavy or kick him in the crotch, and it gave her energy, an attitude to hold on to, Kelly telling herself, You're smarter than he is. Use your head and get out of here.

She said, "You're crazy if you think I'll help you."

"Uh-unh, I'm desperate, so I know you will."

"I'm not Chloe. Anyone can see that."

"You close. We keep the police confused long enough, we home. You live with her, find her signature on something and learn to write it."

"Get another girl."

"It has to be you," Montez said, almost singing it, "no other will do."

Kelly walked to the chair by the window and saw her reflection against a dismal view of trees and shrubbery in different shades of darkness.

Sitting down she said, "I won't help you," and saw Montez appear on the glass pane, his face, and felt his hands on her shoulders.

"Come on now, you know what bullet holes look like. You say okay you gonna do it, but then tell the police you aren't who I say you are? I bet that ugly motherfucker be waiting for you some night you come home. Won't say nothing to you, just shoots you in the head. You might not even see him and you're gone. Understand what I'm saying? I ain't asking do you want to do it, you already in, girl. Now sit down like I told you."

She eased lower into the chair wrapping her coat around her bare legs, a cigarette between her lips. Montez came over with the ashtray and dropped it in her lap saying, "You don't want to burn your nice coat, do you?" Saying, "I want you to get inside your head, tell yourself, yeah, I'm Chloe. Start playing the role, babe. You in there being her when the police ask what happened and who's this girl Kelly you live with, and they realize the sight of it, your friend lying in her blood dead, musta left you fucked up, like you're in shock. Understand?"

For a little while the room was quiet. She felt protected in her wool coat, Kelly sitting low between the chair's round arms lighting another cigarette, Montez by the dresser now to fire up the bong and get into his role.

He wanted her to work it out in her head who she was. But the weed and the alexanders were giving her a buzz, enough to boost her confidence, getting it up to where she could tell herself she was okay. Be herself and not think of Chloe in the chair. She was never self-conscious, in panties, thongs, whatever they put on her. She knew how to pose, how to get attitudes in her eyes. She was Kelly Barr and saw no reason, really, to become someone else.

He wasn't going to kill her.

He needed her.

She turned to look across the room.

"They're gonna smell that."

"Babe, homicide, they don't bother with dope. Where your handbags?"

"In the bathroom."

He got the bags, came back to the bedroom and held them up, both Vuittons. "Which is yours?"

"The black one."

Montez set them both on the bed, opened the one Kelly said was hers, brought out the wallet, looked at the driver's license inside and said, "This is Kelly's. Don't you know your bag from hers? You don't get it straight who you are, girl,

I'm gonna put you facedown on the floor and stomp on your head. Goodbye nose. Goodbye teeth." He picked up Chloe's bag, looked in it and tossed the bag to land in Kelly's lap. "There all your things, your credit cards, your keys. Look in there and find out who you are. Learn what you don't know about yourself. Little Kelly's bag goes downstairs." Montez said then, "Was something I wanted to ask you . . . Yeah. You know if Kelly's ever been fingerprinted?"

"Have I?"

"I said Kelly."

She shook her head. "No."

"Never was ever picked up and printed?"

"You mean arrested? For what?"

"Hookin', being a ho. You never was busted?"

"I'm not a whore, you moron, I'm a fashion model."

"What they call theirselves, except the ones on the street. They selling ass and want you to know it. Listen, the police gonna ask who's this Kelly with the man, hardly any clothes on, showing herself, they can *see* she's a ho. I say yeah, but high class, you understand, or Mr. Paradise wouldn't have nothing to do with her. You both ho's, keep it simple in my mind."

Kelly said, "You know it'll be in the paper."

"Yeah, I guess, and on the TV."

"Pictures of the famous lawyer and the prostitute. They'll find out soon enough it's Chloe. But while they're still thinking it's me . . ."

"What?"

"They'll call my dad."

"He live here?"

"In Florida, he's retired. He'll have to come up to arrange the funeral. He was just here yesterday."

Montez said, "Hmmmmm."

"You didn't think of that, did you?"

"All I been doing is thinking since he flipped the fuckin coin. If I'd known you two were coming tonight . . . See, but nobody told me." He was behind the chair again looking at himself in the window before he said, "Okay," like he was starting over. "The police gonna want to know all about little Kelly. Gonna ask you what she was like. She have a boyfriend was jealous? A pimp was angry at her for something? You don't know much about her, nothing of her family, where they might be at."

"Or her brother," Kelly said, "who'd beat the shit out of you?"

Montez grabbed a handful of her spiked hair and pulled her straight up in the chair, Kelly's hands on the chair arms, gasping until he let go.

"You don't know nothing will help them,"

Montez said, "and I don't either. Kelly? Chloe? Shit, I get 'em mixed up all the time. Names sound the same—you look enough alike it give me the idea."

"We're not exactly twins," Kelly said.

"You got the same hair, the same cute nose— you confuse me, you gonna confuse the police." Montez patted her on the head. "Babe, all I need is time to visit the bank and take this fuckin lawyer suit off and act my age. The time I got brought up for assaulting police officers the man represented me free of charge, put me in a cheap suit of clothes, laid a Bible on the table I read while he argued my case and showed I'd been intimidated. Set up, the man looking for a lawsuit. He got me off and I went to work for him, not knowing I'd become his monkey he dressed up and I'd perform as his cool number one and pimp for him. Understand, he's already paid for what's in the deposit box. What happens nobody claims it, the bank keeps it?"

"So it's okay to take it," Kelly said.

"I'm giving you a way to look at it," Montez said. "The man's not out anything he isn't already out. Understand? See, but now I got to get hold of it quick."

"Like the guy told you," Kelly said, feeling her buzz, "you've got two days, Smoke."

Montez said, "Uh-oh," stared at her and said, "Letting me know you can be a cool little bitch when you feel like it. But see, what you have to remember, we partners now. We don't come through we both get shot in the head."

After the cop with the tobacco breath left—it made her think of her dad—she sat staring at her reflection in the window, a little girl wrapped in her coat. Lost. Alone. She wished she had another alexander. Boy, they were good. She saw herself talking to the cop in that dumb, numb voice playing Chloe in shock. Looked at it the way she would study a proof sheet of poses and thought:

Are you nuts?

A black dude in a pinstriped suit tells you to act like you're in shock, never having ever seen anyone in shock before, and you do it. In front of a no-bullshit cop, not an ounce of sympathy in him, a gun on his belt, handcuffs—

Are you fucking nuts?

She turned halfway around in the chair to look past the back cushion to the doorway. Now there were two black women in the hall, the one in uniform and the other one, older, good-looking hair, very natural, in a long, dark quilted coat and red scarf that wasn't bad. Kelly said, "Excuse me, but what happens now?"

The older one, in her forties, stepped to the doorway and said, "You over your shock?"

"I feel a little better. I don't suppose I could go downstairs."

"Why you want to do that?"

"I want to go home."

"We can take you to 1300, police headquarters, talk to you there."

"Jesus Christ, you think I shot my best friend?"

"And your boyfriend?"

"The old man? This is the first time I've ever *been* here. I met him tonight." Getting a little frantic. She told herself to be cool, and said, "I have no idea what the fuck happened. Okay?"

The woman in the long quilted coat came in the room now saying, "I'm Sergeant Michaels. Why don't we turn your chair around and I'll sit on the bed?"

Kelly said, getting up and starting to move the chair, "Have you talked to Montez yet?"

"We talking to everybody," Jackie Michaels said, helping her with the chair. "The first thing I want to get straight, Chloe, are you a prostitute?"

DELSA STOOD IN THE DOORWAY. HE TURNED ON
the overhead light. The girl in the chair, facing
him, looked up with her Halloween eyes and they
stared at each other until Jackie came out to the
hall and closed the door.

"Frank, that girl's no more in shock than I am.
She's stoned. Musta toked her way out of her
condition. You can smell it out here."

"You feel her up?"

"I lifted her mini."

"Yeah . . . ?"

"She has on a pair of bikinis I couldn't of got
into when I was ten years old. She ask me what I
was looking for. I told her a gun. I went right at
her and she got a little excited, but just for a
minute. It was like she caught herself and turned

it off. She seems alert, then acts a little goofy, like maybe she's stoned."

"Maybe she's pretending."

"Well, at times she seems over the top, if you know what I mean. You wonder if she's acting."

"She a hooker?"

"She says no, and never was. You're gonna like her, Frank."

Alex, the evidence tech, came along the hall with his camera and his kit. Delsa said, "Let's get it out of the way," and brought Alex in with him.

She was standing now, hands on her coat draped over the back of the chair. She looked around and said, "I didn't expect to be searched."

"Now you're having your picture taken. Miss Robinette, I'm Sergeant Frank Delsa, with Homicide. I'm sorry about your friends."

She said, "Only one was a friend," and looked at Alex. "Can I wash up first?"

"After," Delsa said. "We'd like to get you the way you are, part of the scene, the two of you dressed alike."

"Not quite."

"Were you topless, earlier?"

"No, I wasn't."

"Had your underwear on?"

The ceiling light went off.

Alex, his hand on the switch, said, "This is better. Five minutes, I'll be out of the way." He motioned to the girl and Delsa watched her cross from the chair to the dresser. Bare legs and sneakers, the sweatshirt covering her skirt. He watched her take her spot and look at the camera over her shoulder, knowing how to do it.

She said to Alex, "Like this?"

"I could sell that one," Alex said. "What I need is a straight front view, arms at your sides." He got ready to shoot and lowered the camera. "Frank, the bong. It's up to you."

Kelly stepped to the side. "How's this?"

Alex raised the camera again. He said, "That's good," snicked off three exposures and said to his model, "You have any tattoos?" She shook her head. "Then that's it."

"Why don't you do the bathroom," Delsa said, "and a G.S.R. test on her as long as you're here."

She was getting a pack of cigarettes from her coat.

"What's G.S.R.?"

"Gunshot Residue," Delsa said.

"You guys are serious, aren't you?"

"Step in the bathroom and Alex'll take care of it."

She lit her cigarette and then stood listening as Alex said, "I've been meaning to ask you, Frank,

if you watch any of the crime scene shows, like
CSI. All this time I thought we worked for you.
No, I see Homicide works for the techs."

"I saw one," Delsa said, "but I never took
chemistry so I didn't know what was going on."

"I watch them," the girl said. "I think they're
great."

Alex gone, the weird-looking cheerleader back in
her chair, Delsa came over to stand by the bed.

"Where were we?"

"You wanted to know if I was wearing panties.
No, you said underwear."

"Were you?"

"Yes, I was."

"The whole time?"

"What whole time?"

"When you were doing the cheerleading."

"I'd jump up as we finished one and Mr. Paradiso would say, 'I see London, I see France . . .' "

"What'd he say when your friend jumped up?"

She drew on her cigarette before saying,
"What's your point?"

"You call him Mr. Paradiso?"

"I don't think I called him anything."

"You're one of his girlfriends, aren't you?"

"No, I'm not."

"Are you a prostitute?"

"No."

"An escort?"

"What's the difference?"

"Was Kelly?"

"A hooker? No."

"Montez says you both are."

"You believe him?"

"I can find out if it's true. Have you ever been arrested?"

She said, "For what, being a ho?"

And kept staring at him through her makeup.

"I don't get it," Delsa said. "You're playing with me?"

"I thought you might think it was funny."

"Your friend's dead and you want to entertain me?"

She said, "I don't know what I want."

"Are you stoned?"

"I've had three drinks, good ones, crème de cocoa and gin, and a couple of hits on the bong. I'm trying to be careful and sound normal at the same time. I've got a buzz that makes me talkative, so right now I have to watch my step."

He said, "What're you trying to tell me?"

She said, "I'm not sure, Frank. I'm feeling my way along."

It stopped him, the way she said his name so easily. He waited a moment before saying, "You saw the guy who did it."

"I don't know."

"You saw him or you didn't."

"I'm not ready to talk about it."

"Montez says it was a black guy."

She smoked her cigarette.

"Was he?"

"I'm not saying any more."

"You want a lawyer?"

"I want to go home."

"You saw your friend—how're you handling that?"

She said, "How do you think?" Picked the ashtray up from her lap and stubbed out the cigarette. "Can I wash my face now?"

"If you leave the door open."

She said, "I'm not gonna kill myself, Frank. I have to pee."

He watched her walk around the bed to the bathroom, then glance back at him as she went in and closed the door.

Delsa picked up her handbag from the bed and brought it close to the lamp to look at her Michigan Operator License: Chloe Robinette, 6-12-1976, F, 5-8, BLU, Type O, Restrictions: Corrective Lens, a pair of glasses in the bag, an

American Express credit card, several other cards, all platinum; a blue bandana; a packet of condoms; cologne, hand cream, lipstick, blush-on; four hundred-dollar bills, eight fifties and five twenties folded in a silver money clip; loose fives and ones in a pocket; sales receipts from Saks, a hairbrush, a cell phone, a ring of keys. He looked at the photo on the license again that said this was Chloe Robinette. He looked closely at the eyes, the long blond hair. He looked at the bath-room door as it opened. She stood in the light, cream on her face, hair wrapped in a towel, still wearing the skirt but not the sweatshirt, a thin white bra covering her breasts.

"Could I have the bag, please?"

Delsa stepped to the doorway, the operator li-cense still in his hand. They looked at each other. He didn't say anything. She took the brown Vuit-ton bag from him and closed the door.

He sat at the dining room table going through Kelly's handbag, identical to Chloe's exccept it was black.

Michigan Operator License: Kelly Ann Barr, 9-11-1976, F, 5-8, BLU, Type A, no restrictions, sunglasses in the bag, an ATM card, Visa, Saks, Neiman Marcus, Marshall Field's, the Detroit Zoo, Detroit Public Library, AT&T, Blockbuster, more cards than Chloe carried, but not anywhere near as much cash, eighty dollars in the wallet, loose change in a pocket, keys. No condoms.

He brought Chloe's operator license from his pocket and laid it on the table next to Kelly's, both laminated plastic cards.

Here, tonight, both girls had the same mess of semi-spiked hair, and both were blond, right? In real life?

But in the license photos Kelly had light-brown hair that flipped up, and Chloe's was long and blond. The photos, taken two years ago according to the license expiration dates, could be of the same girl wearing different wigs.

He studied the photos again side by side. Good shots for driver's license I.D.'s. Or these two couldn't take a bad picture.

He looked at Kelly.

He looked at Chloe.

He looked at Kelly again and remained staring at her eyes. They looked alike when you weren't looking at them together. But Kelly's expression was more appealing to him, something familiar in her eyes he didn't see in Chloe's and it made him think of the Halloween eyes upstairs, eyes peering out from all that makeup, watching him with a quiet expression . . . The same eyes he saw when the bathroom door opened, cream covering her face but there were her eyes.

Delsa picked up both plastic cards from the table and went into the living room where an M.E. investigator, Valentino Trabucci, at one time with Homicide, an older guy in a jacket and wool shirt was taking pictures of the victims.

He said, "What've you got, Frank, anything?"

"Cause and manner."

"I think we're pretty clear on that."

"Otherwise they're lying to me, as usual."

Val Trabucci said, "That busted-in front door is bullshit. I hope you made a note of it."

"First thing," Delsa said.

"The one I like is Montez Taylor. If he didn't do these two he opened the fuckin door."

"Montez said he saw the guy."

"One guy, alone?"

"That's all, running out of the house."

"Take Montez back to 1300 and beat it out of him."

Delsa handed him Kelly's operator license.

"Tell me what you think."

Val looked from the photo to the girl covered in her blood. "This is the same girl?"

"Kelly Barr."

"If you say so."

Delsa handed him Chloe's license.

Val made the comparison and said, "I could go either way, Frank."

"Can't nail it down for me?"

"I don't have to. We'll print her, locate family . . ."

Delsa said, "Val, you want to call the old man's son?"

"That's one I won't mind doing," Val said. "I imagine you want the bodies out of here first."

"We'd appreciate it," Delsa said.

Val handed over the plastic cards. He said, "I'll have the removal service come in," and walked away.

Now Delsa looked at the two license photos close to the dead girl's face. The eyes closed, she could be either one.

Harris came along leading their boss like they were on a tour of the scene: Inspector Wendell Robinson, his trench coat hanging open over a sweater, and wearing his beige Kangol. Most of the time the man wore a good-looking suit and tie, a Kangol to match, their dude leader, cool mustache, tall, slim, Richard Harris' idol. Every detective at 1300 called him Wendell.

"Frank, you see Val Trabucci?"

"He was just here."

"He tell you who did it?"

"Said Montez Taylor's in it one way or another."

"Write it down. Val came to me from the Bomb Squad fifteen years ago, I was lieutenant of Seven. I never saw a homicide investigator trust his gut as much as Val did. Like you, Frank, only you're quieter about it, put it all together in your head first. Val burned himself out. I told him, go on over to the M.E.'s office, be a death investigator and take it easy. Like being on the job only the hours are better, you have more time to read the paper. You know why he quit the Bomb Squad? His girlfriend was afraid he'd get his hands blown off he's taking some device apart, and she'd have to tend to him he goes to the toilet. I had another guy quit the Bomb Squad for the same reason."

Wendell Robinson turned to the victims.

"Frank, did you flip this girl's skirt up?"

"Somebody did, before any of us got here."

"You think she's been poked?"

"We'll have to wait and see."

"It's sure eye-catching, exposed like that. Richard's been filling me in," Wendell said. "So who did it? Come on, Frank, you must've been here an hour by now."

Delsa handed him the two plastic cards.

"I want to know who's dead first."

Wendell took his time looking from the photos to the dead girl. "I thought she was Kelly Barr?"

"According to Montez. But which one do you say she is, from the photos?"

"I could go either way."

"That's what Val said."

"What about the houseman, Uncle Ben?"

"He goes along with Montez."

"Why would he say it's Kelly if it's Chloe? You got the other girl upstairs. Didn't she tell you she's Chloe?"

"If you're supposed to believe this one's Kelly, you assume the other one's Chloe."

"Frank, I didn't think you assume anything."

"I said, 'Miss Robinette?' She didn't say no, I'm Kelly. I asked if they were prostitutes. She says no, but without acting insulted. I asked if she was one of Paradiso's girlfriends. No."

"Wait now," Harris said. "Lloyd the houseman says Chloe's the regular girlfriend. Kelly, he's not sure he's seen her before tonight. They been other cheerleaders come with Chloe. I put it to Montez, 'These two come here much?' Says whenever Mr. Paradise wants their company. Then how come Lloyd isn't sure about Kelly? Montez says he's old, can't remember shit. Or Lloyd goes to bed before they get here."

"You need to sit this Montez down," Wendell said. "Find out what he gets out of this man being dead. Montez is your focus, and it sounds like he's telling you anything he wants. Says both girls are hookers. The one upstairs says they aren't." Wendell turned to the chair. "If this one didn't sell it, she was sure a fun-loving little girl, huh? You ever see a bush like that wasn't in a garden?" He turned to Delsa. "The one upstairs have her drawers on?"

"Panties and bra," Delsa said. "Montez says she's in shock. Dermot Cleary, first on the scene, thinks so too. Jackie Michaels was with her a few minutes, says she never was in shock. She might've put it on for Dermot so she wouldn't have to talk to him."

Wendell lifted his beige cap and placed it on his head again, loose, low in front. "She act straight with you?"

"Montez fixed her a bong, he said to settle her down. And she's got a buzz on from drinking."

"She a mess?"

"She knows she's half in the bag, talkative, so she's trying to hold herself down. Jackie thought she was a little goofy. I think she's scared to death and using the buzz to cover it up. Like trying to be funny with her friend dead, right downstairs. She knows how it happened or has a pretty good idea, or saw something that ties in Montez Taylor, this guy with fuckin egg all over his face. I think he got to her, warned her to keep her mouth shut."

Wendell was nodding.

"Because if she didn't know anything," Delsa said, "she'd still be scared, but she'd be telling us what it was like seeing her friend dead, how it affected her and go on about that. This girl's watching her step."

"Being threatened could be enough," Wendell said. "You gonna house Montez tonight?"

"I'd rather ask him to stop by in the morning," Delsa said. "Let him stroll in thinking he's a friendly witness, then jump him."

"It's your case," Wendell said.

"The other thing," Delsa said. "I don't want this girl identified in our statement. Not till the one upstairs tells me who she is."

The uniform, leaning against the wall opposite the open bedroom door, straightened as Delsa came along the hall. Her coat was open and she hooked her thumbs in her gunbelt.

Delsa stopped. "You think the girl in there could be a hooker?"

"What, you mean by looking at her? I'll say yeah, she could, without ever seeing any like her in the Seventh."

"What about the girl downstairs?"

"Well, yeah, the way somebody left her, but

you still can't tell for sure. Good girls fuck, too, don't they?"

Delsa sent the uniform downstairs and stepped in the bedroom to see the one who was supposed to be Chloe sitting on the side of the bed smoking a cigarette, light from the bathroom in her hair, soft-looking, no longer spiked, her face in lamplight, the mask of makeup gone, a different girl looking up at him, but with eyes he recognized.

"More questions, Frank?"

He believed he could get used to that.

He shook his head.

"I'm taking you home."

THE WAY IT WORKED, A CONTRACT WOULD FALL
into Avern Cohn's lap and he'd put Carl Fontana
and Art Krupa on it.

Avern was one of those Clinton Street lawyers
who hung out at the Frank Murphy and picked
up criminal cases assigned by the court—where
he first met Fontana and Krupa on separate
homicide arraignments. Avern called himself their
agent and took 20 percent off the top of fifty
thousand, the minimum he charged for a professional hit. The people who wanted somebody
taken out could afford it, all of them in the drug
business. Fifty grand was what, the wholesale
price of two and a half keys to get rid of compe-
tition or pay somebody back.

At one of the early meetings when they dis-
cussed the deal, having drinks at the Caucus

Club, Fontana said, "I thought agents only got ten percent."

Avern said, "What we'll be doing isn't exactly show business. You walk in where I tell you the guy will be, shoot him or throw him out a window and collect the balance, your twenty grand each. What I have to do for half that much is find you the job. I can't advertise, can I? Like I'm one of those personal injury fuckheads. I can't appeal to the little housewife whose husband beats her up every time he gets drunk. And she can't run an ad in the Help Wanted. So I have to deal with people who shoot each other."

It answered Art Krupa's question, why Avern didn't get jobs from ordinary people who wanted somebody whacked. Art said, "But they're out there. Carl knows one."

"Yeah, my wife Connie," Fontana said. "She happens to come to you, turn her the fuck down."

Avern loved these guys he had brought together. They never saw a problem with a job. Walk in Baby Sister's Kitchen, pop the guy eating his farm-raised catfish and walk out. Pop the guy's bodyguard while they're at it. They didn't do drugs to excess, and they were both racist enough to feel more than comfortable about taking out black guys and ethnics, like Chicanos and Chaldeans.

Avern had represented Carl Fontana for killing a man with a slug barrel mounted on his Remington. What happened: this guy Carl knew from church shot a deer up by Northville. It was out of season so they left right away, brought the deer to the guy's house and hung it on the garage over a washtub. They drank a bottle of Jim Beam while the deer bled out. Carl's statement: "Here's this guy doesn't know shit about dressing a buck, he's hacking at it with this big fuckin Bowie knife. All I said to him was, 'You don't cut the steaks till you have him dressed out, asshole,' and he come at me with the knife."

Not a week later Avern represented Art Krupa for the fatal shooting of a black guy during an argument—in a Seven Mile bar on Martin Luther King Day. Krupa was connected to the Outfit at the time, collecting street taxes from bookmakers, but the shooting had nothing to do with his job. Krupa said it was just one of those things. "I had no intention of taking the smoke out when we started talking. The guy must've been offended by something I said about Dr. King, broke off a beer bottle and I had no choice."

Manslaughter with a firearm could get them each fifteen years. Avern worked a deal: they drew the Southern Michigan Prison at Jackson, Fontana forty-two months, Krupa, forty.

While they were down a client came to Avern complaining about drive-bys fucking up his business. "Man, nobody wants to walk in a crack house all shot up." Avern thinking about a professional hit man service: relieve the client, who'd be an immediate suspect, from being involved. Hire bad guys to hit bad guys. Why not? Contracts without contracts. He could reach in his files not even looking and pull out shooters, but they were mostly all kids, gangbangers, hard to control. He thought of Carl and Art, both at Jackson in D Block, grown men, white, unaffiliated. Not big guys but tough monkeys, both of them. He'd tell them to look each other up, and if they hit it off come see him, he had something for them.

Carl Fontana was fifty-two, five-seven, wiry, losing his sandy hair, a bricklayer who hated doing patios with designs to figure out. But thirty years ago in Vietnam Carl was a tunnel rat, his size getting him the job. Crawl into a hole with a .45 and a flashlight. Carl said, "I can't tell you how fuckin scary it was." But he did it, he went in. He came home and did county time for raising hell, a couple of aggravated assaults, before settling down with the bricks. Carl told Avern you didn't just lay 'em one on top the other, each brick was different.

Arthur Krupa, forty-eight, five-nine, stocky, came out of high school wanting to be a gangster or a movie star who played gangsters. He didn't know anybody in Hollywood, but had an uncle who was connected. Art pulled a store burglary to prove himself and his uncle got him in. But, Jesus, it was boring collecting from the books, have to listen to 'em bitch and call him names in foreign tongues. Art thought he looked like John Gotti, but no one else did.

That time at the Caucus Club Avern ordered another round the same way, martini with anchovy olives, a couple of Molsons with shots of Crown Royal on the side. These guys were blue-collar down to their white socks.

Avern said, "If I can get you five a year that's a hundred grand each. But five might not be possible. You're gonna have leisure time in between. You might want to look into home invasions, see if you like it."

Art said, "I've done it."

Avern said, "You'll be shooting criminals if you need to think about it."

Art said, "I 'magine mostly smokes."

Avern said, "You don't see a problem picking up guns?"

Art said, "In this town?"

Avern said, "Barbra Streisand sang here at the

Caucus when she was eighteen years old." Avern was sixty-one, active in a theater group. "I remember her doing 'Happy Days Are Here Again' real slow."

They'd been in business now a year and a half, five home invasions that paid okay, but only four hits. They blew another one trying to pop the guy in his car, firing at him doing sixty up Gratiot and the fucker spun out of control and got hit by a truck. They had a shotgun now for when they'd try him again. The hits were three black guys— first you had to find the fuckers, never where Avern said to look—and a Chaldean drug dealer who owned a gas station/convenience store. There were a bunch of Chaldeans in Southfield, Carl said, from Iraq, towelheads but they weren't Muslims. Art had dealt with Chaldean bookies. He said what's the difference, a fuckin towelhead's a towelhead.

Avern told them about the next hit saying it would be the easiest one yet. "The front door's unlocked. Walk in and shoot the old man and walk out. Make it look like you broke in. The houseman, Lloyd, will be in bed. Montez, the contractor"—Avern no longer called the one paying for the hit a client—"lives there but won't be around. He says he'll pay you in two days, meet you at a motel on Woodward." Avern saying, "I got the name of it here someplace."

They were in Avern's office on the twentieth floor of the Penobscot Building, drawings of old guys in wigs and robes on the wall behind him, like cartoons but weren't funny. Carl watched him looking for the note on his desk and asked why this Montez couldn't have the money ready, at the time.

"I just told you he won't be around, doesn't want it to look like he's involved in any way." Avern said, "Here it is," and handed the note across the desk to Art. "The University Inn, near Wayne."

"This Montez isn't a dealer," Carl said, "but can put his hands on forty grand, cash?"

"Don't worry about it."

"Yeah, well, you're all set," Carl said. "How'd he know you could get this done for him?"

"I'd see Montez at Randy's, different places. When he was a kid I used to represent him at Frank Murphy arraignments, get him a plea deal. Now we have a drink and talk. He asks my advice about things, his future."

"He ask you how to get his boss knocked off?"

Carl felt Avern was holding back, not telling the whole story. He listened to Avern saying the old man was feeble, incontinent. Changing his diapers, feeding him, had become a full-time job. "The old man wanted Montez to whack him, put him out of his misery, but Montez couldn't do it. He was ready to die, so Montez agreed to find somebody. I accept that as his reason," Avern said, "and thought, why not help out, make a few bucks."

Art said, "Come on, let's go."

Carl said, "Montez is getting something out of this."

Avern said, "Well, yeah, he's in the old guy's will. He must be."

But didn't say a word about a girl sitting in the chair with him topless, her jugs and her face painted.

From the start Carl had a bad feeling about this one. First listening to Avern making it look simple, and now in the Anchor Bar, talking to Connie on the phone till she hung up on him. Going back to the table, Art sitting there with a rum and Diet Coke watching the hockey game on TV, Carl wanted to blame Connie for how he felt.

Art said, "Fuckin Wings, man. Yzerman scored, they're up four two over the Rangers."

Carl sat down and picked up his Seven and Seven. "I got two calls, but she won't tell me who they were."

"Connie?"

"I told her I'd drop off a bottle of vodka and I forgot. She goes, 'You don't do nothing for me, I don't do nothing for you.' "

Art said, "She's got a car, for Christ sake."

"They took her license again, third D.U.I. in the last year and a half. I tell her, 'Jesus Christ, can't you drink without getting smashed every time?' She goes, 'What would be the point?' "

"It might've been Avern," Art said. "You want to call him?"

"He won't be there," Carl said.

Art brought his watch up to find some light in this joint and raised his face to look at it, his hair combed back like John Gotti's, no part in a full head starting to turn gray. "You ready?"

Carl lit a cigarette. He picked up his drink saying, "This old man isn't a criminal. Avern said we'd be shooting bad guys."

"We get in there," Art said, "check the liquor cabinet, pick up a bottle of vodka. We could look around some, see if there's anything we like."

"I'd just as soon go in and get out," Carl said.

Art said, "You aren't in the mood now, are you? Any time you talk to her you tighten up. You have to explain to me sometime why you don't fuckin walk out on her. Connie, you *know*, 'cause I heard you say it, isn't even that good-looking. The only thing she's got going for her is that red fuckin hair, man, the way she fixes it. You stay at my place more'n you stay with her." Art checked his glass, rattling the ice.

"Let's go do it."

They took Fontana's red Chevy Tahoe across downtown to the parking lot behind Harmonie Park. On the way back to pick it up they'd stop in Intermezzo right there and have a few to unwind. They walked up to Madison and then east a short way to the Michigan Opera Theatre and stood on the empty sidewalk smoking cigarettes pinched between the fingers of their black kidskin gloves, waiting for the performance to let out.

Art said, "*Tales of Hoffman,*" looking at the poster. "You ever see one?"

"What?"

"An opera."

Carl said no and that covered the subject.

"They're starting to come out," Art said. "Hey, but if you rather boost one it's okay with me."

Carl said, "This is too fuckin easy."

They put their hands in the pockets of their black raincoats and walked around to the side of the opera house where attendants were bringing cars to people coming out from the cashier's window inside. Carl and Art stood among the dressed-up operagoers in the dark, Art with a five ready, watching headlights coming along in two lanes bumper to bumper, the attendants in jackets and gloves in a hurry, keeping 'em coming. An attendant got out of a white Chrysler to stand waiting, holding the door open, looking at the crowd through the mist of his breath. Art said, "There it is," and they stepped out of the crowd. Art handed the attendant the five and got in behind the wheel. Carl strolled around to the other side. Once they were out of there, working through downtown south to Jefferson Avenue, they brought Detroit Tigers baseball caps from their raincoat pockets and put them on—the Tigers road caps with the olde English *D* in orange—Art looking at the mirror to set his just right.

They were quiet now coming to the house on Iroquois lit up with spots, no way to miss it. They'd checked it out earlier. Art pulled into the drive, right up to the door and cut the lights. They sat there not talking. Now they brought out semi-automatics and racked the slide to put a load in the chamber, Carl's a Smith & Wesson, Art's a Sig Sauer. They were told the old man would be in his bedroom upstairs, end of the hall, if he wasn't downstairs somewhere. Avern guaranteed he'd be alone.

Still not saying anything they got out of the car and went in, the door unlocked, and heard the

TV on in the living room, directly ahead of them, a big chair facing the set. They crossed the room to come up on either side of the chair.

The blond sitting with the old man was topless, her jugs and her face painted, looked up at them holding guns, but didn't scream or freak or anything. She said to the old man, "Friends of yours?"

The old man squinted at them like he was thinking. Are they? But then, trying to sound tough, in charge, he said, "Take what you want and get the hell out of here." He said, "I don't have a safe, so don't waste your time looking for one," the old man not sounding at all feeble; he knew what was going on.

Carl pointed his Smith at the old man, shot him in the chest and shot him in the head.

It caused the blond girl to suck in her breath, a hard gasp, and sit rigid, her painted eyes wide open—Carl and Art watching—now her mouth opened and she was touching the tip of her tongue to her lips, reached down to bring her skirt up, exposing herself—Carl and Art watching—and said, "You fellas aren't mad at me, are you?"

Art shot her.

Hit her just above her breasts and in the center of her forehead. He stooped to pick up his casings and then felt around till he had Carl's. Art stood up hearing cheers, crowd noise, coming from the TV and took a look at the football game that was on. He watched for a half minute, turned to Carl and saw him looking at the girl. "They're watching the Rose Bowl Michigan won," Art said. "Here, Washington State's on Michigan's twelve. Woodson's about to pick off a pass in the end zone, save the Wolverines' ass. I remember the game, I won a hunnert bucks." He turned to Carl again and said, "She's dead."

Carl could see that.

Art said, "You know I had to do it."

"I know."

"I was afraid if we started talking to her—"

"I know what you mean," Carl said.

"Man, she was cool," Art said. "I'd like to've known her. Sure as hell if we started talking to her . . ."

Carl turned from looking at her to see Art pointing his .40-caliber Sig at the hall.

At a dressed-up black dude saying, "Don't shoot, man, I'm the one paying you." Coming toward them now, his eyes on the chair till he reached it and was looking at his boss and the girl. His eyes closed and he said, "Oh, shit," sounding like a groan dragged out of him. He said, "You didn't have to," shaking his head now.

"I mean it, you could've let her go and she wouldn't of said one fuckin word. Man, you don't know what you did."

Art looked at Carl staring at Montez, Carl saying, "He was suppose to be alone."

"And you suppose to be where I can reach you," Montez said. "I call the number, this angry woman hangs up on me." He looked at the dead girl shaking his head again. "You blew it's what you did."

Carl raised his Smith, putting it in the guy's face.

"You want to fuck with us?"

Montez said, "You want to get paid?"

Art said, "You have it?"

Montez said, "You get it when you suppose to."

Art walked up to him raising the Sig Sauer in his right hand, got Montez looking at it and hit him in the face with a left hook, hard. It staggered Montez but didn't put him down. Art said, "You don't show up with it the day after tomorrow, Smoke, we'll find you."

Montez worked his jaw but didn't touch it with his hand, staring at them like he was deciding whether to stay in the game or get out. What he said was, "Go on take something, the silver, those old paintings, take *some*thing, anything you want."

Carl had that feeling again that bothered the hell out of him. "You want it to look like a robbery."

"A home invasion," Montez said, "that went bad. You come in thinking nobody's home—"

"Come in," Carl said, "and a fuckin party's going on. A surprise party. Nothing wrong with the old man. Has a broad with him. You show up in your pinstripe suit, start telling us what to do . . . Why you want him dead anyway?"

" 'Cause he's old, tired of his misery. You want the truth, it was his idea. Go out with a bang."

"I get old, I hope I'm this fuckin miserable," Carl said. "Watch a football game with a naked broad. What do you get out of this? You don't pay fifty grand to get hold of his suits."

"How about the next time," Montez said, "we skip the conversation. I hand you the money, you don't even have to thank me."

Carl wanted so bad to shoot him he had to keep the Smith stiff-armed at his side, telling himself to take it easy. The sound from the TV went off. He heard Art say, "Twenty-one sixteen," and then, "there's your vodka," and Carl grabbed it out of the ice bucket, a brand he'd never heard of.

Going out to the hall Art said, "I remember that Rose Bowl like it was last week, Michigan finally taking one."

Carl said, "I almost shot that jig."

"I know what you mean," Art said. "He sure has a mouth on him." At the door he aimed his piece at Montez, still in the living room, and reminded him of the day after tomorrow. Montez yelled at them to break the glass. Outside, Art smashed a pane with his gun and said to Carl, "You think the cops'll buy it?"

Carl said, "It ain't our problem."

DELSA SAID, "YOUR DRIVER'S LICENSE," HANDING
it to her in the foyer. They both had their coats
on now; he was taking her home.

She said thanks, but didn't look at it until
Delsa turned to the door as the uniformed cop,
the one who first questioned her upstairs, came in
from outside and she checked the license, Chloe's,
and slipped it into her coat pocket. She heard the
uniformed cop say now was a good time, the
chief had shown up and the TV crews were all
over him. Delsa told her to stay close to him.

They went out the door and walked past the
police cars in the drive to the street where video
cameras were aimed at the Chief of Police of the
City of Detroit and round black microphones
were held in front of him. Kelly said, "What's he
doing here?" Still feeling a confident buzz, talka-

tive. Delsa said he was making an appearance. Kelly said, "Yeah, but why?" Delsa said she'd have to ask the chief that one. They walked past the TV news trucks to a dark blue four-door facing this way. Delsa unlocked his door and she walked around to the other side and got in. They were quiet until Delsa turned onto Jefferson, heading toward downtown now. Kelly said, "It's not far." He said River Place. They were quiet until he turned toward the river. Coming to the complex of old buildings revamped, headlights on red brick walls and tall oval windows, he said the Stroh Brewery headquarters was right here. He said Stroh's used to be the most popular beer in town but he never cared for it much. "You want history?" Kelly said. "The building I'm in used to be Parke-Davis, where aspirin was first made. I could use a couple right now." Delsa said he was thinking of looking for an apartment downtown, closer to the job. Kelly said, "You have a family?" He said no. Then told her his wife had passed away. Kelly said, "Oh, I'm so sorry," and wanted to ask about her but wasn't sure how to do it. They stopped in front of her building and he said he'd like to go in with her, look at her friend's things if it was okay. Kelly said, "Of course." He said he needed to learn everything he could about her. She said, "Well, if

I can help . . ." She had to remind herself Frank Delsa was a homicide detective and quit thinking about his cool dark eyes and the quiet way he spoke. They got out of the car that was like an icebox, the heater still blowing cold air. Kelly opened Chloe's bag now to find the keys.

Her hand came out with all kinds of keys and a St. Christopher medal on a silver ring. She fingered through them wanting to see a front door key, please, that looked like hers. She found it, walked up to the entrance with him, put the key in the lock, tried to turn it . . . She said, "I must still be a little blitzed, I can't even pick the right key," and knew it was the wrong thing to say. Delsa waiting, watching her, Delsa saying why not let him try, and took the keys from her. He chose one, slipped it in the lock and opened the door. Kelly said, "Hey, you're good with keys." Sounding stupid and thinking, Keep your fucking mouth shut, okay? Jesus. They rode the elevator to the fourth level. In front of Kelly's door now he wanted to see if he could do it again. He unlocked the dead bolt, no problem; Kelly not exactly wide-eyed, more like the dumb girl watching. He tried two keys in the spring lock before the door opened. She said, "How do you do that?" Sounding amazed, still the dumb girl. She couldn't help it. He told her you try to match the key to the lock. "And if that doesn't work," Kelly said, "kick the door in?" He was a nice guy, he smiled. But then asked why she had so many keys. Yeah, well . . . "They seem to accumulate," Kelly said. "Two or three, I don't even remember what they're for. Well, I do—one's for the locker downstairs, but I don't store anything in it. Another one gets you up on the roof. There's a sundeck . . ." Talking to be talking, filling the silence as he watched her.

He held up the ring of keys and picked out the ones he had used. "This is your front door key, and these are for your apartment, your loft. Okay?"

Smiling again, still the nice guy.

But the smile this time telling her he knew who she was.

Then why didn't he come out and say it?

Delsa, in no hurry, wanted her to tell him.

He followed her into a brick foyer and along a hall of closets, doors to a study, a bathroom. She snapped a switch and track lighting came on over the living area. She said, "Both the bedrooms are over here. The kitchen's over there and everything else is in between."

Everything being whatever two girls with style and money wanted, half a basketball court in muted tones and splashes of bright color, plants and weird paintings, a soft look to the rumpled sofa, chairs with bamboo arms, bare windows in brick walls, red Orientals on the tan-painted concrete floor, a ficus that filled a corner and reached almost to the ductwork in the fifteen-foot ceiling, a round dining table with a slate top, an exercise bike, a tiled counter separating the kitchen. Delsa took it all in before his gaze returned to the dining table and the mail and magazines waiting there.

"You don't have a computer?"

"In the study."

He had to ask, "How much does a loft this size go for?" She told him four hundred, and he said, "Four hundred thousand?" even though he knew it was what she meant—for the corner of an old laboratory where they used to make aspirin. He said, "It's nice," nodding his head.

She said, "You live in the city?"

"Cops had to until a few years ago. I'm still here, on the east side." He walked over to the slate dining table.

"Which one of you owns the place?"

The table held a few magazines, a pile of catalogs, a Victoria's Secret, a few bills, a large black envelope, ten by twelve. He turned to see her with a bright expression, eyebrows raised as she worked on an answer that should be easy, but having a tough time being Chloe.

"Whose name is it in?"

She said, "Mine," right away this time.

"You hold the mortgage?"

Delsa waited.

She said, "It's paid for."

Delsa let it go. She was probably telling the truth. Chloe owned the place—not out of reach for a nine-hundred-an-hour call girl; he assumed that, too—and Kelly, who hadn't moved from that spot since they came in the loft, shared expenses.

He said, "You get a lot of mail, don't you?"

She said, "Mostly junk."

He picked up the Victoria's Secret catalog and showed her the cover. "Are you in here?"

She said, "Kelly is," and after a moment, "page sixteen."

Delsa found it and looked at the girl in the black bikini panties well below her hip bones, brown skin, no stomach. None.

She came over in her coat and looked at the page. She said, "Yeah," in a quiet voice, close to him, "that's Kelly. It was shot last summer."

Delsa leafed through the magazine—she was playing with him again, wanting him to see her—and stopped. He said, "Here's Kelly again. In her underwear. Wait a minute. Or is it you?" Offering her a break.

She looked at herself wearing low-rise panties and thongs. "Yeah, I forgot, that is me, right."

"The thong," Delsa said, "doesn't look too comfortable."

She said, "I can't wait to get it off."

Delsa told himself she was agreeing that it was uncomfortable, not making a move on him, putting anything into what she said. Otherwise he'd get out of here now and come back with Jackie Michaels, not take a chance fucking up seventeen years on the job. She was a witness. Maybe the best-looking girl he had ever seen this close, or outside of the movies, or even counting the movies, but she was still a witness.

He picked up the black envelope and looked at the label, addressed to Kelly Barr, from a photographic studio. He turned to Kelly-as-Chloe, almost as tall as he was.

"You think this will tell me something about her?"

"They're just photos."

He walked away, bringing the catalog and the black envelope to the counter, took a kitchen knife from a rack and slit the envelope open.

"We'll need pictures of the complainant."

"The what?"

"The victim."

"They're swimsuit shots."

"Taken recently?"

"Last week."

Delsa pulled out a half dozen color prints and a proof sheet and laid them on the counter: Kelly full length in bikinis, tiny ones.

She came to the counter to look at herself, leaning in on her arms to study the proof sheet.

She heard him say, "Your glasses are in your bag. You don't need them?"

She straightened and turned to him.

"You figured it out."

"Even without the glasses."

"You saw her in the chair, her skirt up. You look at these shots . . ."

"And I know Chloe doesn't model swimming suits," Delsa said.

"Yesterday we happened to be looking at this catalog and she said, 'If you want to know why I never wear a thong, ask Mr. Paradise.' You know what she meant?"

"He didn't go for the Hitler look," Delsa said. "Just an old-fashioned guy. Are you gonna tell me who you are?"

"You already know."

"I'd like to hear you say it."

She shrugged in her cinnamon coat.

"Okay, I'm Kelly Barr. Now what?"

He told her she had gone through enough for one day. He'd pick her up in the morning and take her statement at 1300, police headquarters.

She didn't like the sound of that. Take her statement? She said did he mean, like, what she was doing when it happened? He said, from the time she arrived at the house. Okay? He hadn't taken his coat off, he was ready to go . . .

Later, it reminded her of the thing Peter Falk used to do playing Columbo. Gets to the door and turns with one more question.

Delsa was still at the counter fastening his toggles. He said, "The main thing we'll get into, why you wanted us to think you're Chloe."

She knew it was coming and had to say something because he was looking at her, waiting. She had to give him an answer and had made up her mind to tell the truth. Up to a point.

"Montez threatened me. He said I had to do it if I wanted to stay alive."

"What was his reason?"

"He didn't tell me."

"All that time you were together—you didn't ask him why?"

"Of course I did. He still wouldn't tell me."

"Have you thought about it since?"

"Have I *thought* about it—all I keep thinking, I never should've been there in the first place."

"Chloe asked you to come and you couldn't say no?"

"She talked me into it. Help her out with the fucking cheerleading because the old man loved it."

"Were Chloe and Montez friends?"

"She said they got along okay."

"They have something going?"

"No. She would've told me."

"You were close? You confide in each other?"

"We were good friends."

"But she was a prostitute."

"She gave it up for Mr. Paradise."

"There was a time before that—"

"She never brought them home. She told really funny stories about weird things that guys liked. I asked if she ever beat them. She said, 'Hon, I even pee on some.'" Kelly picked up her pace saying, "We met doing a runway show for Saks. I'd see her at studios—photographers loved her hands—or we'd meet for a drink. We laughed a lot and she invited me to move in." Kelly took hold of Delsa's dark eyes saying, "She got tired of fucking strangers, especially the regulars. Mr.

Paradise made her an offer and she quit being a ho."

This time he did smile, though she didn't.

Smiled and let it fade and said, "How'd you happen to be upstairs with Montez?"

She told about the old man flipping the coin. "To share his ladies with Montez—his exact words—and not play favorites."

"He thought you were a hooker. Did you tell him you weren't?"

"I didn't want to start anything with the old man, Chloe in the middle. I'd go upstairs with Montez, and as soon as he had his pants off, I'd run. Out of the house."

"What about Chloe?"

"She's okay. It's her boyfriend's party."

"What'd Montez say?"

"Upstairs?"

"Before, when you got him."

"He got *me*. Took me upstairs by the arm."

"What'd you do then?"

"I smoked a cigarette and went to the bathroom."

"Did you talk?"

"Nothing that I remember."

"He take his pants off, undress?"

"I came out of the bathroom and that's when we heard the shots. Two and then two more."

"They all sound the same?"

"I think so."

"What'd Montez do?"

"Ran out of the room. I put on my coat, picked up Chloe's and started down the hall. He was at the top of the stairs, so I hung back, I didn't want him to see me."

"Why not?"

"I wanted to leave, not be involved."

"You knew they were dead?"

"*No.* It was like I knew it without actually knowing it. All I wanted to do was leave, get out."

"You said not get involved."

"With the police, as a witness."

"Don't you want to help us?"

"Of course, yeah, now. But when it was happening, no. I wanted to go *home.*"

"You say Montez was at the top of the stairs. What did he do then?"

"He went down to the first floor."

"How? I mean, was he cautious after hearing the shots? Not knowing who was in the house?"

"He ran down the stairs."

"He call out anything, a name?"

Kelly shook her head. "I went to the railing and looked down. He wasn't in the foyer."

"You hear anything?"

"I might've heard voices, but I'm not sure. I thought about running out of the house."

"What stopped you?"

"I didn't have my bag, goddamn it. I forgot it."

"Why didn't you get it?"

"I heard voices and looked down. Two men I'd never seen before, in dark coats and baseball caps, were in the foyer."

"White or black?"

"White. Not young, not old, both average height—it was hard to tell looking down at them. One was heavyset. He had a gun in his hand, like an automatic. The other one was holding a bottle of vodka."

"What kind?"

"Christiania, what the old man was drinking."

"And you and Chloe had alexanders," Frank said. "How're you feeling?"

"I'm worn out."

"Starting to droop a little. What'd the two guys do?"

"They left, out the front."

"Was the glass in the door already broken?"

It surprised her. "No, they did it when they were outside, smashed it with something. I suppose so you'd think that's how they came in."

"How did they?"

"I have no idea. Unless they broke in."

"Or the door was unlocked," Delsa said. "The two guys are in the foyer, where was Montez?"

"I don't know."

"You didn't see him with the two guys or hear them talking?"

"They left and a few minutes later he came upstairs. He could've been hiding—I don't know."

"Didn't you say anything?"

"I asked him what happened, if he saw the two guys. But he didn't say a word until he took me downstairs. In the living room he said, 'You know what you're gonna see. They're both dead, Mr. Paradise and your friend Kelly.' I thought he had us mixed up. I said I'm Kelly, and he said, 'Uh-unh, you're Chloe.' "

"Then what?"

"He made me look at the bodies."

"Was Chloe's skirt raised?"

Kelly nodded. "I was about to pull it down and he stopped me."

"He told you you were Chloe and you said okay?"

"Montez said, 'You know what bullet holes look like.' He said if I don't do what I'm told, that ugly motherfucker will be waiting for me some night."

"Who's the ugly motherfucker?"

"Someone who'll shoot me in the head."

"You're sure you saw two white guys."

"Positive."

He asked if there was anything unusual about them. Kelly said she thought of them as working-men, blue-collar. He asked about their baseball caps and she remembered the orange *D* and he said they were the caps the Tigers wore on the road. He told her to go to bed, he'd call her in the morning.

She said, "What if Montez calls during the night?"

"He won't, I'm gonna have him picked up." Delsa said, "Anything else you want to tell me?"

Not right now.

Kelly didn't say that. She said, "Not that I can think of," with a little shrug. She had decided there was more to think about here than just getting it over with. Montez would deny everything she told Frank. Her word against his. In a corner Montez might even say it was *her* idea. It was kind of cool to be in this with your eyes open, letting it happen. Maybe she should try acting, modeling with lines, hitting marks . . . Frank Delsa looked at you with those quiet eyes asking questions, and you answer, you know he's getting more out of it than what you're saying. She wondered when he first knew she wasn't Chloe. Before she fumbled the keys, probably in the bed-room. He listened, he paid attention . . . For the next two days she'd hold off saying anything more and see what happened next.

She loved his eyes.

AUTOPSY ATTENDANTS WERE PREPARING FOUR
bodies this morning for pathology: Tony Paradiso,
Chloe Robinette, and the two guys from Orlando's
basement who'd been shot but not dismembered.

Delsa, hospital booties covering his shoes,
watched the diener working on Mr. Paradise,
snipping free the old man's rib cage with a long-
handle pruner. Chloe's organs had been removed,
weighed, tissue samples taken, the organs returned to her body in a plastic bag. Chloe was
now being stitched back together, the section of
skull refitted, her blond hair in place again. They
had traced her to Montreal, to strip clubs in
Windsor, a Web page on the Internet, this girl
who'd made nine hundred dollars an hour lying
naked on an autopsy table, a weak sun shining on
her through the skylight.

She didn't show up on LEIN; neither did Kelly. Montez and Lloyd both had sheets. They'd pick at Lloyd, see about tying him in, but concentrate on Montez. Throw the two white guys at him. Get a copy of his 9-11 call.

He noticed a note on the board that said, hand-printed, "Howard, you will be responsible for brain bucket cleanup Monday."

Richard Harris tapped on the glass partition of the observation room, Richard on the other side where you could watch autopsies from a distance and not become too grossed out. Delsa went out to him because Richard refused to come anywhere near an autopsy. He said, "We got an I.D. on the one was cut up. His name's Zorro, the fox, with the Cash Flow Posse."

"How'd you get it?"

"The man's family, his mom and daddy, they both in the business. Zorro didn't call when he was suppose to. You understand this was a dangerous man, knows this other posse wants him out of business. If he doesn't follow up and call by a certain time? He must be dead. They're out in the viewing room, the family. The M.E. photo guy's trying to shoot Zorro's face without it looking so burnt.

"And, Mr. Tony Jr.'s in the lobby bitching. Wants to know what all the fuckin Chicanos are doing in the room, the viewing room, where they show the complainant on that monitor. Tony wants to talk to you. I mean he's demanding to speak with you."

"What about Tyrell?" Delsa said. "You take him down?"

"Him and two of his crew with outstanding warrants, violated their probation. Yeah, I went in and ordered breakfast—give me time to check the place out, glance in the kitchen. Sit at the counter you can watch the activity, Tyrell in there frying eggs. I got him lined up, my phone nudges me. It's Manny outside with Violent Crimes. 'Is he there? What're you doing? We going in or not?' I told him soon as I finish my breakfast."

"Manny Reyes."

"Yeah. The way it went down, Manny comes in and we approach Tyrell in the kitchen. He sees us and runs out the back to a car, his baby's mama and his baby sitting in the front seat, like they waiting for him to get off work. Now he sees our guys, he snatches up the baby and runs around to the driver's side, using the child as a shield, his own baby girl. You hear what I'm saying? We ganged on him fast. After, Manny said, 'I learn something today. You can fit a Glock Forty up a guy's nose.' "

Delsa had called Richard last night, still at the

Paradise scene, told him the girl in the chair with the old man was Chloe, not Kelly, and to house Montez for questioning about the false I.D. Delsa said last night, "But don't tell him we know."

Today at the Medical Examiner's he said, "Pick up Montez when you're finished here and I'll see you up on five."

Richard said, "You gonna run into Tony in the lobby."

"How's he know I'm on the case?"

"Must keep track of you, man, since you beat him on that wrongful death. I remember I was with Violent Crimes at the time, everybody talking about it. What was it the man was asking, thirty million?"

Late November four years ago at Eastland with Maureen, ten past eight driving up and down aisles in the dark, headlights looking for a parking space—one close to Hudson's, before it became Marshall Field's. Maureen said, "There's one," but Delsa had to creep behind two lanky, slow-moving guys walking up the aisle.

They turned into the open space—scruffy-looking white guys, mid-twenties—maybe to cut through to the next aisle, the parking space facing this one also open, and Maureen said, "*Move, will you?*" Out loud but for her own benefit,

Maureen not the most patient woman, high on energy, worked out with weights while Delsa watched television. She reached over and blew the horn at them.

As Delsa expected, the two guys turned and stared into the headlights—at that time a black Honda Accord with 94,000 miles on it—one of the guys calling to them, "You in a hurry?"

Delsa remembered Maureen saying, "What do you bet you get a LEIN hit on both of them." And telling her, "That's why I wish you hadn't blown the horn."

She said, "You know what they're doing, looking for a car to boost." Then reminded him that the Honda Accord was the most frequently stolen motor vehicle in the U.S.

Delsa remembered saying if they didn't get to Hudson's soon it would be closed. They were here to buy her dad a couple of sweaters, one for his birthday and one for Christmas, kill two birds.

But now the guys were coming toward the car, grungy jackets hanging open, caps on backwards, and that vacant stare that made them rockheads.

" 'Night of the Living Dead,' " Maureen said. "Let's roll down the windows. I want to see what these assholes have to say."

Delsa had to agree, these guys could be dirty,

looking for action. He released his seat belt, zipped open his jacket and reached inside to unhook the snap on his holster, the Glock resting against his right hip, part of him. Maureen's was in her handbag, open on her lap.

The guy who came up on Delsa's side laid his arms on the sill and hunched over to get in Delsa's face. He said, "You drive like a fuckin nigger."

Delsa didn't know what he meant and didn't ask. He said, "You're almost in serious trouble." He said, "Step away from the car," and shoved the door open in the next second, putting his shoulder into it, the top edge of the door frame hitting the guy in the face and he went down. Delsa was out of the car by the time he heard Maureen—"Frank, he's got my bag!"—and saw the other guy running with the brown leather shoulder bag through the open parking spots and across the next aisle to the rear end of a pickup truck, headlights on him as a car approached and went by. Now the one Delsa had flattened was up and running toward the pickup. He stopped in the next aisle, looked back and yelled, "You're fucked now, man." Delsa was out of the car and heard Maureen—"He's got my gun!"—but kept his eyes on the one who'd yelled, letting Delsa know it wasn't over. The guy was at the pickup cab now, the inside light coming on. Delsa pulled his Glock and racked the slide. The light in the cab went off as the door slammed and the guy was in the aisle again with a shotgun, pumping it with that ratchety sound as Delsa raised his Glock and took aim the way he was taught and shot the guy in the chest, sure of it, the shotgun going off at the sky as the guy dropped to the pavement. Delsa put the Glock on the other guy shoving his hand in Maureen's bag, the hand coming out of the bag with her .40 caliber and shot him dead center and he went down. Delsa walked over with Maureen to stand looking at them as Maureen checked each one for a pulse. It was the first time he had fired his weapon at anyone. Maureen called 9-11 while he drove the Honda around to that aisle and put his headlights on the scene.

The two were brothers, convicted car-jackers on lifetime probation, six months in violation for not reporting, high school dropouts . . . "So the boys could find work and support their mom while their old man was doing mandatory life," Anthony Paradiso Jr., representing the mom, told the press. He had filed a wrongful death suit in civil court against the City of Detroit, the police department and Frank Delsa, asking thirty million in restitution. Tony's argument: Delsa's action was overly aggressive, irresponsible in the excessive use of deadly force. Aside to the press Tony said, "It's okay to kill two young boys trying to jack an old Honda? Ninety thousand miles on it?"

Civil court reviewed Tony's suit and threw it out. A board of police executives looked at evidence prepared by Central Affairs, determined that Delsa had gone by the book and returned him to active duty. The department psychologist said that Delsa's reaction was positive, he wished he hadn't had to fire his weapon. He did express some relief that the two he shot were "white guys" and there was no chance of it becoming a "racial thing."

Both of the wide, curving benches in the Medical Examiner's lobby were done in a bright blue fabric within a bright yellow wood frame—that Delsa thought of, for some reason, as high school colors. He could imagine a banner on the wall that said "Home of the Fighting Pathologists." He saw Tony Paradiso right away:

Tony occupying a section of the closer bench, arm extended along the backrest, Tony at ease, comfortable, a guy who was pleased with the way he looked, wore expensive suits and boots with a heel that would get him up to five-ten; a guy who could tuck a dinner napkin in his collar with a certain flair and get away with it. Delsa ran into him at Randy's after the wrongful death suit was thrown out and Tony bought the lunch. He had personalities to fit the occasion, able to soothe the wives and mothers of the dead, scream in the face of an opposing witness. Delsa thought he overacted and didn't care for his type, but got a kick out of watching him show off in court and didn't mind talking to him. Tony was a lawyer, so you had to accept the fact he was opinionated and full of shit. Delsa had never thought of him as a prick, though he probably was if you got to know him. He was a high-priced defender, fifty-three, with dark hair carefully combed and a big ass.

He saw Delsa and said, "Frank, come here, will you? Help me out." But didn't get up. Delsa walked over. Tony said, "They won't let me see Dad." A solemn tone but hope in his eyes looking up at Delsa.

"I guess the viewing room's in use."

"Bunch of Mexicans. Who's dead?"

"Guy named Zorro, with one of the posses."

"Never heard of him. Was it a cop pop?"

Delsa shook his head. "Nothing there for you."

Tony said, "Is that resentment I hear? You still holding a grudge against me?"

Delsa said, "I never did."

Tony said, "Frank, it wasn't personal, I explained that to you after. We could've settled, the city pays out a few bucks, it wouldn't of cost you a dime."

"You didn't offer me a cut."

"Come on, you know I don't do that. The only reason I thought you were quick on the trigger, you weren't gonna let that asshole shoot you with your wife's gun. But I didn't bring that up, did I? Listen, I was sorry to hear about your loss, Frank. Now I've lost Dad, and they won't let me in to see him."

"You don't want to right now," Delsa said, "they're doing a post."

"What I'm saying, I'm not gonna identify him looking at that fucking TV, I want to *see* him. You have to sit on the floor in there to see the goddamn screen. Boxes of Kleenex all over the room. Go near the door you hear those fucking beaners in there carrying on—a very emotional people, Frank. They give you anything to go on?"

"Not yet. Harris's on it."

"I saw him last night. He said you were there but left. How do you see it, home invasion?"

"For the time being. Tony, there were two young women in the house. What I need to know, which one was your dad's girlfriend."

"The one sitting with him, Chloe. Wasn't it?"

"You assume that."

"It wasn't Chloe?"

"She was identified as Kelly Barr. By Montez."

"Nobody told me that," Tony said. "Kelly Barr? I never heard of her." He said, "Wait a minute—Chloe's alive?"

Delsa told him no, it was Chloe in the chair. He said, "Montez made a mistake," and watched Tony frown at him.

"What're you talking about? He knows her, picks her up, takes her to the house."

Delsa said, "How well did you know her?"

"Me? I kept checking Dad's will," Tony said, "waiting for her name to show up on a codicil. That's how well I knew her."

"You figured she had to be after his money."

"Frank, she was a whore."

"Your dad knew it, didn't he?"

"She walks in the house taking off her clothes —sure, he knew it. Found her on the Internet under pussy. He liked her—why wouldn't he? She helped him get his eighty-four-year-old rocks off, if that's possible. But that didn't qualify her for his will."

"Did he ever propose adding her name?"

"No, but I saw it coming. I was seriously thinking about getting power of attorney. He was losing it, Frank, the early stages of Alzheimer's fucking with his judgment. He was already giving her five grand a week that I knew of."

"Maybe he had another way of taking care of her," Delsa said, "after he's gone."

"What good's it do her? She's gone, too."

That wasn't the point. Delsa said, "What if it was already set up? Say, an account in her name?" And saw six, seven, eight people filing out of the viewing room, each of the three women holding a handkerchief to her face. He watched Harris approach one of the men, an older Hispanic.

"If he left her anything," Tony said, "I don't know about it."

"You mentioned your dad got Chloe off the Internet. He knew how to use a computer?"

Tony thought a moment and said, "You're right, it must've been Montez got her for him. It's what he was there for, get Dad anything he wanted. Dad planned on leaving Montez the house, but then my daughter Allegra thought it would be fun to live in the city, so Dad put it in his will. She gets the house, but now I don't know. Her husband wants to move to California and buy a winery. I can't keep up with him, John Tintinalli. Right now, he's selling bull semen on the Internet, acts as a broker. They sell it to dairy farmers who impregnate their cows every year to keep the milk flowing. Yeah, John represents a number of Grand Champion bulls, Attila, Big Daddy, some others."

Delsa had to ask, "How does he get the semen?"

"As I understand it," Tony said, "they use an artificial cow's vagina and get the bull to ejaculate into it. Or they give him a hand job or stick an electric rod up his ass. There're different ways. You'd have to talk to John about it."

Delsa had trouble picturing the second method. He said, "So your dad and Montez got along."

"Yeah, fine. Dad would sometimes refer to him as his pet nigger. He was not only the boss, he was the white boss. You know, that generation, he still thought of Montez as colored. He was definitely not in the old man's will, but they'd play games with each other. Dad would mellow after a few drinks, start talking like all men were created equal, and Montez would hustle him saying, 'Yes, suh, Mr. Paradise.' Dad loved that Mr. Paradise shit. Now Lloyd, Lloyd was even better at it."

"He didn't tell us much. Said he was asleep."

" 'Cause Uncle Lloyd's smarter than Montez, he keeps his mouth shut. 'No, suh, don't know nothin' about that.' "

"Why'd your dad have him around?"

"I just told you, Lloyd doesn't know, hear or see anything. Even scratches his head on cue. And he's not a bad cook. Worked as a sous chef at Randy's after he got out of the joint."

"What was he down for?"

"I thought you were the ace investigator."

"I haven't seen his sheet."

"Lloyd was into armed robbery, big time. Took part in a payroll heist and got finked out. Lloyd in his prime, Montez'd be working for him. What I want to know is, why Montez said it was the other girl, with Dad."

"I'll get into that with him."

"The other girl was still around, after?"

"Yeah, in the house."

"He could see she's not Chloe, right?"

"Good point," Delsa said. "I'll ask him."

And got out of there.

MONTEZ SAT IN THIS ROOM NO BIGGER THAN A
closet, a wood table the size of half a desk, two
straight chairs facing each other, no window, pink
walls with nothing written on them. Montez was
thinking that if brothers had sat in here and over
time made to wait like he was, there ought to be
things written on the walls, names like Shank, Bolo,
"V-Dawg was here." Inscriptions like "F-1": for
Family First. "SMV," same as a tat the Seven Mile–
Van Dyke gang wore on their arms. Could even be
swastikas and "White Power" shit written there by
Aryan Nation assholes. The walls were clean,
Montez decided, 'cause nobody brought anything
to write with in here. Coming into 1300 there were
brothers coming out carrying their shoelaces.

He had told his story over and over how he
was confused.

The door opened and here was the brother in a striped shirt and gold cuff links, tiny knot in his tie up there tight, starch in the shirt, the one last night the tech called Richard, Richard Harris sitting across from him at the table now and asking, "How long have you known Chloe Robinette?" Gonna ask him all this shit again, leading to why did he say it was Kelly with the man when he knew it was Chloe?

"I already told your boss and I told that woman they call Jackie? Man, ask them."

Harris said, "Yeah, but what you told them's all a fuckin lie. I want to know why you told Kelly she was Chloe."

"I never told her that."

"You knew she was Kelly."

"I *didn't* is the thing. I look at the girl dead, messed up, all the blood on her. Yeah, I know Chloe, but this dead girl don't look any fuckin thing like her. Man, seeing them like that can fuck with your head. You understand? Once I decided this one in the chair's Kelly, since it don't look like Chloe, then the other one had to be Chloe, upstairs in the bedroom, dark in there. After while I become mixed up, this Chloe or Kelly? They look alike, they dressed alike, same hair. I breathed on the bong a few times to settle me. Know what I'm saying? Now it could been either one in the chair. I said fuck it."

"We had a window in here," Harris said, "I'd hang you out there, five floors to the concrete, till you told me the truth. Ask you the question—you're hanging outside in the weather—I say, 'What was that, motherfucker? I can't hear you.' The girl says to you, 'I'm Kelly, you ignorant fuck.' You say to her, 'No, you not, you Chloe.' " Harris leaned over the table on his arms, close to Montez now. "Why'd you tell her she was Chloe?"

"She lied to you, man."

"Why do you want her to be Chloe?"

"Ask the bitch why she lied."

"What do you get out of her being Chloe?"

"I swear to God on my mother's grave—"

"Where'd you pick that up, the movies? Your mama passed? Her ass rotting in a grave? Where's this grave at? You swear to God, then gonna give me the same shit you been telling us."

Montez held up his hands to show his palms. "Man, you got the advantage on me. What can I say?"

"What's your phone number, your cell?"

"Why you want that?"

"Tell me right now or use it to call a lawyer."

Kelly said, "He's in there? I thought it was a closet."

She sat at the side of Delsa's desk, turned in the chair to look over her shoulder.

"It's our interview room," Delsa said. "Richard Harris is with him. He was there last night. As we were leaving Harris was talking to the tall guy in the trench coat and beige cap? That was Wendell Robinson, our boss. He might want to talk to you when we finish with your statement." Delsa watched her glance toward the back of the squad room again, not comfortable being near Montez. Delsa could understand why, but maybe there was more to it.

"What if he comes out and sees me?"

"He won't."

"If Harris leaves him alone?"

"He knows he has to stay in there, and he will, he's trying to make a good impression, can't believe we find fault with his story. I meant to ask you," Delsa said, "he knew you were coming last night?"

"He picked us up. Chloe arranged the visit. She wanted me to go with her the night before but I had to take my dad to the airport. He said the reason he came up, he missed his little girl so much, but it was really to borrow money. My dad drinks."

Delsa said, "Did you know that people who come from money call their dad 'Dad,' and people who don't come from money call him 'my dad'?"

Kelly said, "Can you prove it?"

"I feel it, I don't know it."

"Dad lives in West Palm Beach," Kelly said. "He's a semi-retired barber. Not a hair stylist, a barber. He drinks and chases women."

"Your mother's not with him?"

He was used to asking questions with obvious answers.

"She died just about the time I started modeling, I was sixteen. She pushed me into it but didn't live to see it pay off. My dad says he drinks because he misses her, but you know he's been drinking all his life." She said, "He's not a bad guy. I can take him for a couple of days."

She had a soft, almost lazy way of speaking, and he said, "You're not from Detroit."

"Actually I am, I was born here, Harper Hospital. We moved to Miami when I was little. I was twenty, I came up to do an auto show, met a guy and decided to stay. The guy turned out to be a mama's boy, left his clothes lying around, but now I was *here* . . . I can live anywhere I want, really."

"And you stay in Detroit."

"I'm too lazy to move. No, it's okay. A lot of music, not a lot of traffic, you can drive fast. I have a VW Jetta, black, always starts, easy to drive in snow and ice . . . What else do you want to know?"

"Montez picked you up . . ."

She hesitated. She said yeah. "But now that I think of it, he didn't know we were coming. In the car he said no one told him. He made a call on his cell but didn't speak to anyone."

"He leave a message?"

"No, he was mad when no one answered and threw the phone down." She said, "Have you talked to him?"

"This morning? Yeah, I was first, then Jackie Michaels—you met her last night."

"She threatened me."

"Woke you up. Now Harris is on him."

"And Montez, what does he say about it?"

"You're lying. You made it all up."

"Does he know everything I've told you?"

"We're giving him a little bit at a time and let him think about it. We haven't mentioned the two guys," Delsa said. "You're sure he doesn't know you saw them."

"Almost positive."

"They left and Montez came upstairs."

"A few minutes later," Kelly said, what she had told him in the loft, in the kitchen. "If he thought I saw them, wouldn't he ask me? He said it was a black guy. He said, you know what bullet holes look like. He said if I didn't do what I was told the ugly motherfucker would shoot me in the head. You can understand why I'm a little freaked. Right?"

Delsa couldn't keep his eyes off her.

Kelly asked if she could smoke and he brought his ashtray out of the desk drawer and watched her light one of her Virginia Slims 120's and raise her perfect face to blow a stream of smoke into the fluorescent lights. She wore a sheepskin-lined coat with her jeans, an outdoor girl this morning, black cowboy boots, old and creased, but with a high shine.

"Did you hear Montez call nine-eleven?"

"He was downstairs."

"What about Lloyd, was he around?"

"Not after."

"Jackie's gonna have a talk with him."

"He seems harmless."

"But he was there," Delsa said.

"You know Montez is your guy. But it comes down to my word against his," Kelly said. "Isn't that right?"

"So far."

"If he doesn't admit being involved you'll have to let him go?"

The way she said it Delsa wasn't sure if she was

hopeful or apprehensive. But if being near him freaked her, she wouldn't want to meet him on the street. Would she?

Maybe get Jackie to have a word with her.

"If we keep talking to him," Delsa said, "he'll want a lawyer. And if we can't arraign him on a warrant, he walks. We're looking for a motive. Who stands to gain from the old man's death, other than family? We rule out robbery—nothing was taken but a bottle of vodka, an expensive brand, Christiania, but not worth a home invasion. So we focus on Montez, a guy with felony indictments on his sheet but clean for the past ten years. If he isn't somehow involved, why is he lying to us?" Delsa threw in, "Assuming you're telling us the truth," and saw it give her a nudge.

Kelly, about to draw on her Slim, lowered it to the ashtray. "I told you who I am, I straightened that out."

"Not right away."

"No, and I explained why."

"Afraid of being too talkative."

"We got to the loft, I felt more secure. I told you everything I know."

"The house full of cops, you didn't feel safe?"

"Frank, I was semi-stoned, I wasn't sure what I felt. I didn't want to have to think and answer questions till I had a clear head."

On the defensive but cool now, using his name, comfortable in the chair.

"Okay," Delsa said, "we put the focus on Montez. If he's not involved, why is he lying? Why does he want you to be Chloe? There has to be something in it for him, a payoff that's worth becoming a suspect. He isn't in the old man's will. Neither is Chloe. So I wonder if Mr. Paradise had some other way of taking care of her, after his death. She ever mention anything like that?"

"He was giving her five thousand a week," Kelly said.

"Very generous man, but made no attempt to put Chloe in his will."

"Because of his son," Kelly said, "Tony Jr."

"So you did talk to her about it."

Delsa watched her tap the cigarette in the ashtray, twice, three times.

"Yeah, well, for the reason you said, the guy was so generous, I thought she'd be in his will. She told me why she didn't expect anything and really didn't care. Even the five thousand a week, Chloe could make more than that turning tricks."

Delsa said, "Amazing, isn't it?"

Kelly seemed to shrug, smoking her Slim.

"In the meantime," Delsa said, "we're working to get a lead on the two guys. We have to believe they were hired to hit the old man. The flip of a coin put Chloe there instead of you and they had to take her out."

"I think about that all the time," Kelly said.

"And Montez is part of it." He held her eyes for a few moments, looking to see what he might find in there. He said, "Give some thought to the two guys in the baseball caps. Tell me again what they looked like."

CARL FONTANA AND ART KRUPA WERE AT NEMO'S
on Michigan Avenue at a table, half past five, the
bar side packed. They felt at home here, a block
from Tiger Stadium, where they used to stop for
a couple before a game and both rooms in the
place would be full of fans. Carl was showing Art
the front page of the paper, the headline:

LAWYER GUNNED DOWN IN INDIAN VILLAGE

Art said, "It doesn't look like him."

"It's an old picture," Carl said. "Must've been
taken when he was about fifty."

Art read, " 'Paradiso Sr., unidentified woman
found dead in his living room.' " And said, "Why
don't they know who she is? All they had to do
was ask Montez."

"He prob'ly left," Carl said. "You know, so he can walk in with all the cops there, dumb look on his face, 'Hey shit, what's going on?' "

"Next thing," Art said, "they're checking his fuckin hands for gunshot residue."

The bartender motioned to them. "Art, telephone."

Art left the table and a minute later Avern Cohn came in the front looking around. Carl waved him over. Avern sat down saying, "How do you get a drink in this place?"

Carl said, "Fuck your drink. The guy was suppose to be alone. There's a half-naked broad sitting in the chair with him."

"The unexpected can happen," Avern said. "You did what you had to do."

"How come they don't say who she is?"

"I guess the cops don't want us to know."

The waitress came along the aisle. Carl stopped her. He said, "Geeja, keep an eye on us, will you, for Christ sake?" She stood with the edge of her tray against her cocked hip, not saying a word. Avern ordered a Chivas with one cube of ice. Carl said, "The same way without the tequila."

Picking up the empty beer bottles Geeja said, "Just the Coronas?"

"Isn't that what I said?"

"I was making sure," Geeja said. "What's the matter, Connie giving you a hard time?"

She left. Carl said, "I met Connie here. She use to work at the ballpark, behind a counter, and I'd meet her here after. Geeja's a friend of Connie's."

Avern was watching him, waiting and then saying, "I'm gonna tell you something that strikes me as fascinating, mysterious, like a portent. You're drinking Mexican beer, which I've never seen you do before, and I have a job prospect that comes out of the fatal shooting of three Mexicans, the night before last. It's in today's paper, page three. But the victims aren't identified, not even as Mexican. Their bodies were burned, one of them dismembered."

Carl said, "Why?"

Avern said, "Who knows. The house's only three blocks from here, the other side of the ballpark. Empty, half burned, you can go in and look around."

"For what?"

Art came back and sat down saying, "That fuckin smoke."

Carl said, "How'd he know to call you here?"

Avern held up his hand to Art and said to Carl, "I told Montez I was meeting you. I told him any hitch in the program, he'd have to tell you about it himself. I'm out of it." He said, "Unless, the way it's going, I end up representing Montez. He hasn't been arraigned, but it's a possibility."

Carl said, "They think he did it?"

"They'd like him as an accessory, at least. He falsely I.D.'s the girl you shot. But they can't prove he did it with malice, so they have to cut him loose."

Carl said, "Who'd he think she was?"

"Another girl was there and he made a mistake."

"There's nothing about that in the paper."

"I got it from Lloyd, the houseman."

Carl said, "You know the old guy, you know Montez, you know everybody in the house?"

"Hang out at Frank Murphy," Avern said, "you get a line on all the players. I've known Lloyd since he was holding up grocery stores. I represented him a couple of times. We'd run into each other and have a drink, tell stories. We try to top each other on the dumbest criminals we've known." Avern smiled, said, "That Lloyd," and shook his head. "He could write a book on playing a house nigger—eyes and ears open, mouth shut. I asked Lloyd to watch Montez for me. This was even before Montez came with the contract. He's working for old Tony all these years and has kept himself clean? It didn't sound like Montez. I said to Lloyd, 'He's getting something out of his faithful service.' And Lloyd said 'Yeah, he's getting the house when the man passes.'"

Carl said, "You pay Lloyd?"

"He owed me, I got him off on those early beefs in his youth. But now a few weeks ago Lloyd tells me the situation's changed. Montez isn't getting the house after all. He acted uppity and it pissed off the old man. Now his granddaughter gets the house. Then this morning I'm talking to Lloyd, he tells me there were two girls there last night. Chloe, the old man's girlfriend, and Kelly, her roommate. I spent four hundred and fifty bucks on Chloe one time and it was a highly memorable occasion." Avern touched his thinning gray hair, smoothing a spot. "She was in *Playboy* and her rate jumped up to nine hundred an hour."

Art said, "The fuck're you talking about?"

The waitress came with their order, the table quiet as she served them, a pause in the conversation. Geeja said, "What're you guys doing, telling dirty jokes?"

She left and Carl said to Art, "So Montez called . . ."

"Fuckin smoke says he won't have it tomorrow."

Avern stepped in.

"But he *will* pay, believe me. I have to wait for

my end the same as you. But I know Montez and I'm absolutely sure he'll come through. The money's from the old man, paying for his own hit. He put stock in Montez' name. Montez sells it for enough to cover expenses. But his broker wants him to wait just another day or so, make a few more bucks."

Carl said, "He's in the stock market?"

"Everyone is," Avern said, "or was. Tony gave him some blue chips he's been sitting on. I said to Montez, well, okay, but he'd have to add another ten to the contract or you guys'd be after him."

Carl said to Art, "He tell you that?"

"Yeah, and I told him it had to be another ten each. He said okay."

"You believe him?"

"I told him he don't come through he's a dead nigger."

"Both concise and reasonably coercive," Avern said. "Now then, if you'd like to hear about the next one—"

"Three dead Mexicans," Carl said to Art. "Somebody's looking for a payback."

"I'm negotiating with him now," Avern said.

"One of 'em cut up," Carl said to Art. "I imagine with a machete."

"A chain saw," Avern said. "I'm talking to the

head of the gang, the posse the three guys belonged to. I explain to Chino—"

Art said, "That's his fuckin name, Chino?"

"It's what he's called."

"How do you know him?"

Avern was patient with his ethnic hitters, his guinea and his polack. He said, "Again, hanging out at Frank Murphy, where the action is. I explained to Chino how he can enjoy satisfaction for his loss without becoming involved. I said, 'Why take a chance with heat on you? Gang squad cops waiting for you to retaliate.' "

"I live down there," Carl said, "by Holy Redeemer? You go in that Mex neighborhood, cruise down Vernor, you see a big maroon Lincoln prowling the streets, always three to four detectives in it."

"Special ops," Avern said, "known as boosters. The old days they were the Big Four. Rode around in a Buick—four big cops with shotguns, armed to the teeth and looking for trouble. Okay, back to the gay caballeros."

Art said, "The dead guys were queers?"

"Forget I used that expression," Avern said, "it doesn't mean anything."

Art said, "What'd you say it for?"

"I wasn't thinking," Avern said. "Okay. The

three Mexicanos delivered a hundred pounds of weed to a dealer's house, a black guy they've been doing business with. But something happened and they end up dead in the guy's basement. Check the house. It might have police tape around it, but no one's there now. It could give you a lead on the guy. I got his name from a kid who works for Professional Recovery Service— they picked up the bodies."

Carl said, "You met this kid at Frank Murphy one time?"

"Actually he's the brother of a guy I once represented," Avern said. "The guy you want to pop, his name is Orlando Holmes."

Carl and Art ordered a couple more Coronas and decided, yeah, they'd do the tequila again. What was on Carl Fontana's mind weren't dead Mexicans or this jig Orlando, it was the guy who'd just left.

"He knows everybody in town," Carl said, "as long as they're felons. Friendly man, isn't he? Runs into Montez, they have a drink and he gets a contract. Runs into Lloyd and has a drink, gets information. Runs into Chloe, who wasn't suppose to be there—"

"And gets fucked," Art said. "What might be happening to us."

"Well, now you're catching on," Carl said. "I never felt right about this one, now I'm starting to see why. Avern says walk in and shoot the old man 'cause Montez Taylor feels sorry for him and will cash in stock the old man gave him to be out of his misery sitting there with that naked girl."

Art said, "I never heard of a smoke owning stock."

Carl said, "I think Avern wants to put us on his dumbest criminals list and tell Lloyd, have a good laugh over it."

"You ever see him?"

"Who?"

"Lloyd."

Carl shook his head. He took a swig of Corona from the bottle. Art did too.

Carl said, "I think Avern had to make that story up in a hurry, about the stock. Threw it out there and kept talking, couldn't wait to get to the dead Mexicans."

Art said, "The one chainsawed, I imagine they cut him in five pieces."

Carl said, "I think Avern and Montez might be partners in this deal."

Art said, "I mean six pieces."

Carl said, "Shit, or it was Avern's idea to kill the old man in the first place. Avern gets his cut as our agent, but what's Montez get out of it?"

"You hear him?" Art said. "Avern hasn't been paid his end either?"

"You believe it?"

"I think he would've tore up the unwritten contract."

"Yeah, but you hear how he talks about Montez? How he trusts him, knows we'll get paid? Shit, Avern's running it. We got to find out what the deal is here."

They picked up their tequilas, flipped the shots down and took swigs off their Coronas.

Carl said, "You want another?"

"I wouldn't mind."

"You mentioned this Lloyd a minute ago."

"I asked did you ever see him."

"If you haven't, I haven't."

"He must live right there."

Carl said, "If he's the houseman. Avern says Lloyd owes him a couple, so he's got him keeping an eye on Montez, find out what he's up to. I believe that. I think part of what Avern said when he was lying was true. See, then when Montez came to him with the contract, shit, Avern knew Montez was looking at a payoff."

Art was listening, nodding his head of John Gotti hair.

"Pissed 'cause he wasn't getting the house. He

told Avern what the deal was, to get his help, or he told this Lloyd and he told Avern."

Art squinted with a faint smile. "How'd you figure all that out?"

"Like laying bricks," Carl said.

"All this time," Art said, "I thought it was Connie had you acting weird."

Carl said, "Jesus Christ, don't bring her up." He thought about the situation again before saying, "We put a gun to Avern's head, he'll think up another story and we might believe it. We can't call Montez on it, we shoot him we don't get paid." Carl said, "Shit, I think what we have to do is talk to this Lloyd."

Art waved to Geeja to come over.

Carl said, "How you figure the Mex was cut in *six* pieces?"

DELSA BROUGHT JACKIE MICHAELS ALONG WITH
an empty cardboard box to drive Kelly home,
telling her, "Jackie can look through Chloe's
things, maybe see something I'd miss." He
swapped handbags with her, giving Kelly the
black Vuitton and taking Chloe's brown one.
Kelly didn't say a word in the backseat of the car.
They parked at the front entrance and went up to
the loft. Delsa noticed the photos still on the
kitchen counter. Jackie went into Chloe's bedroom with the box.

And now Kelly said, "Frank, would you help
me off with my boots? I forgot when I put them
on, you need a roommate to get them off." To
Delsa they looked old and worn enough to slide
off her feet. She sank into the sofa on her spine
and told him to straddle the leg she extended, his

back to her, and pushed against his rear end with the other foot as he pulled off a boot and then did it again. Kelly said, "You suppose cowboys help each other off with their boots—out on the lone prairiee?"

Delsa tried to picture it and said, "Maybe some." He straightened feeling awkward and watched her pick up a book from the bamboo coffee table, what looked like an old book but still wearing a dust jacket.

"I want to read something to you, get your re-action."

She opened the book to a page with a corner turned down and leafed back a few pages.

"Here it is. The girl says, 'If you want me to, I'll love you. I know you better now.' "

She looked up at him, Delsa in his duffle coat hanging open. "They've just met, but she knows about him. He's a playwright with a recent opening in New York. What she's saying is, if you want to get it on, let's go. Have an affair in this small town in Vermont. And he says"—Kelly looking at the book again—" 'Don't love me, Sheila. I can't reciprocate.' "

She looked up at him and Delsa said, "Yeah . . . ?"

"Would you want to see one of his plays?"

"When was the book written?"

"I checked after I read the line, 1967. Did people talk like that then?"

"I was a year old."

"In that situation would you say you can't reciprocate?"

"What's the situation? Do I like her?"

"You barely know her, but she's attractive, easy to talk to, intelligent. She's cool."

"Then I'd probably reciprocate," Delsa said, "before too long."

Kelly said, "Why not, uh?" She said, "How long have you been alone? I mean since your wife died?"

"A year in July."

"I remember you said you don't have kids. What was her name, your wife?"

Where was she going with this?

He said, "Maureen."

"She have a job or was she a homemaker?"

"She was a cop," Delsa said. "She ran Sex Crimes."

Kelly said, "Wow," barely above a whisper.

"You want to know if I'm looking around?" Delsa said. "I thought I ought to wait at least a year."

Kelly said, "Why? Are you Sicilian?"

She didn't smile. Still, he knew she was kidding. What she was saying was why wait.

Jackie came out of the bedroom with a copy of

Playboy she handed to Delsa, open. "An interesting shot of the complainant. I put some things in the box, credit card bills, bank statements, a few letters that should give us next of kin. Why don't you have a look in there. You can put the magazine in the box."

Delsa walked off and Jackie stood looking around the loft. She wore a long black quilted coat and wished now she'd worn extensions, a bunch of dreadlocks to come on with a more fierce look.

"You have a killer pad here," Jackie said. "All this space, you can have parties with live music, play touch football naked, do anything you want. You have a lot of parties?"

"Hardly ever," Kelly said, on her feet now.

"Like the quiet affairs better. Some friends you can be yourself with. Some exotic incense burning, a big pitcher of alexanders. You like gin or brandy in yours?"

"Gin."

"Montez over here much?"

Looking up at the ficus as she said it and hearing Kelly's surprised voice say no. "Why would you think that?"

Looking at her now. "All the time you've known him?"

"I didn't know him. I met him last night."

"You leave when he comes to see Chloe?"

"He was never here."

"Okay, but she must've talked about him, as roommates do, confide things? You know what I'm saying?"

Had her on the ropes. The girl frowning.

"You tell me he's never been here," Jackie said, "we'll be getting off to a bad start."

In the car driving back to 1300 Jackie said, "I thought I had her, but she stood up to me. Does not know Montez. Never saw him at the loft or before last night."

Delsa said, "You believe her?"

"I want to believe she's got nothing to do with Mr. Montez Taylor."

"He makes her nervous."

"You know what I mean. The girl's holding back. Tells us—maybe I should say *admits* Montez wants her to be Chloe."

"Needs her to be Chloe," Delsa said. "Needs to use her, I'm pretty sure the old man left Chloe something on the side, not in his will, that Montez knows about. And he's using Kelly to get his hands on it."

"Yeah, but you see where you're going?" Jackie said. "It means Kelly knows about it, too, but hasn't told anybody."

Delsa nodded looking straight ahead past the windshield wipers working at the Renaissance Center, seven hundred feet of glass standing against a sky full of sleet.

"She cops on Montez," Jackie said, "to get her name back. No harm done, it's her word against his. He's on the street and she can become Chloe again any time she wants. But this chick's spotless. Looks like a movie star. Is she willing to commit fraud, risk going to jail? Risk her *life* dealing with Montez? Frank, what's her game? She has to make all kinds of money showing herself in her underwear. Is she crazy? If she's only naïve, that's worse."

Delsa said, "She hasn't done anything yet."

"But thinking about it every minute. Watch her expression she doesn't know you're looking." Jackie said, "Yeah, like that would be a problem. You can't keep your eyes off her."

They turned north on St. Antoine, toward the jails and the court and 1300.

She said, "Frank?"

Now she'd tell him to watch his step with Kelly, don't get carried away and fuck up. He was sure of it.

"What?"

"I interviewed Uncle Lloyd."

Delsa put his mind back on the case. "Tony Jr. says Lloyd's paid to see no evil."

"But he's out of work now. I went after him hard-nosed," Jackie said. "I did learn the old man was giving Montez the house and then changed his mind. Montez, as you can imagine, had a fit. Lloyd seemed pleased to tell me this."

"But will he testify to it?"

"I doubt it. I'm gonna study Lloyd's sheet and go see him again," Jackie said. "He offers me a drink this time I might take it."

They walked in the squad room and Richard Harris was on his feet telling them the inspector had stopped by to take a shot at Montez.

"Wendell got in his face saying the sooner he started talking the less time he'd do. I was surprised he threw the two white guys at him. You know, like we knew who they were and Montez, you could see, was becoming edgy. But he hung in, shaking his head, finally said that was it, he wanted his lawyer and was ready to call him. He took a card from his pocket and laid it on the desk. Avern Cohn. Wendell looked at it and said, 'I thought Avern had been disbarred by now.' He told Montez to go on home and think about doing time. He left and Wendell said, 'That man's so tightened up I doubt we could pound a peanut up his ass with a jackhammer.' "

Delsa said, "Avern Cohn . . ."

"Wendell said he use to represent Montez before Tony Paradiso took him over. Hey, but wait." Harris got a wanted sheet from his desk and handed it to Delsa.

Delsa looked at it, at the mug shot of the wanted man, and smiled. He sat down at his desk, his coat still on, and called Jerome Juwan Jackson.

"Man, I need you to stop by the squad room."

"Man, my mother's car ain't running. Have to go look at it, see what's wrong."

"Where's your mom live? I'll come by."

"But see," Jerome said, "I don't know when exactly I'll be there. Tomorrow's Nashelle's birthday, my girlfriend? I said I'd take her to the mall, she can pick out her present."

"Jerome," Delsa said, "let me read something to you. It's a poster that says 'WANTED' in big letters at the top. It describes the guy as a black male six-foot, two-ten, his hair in rows, beard with mustache—but it's a shitty beard, Jerome, bare spots in it. Name on the poster, Orlando Holmes."

"Yeah, you mentioned that one to me," Jerome said, "Orlando, with the dead Mexicans in his basement."

"That's right," Delsa said. "Then at the bottom of the sheet, Jerome, it says 'REWARD $20,000' for information that leads to his arrest."

Jerome said, "How long you gonna be there?"

Forty minutes later Delsa was telling Jerome, sitting at the side of his desk, "Now is when you use your street connections. Ask around—who knows what happened to Orlando? Try to find his girlfriend Tenisha through her mother. I'll get you her name and address. Get next to this lady if you can. I think she could help you out."

"What if I go to Orlando's house and look around?"

"You could. We've been through it. The trouble is, I find a phone number and call it? You know what I get?"

" 'Orlando who?' " Jerome said. " 'You mean the dude with the rows and the shitty beard? Never heard of him.' "

Delsa liked the way Jerome was showing his sense of humor, at ease in the squad room.

"What you do," Delsa said, "you find a number you call it, say you've been looking all over for Orlando. You have a deal going with him. Or, you say you want to know how he likes the Love Swing you gave him."

"Man, you crazy? Give him one of those? Get

tangled up in it . . ." He said, "That's all I'm looking for, phone numbers?"

"Jerome," Delsa said, "a good investigator doesn't know what he's looking for till he sees it."

Jerome said, "A good investigator," nodding, going over the rest of it in his mind before he grinned and said, "Cool."

Delsa said, "Go to the scene during the day so you can see what you're doing. The police tape's gone, the woman next door moved out. Look on walls where there might've been a phone. On kitchen cabinets . . . Start there and find out what you're looking for."

Jerome held up the wanted poster. "Can I keep this?"

"It's yours," Delsa said.

Jerome looked from the poster to Delsa.

"Can police collect on this, they catch Orlando?"

Delsa shook his head.

"No, we're paid to do our job. Rewards, Jerome, are compensation only for concerned citizens, like yourself."

Jerome said, "Uh-huh."

He took his coat off, hung it on the rack, came back to his desk and phoned Kelly Barr.

"How're you doing?"

"The phone rings and I jump."

"We'd like you to come in tomorrow for a few more questions. It won't take long, I can pick you up and drive you home right after."

"So you're not arresting me."

"For what?"

"I was kidding."

"Yeah, but what were you thinking when you said it?"

"You want to grill me on the phone?"

"We'll save it for tomorrow," Delsa said. "Unless I can pick you up right now. What time is it?" He looked at his watch. "Almost six."

Kelly said, "Why don't we do it here?"

"I can wait."

"You asked me what I was thinking. You're dying to know, but you can wait?"

"Will you tell me?"

"By tomorrow I might've forgotten. Frank, I'm sitting here by myself scared to death not knowing what's gonna happen."

He said, "All right, I'll be over," not giving himself a chance to think about it.

She said, "I'll answer your questions, but can't we kick back a little, not be so formal about it?"

Delsa said, "This is serious, Kelly, and you're a witness," hearing his serious tone, always serious, so he'd keep looking at her as a witness. But he wasn't himself, only a cop asking her questions. He said, "I can come now if you want."

She said, "Make it seven-thirty. I have to shower, straighten the place up, put the right music on—"

He said, "Kelly . . . ?"

She said, "See you, Frank," and hung up.

An hour and a half before he'd see her again after staring at her in the squad room this morning smoking her Slim, after sticking his butt in her face to pull off her boots and answering her question about reciprocating, staring at her and wanting to touch her face. He could miss Maureen, feel love, sorrow, and he could stare at a woman sometimes and wonder about her, not many, not any the way he stared at Kelly Barr and wanted to touch her. *Touch her*—Christ, eat her up. He had refused to admit it this morning and this afternoon, but now, hearing her voice in his mind, *See you, Frank,* he had to tell himself, You're fucked, you know it?

Nothing he could do about it. He wanted to be at ease with her, but she could be involved in the case and he didn't want to find it out unless she told him.

Maureen in the hospital said she knew he'd marry again, saying, as he shook his head, "You know you will, you like girls. You know how to talk to them. You like to flirt. I know you do, you can't help it." He told Maureen, swear to God, he had never cheated on her, not even thought about it in the nine years. She said, " 'Cause you know I'd shoot her, the cunt, whoever she is." Maureen said, "You like being married. You'll do it again and I'll take it as a compliment, I made you happy." She said, "But go slow, see if you can talk first. There's a lot more talking in a marriage than screwing." She said, "You know why girls like you? You're gentle. They like the way you smile with your Al Pacino eyes. It's okay if she's a little smarter than you are. It didn't hurt our marriage. If she's a brain she wouldn't marry a cop anyway." He wondered what Maureen would've thought of Kelly. Maureen, with her Sex Crimes experience, had interviewed hundreds of rape victims, real ones and phonies, Maureen with her critical eye. She'd like Kelly but would find fault, pick at some mannerism, think she was a bit theatrical, low-key but still acting.

Now he was blaming Maureen for what he felt.

He thought of Jackie saying she was going to talk to Lloyd again. Maybe let down her dreads this time, have a drink if he offered her one, see if that worked.

Delsa was leaning that way now.

SHE HAD THE TRACK LIGHTING SET MEDIUM-LOW
for mellow, Sade on the sound system doing
"Smooth Operator" at the moment with Lauryn
Hill standing by, Missy Elliott and her jungle hi-
tech ready to bump up the mood if needed. He
came at twenty to eight wearing the same outfit
he'd had on earlier today, the dark turtleneck and
duffle coat that made him look like a seaman.
He'd shaved. The lotion wasn't bad. She told him
he'd look salty with a beard, saying her dad had
grown one in the navy and she had pictures of
him she loved. He told her it was still cold out,
wiping his feet on the Oriental inside the door.
He said it was supposed to go down below freezing tonight and tomorrow afternoon it could be
fifty degrees. Why does anyone want to live in
Detroit?

She said, "Why do you?"

He said when he was away for a while he was always glad to get back.

"And you don't know why," Kelly said.

She helped him off with his coat, smelling his aftershave again, hung the coat in the hall closet and brought him into the loft the black woman cop, Jackie, said you could play touch football in naked if you wanted. Now he was taking it all in, the lighting, Sade's soothing voice, the crystal pitcher of alexanders on the coffee table. She said, "Don't be nervous, Frank, I'm not trying to seduce you."

"You mean it's always like this?"

"Pretty much."

"Two glasses on the table?"

She said, "Come on," and steered him to the sofa, got him into the deep cushions that were hard to get out of, poured alexanders into the stem glasses and placed one in front of him on the glass top of the bamboo coffee table. Kelly, standing on the other side now, raised her glass. She said, "Here's to your getting the bad guys," and watched him look up at her. Reading something into her toast? Maybe. He took a sip of his drink, then another that almost finished it.

He looked up at her again and said, "That's not bad."

She topped off his glass, feeling him watching her. He asked her what she did when she wasn't modeling. She straightened and looked down at him trapped in the ochre-colored cushions.

"I like to go to clubs and wave my arms in the air, thrash around, get down with the beat. I think there's more energy in it here than in New York, a working-class audience getting their release. You know what I mean? I've seen Eminem at the Shelter, in the basement of St. Andrews? Iggy at the Palace, back with the Stooges. Hush, white hip-hoppers, and the Almighty Dreadnaughtz at Alvin's. Karen Monster, a cool chick, the Dirt Bombs, they're high-speed Detroit punk. The Howling Diablos any Sunday out in Berkley. There's a new band called the Go, kind of glam but they're okay. Aerosmith I love, they keep coming back to town. I was never a groupie," Kelly said, "but I've always sort of envied those chicks, they're so aggressive."

"I worked security at concerts," Delsa said, "a long time ago, on the side. A girl would come up to me, 'I'll show you my tits if you let me go around back.' You know, to meet the band. This was at Pine Knob."

"Would you let her?"

"If she was nice about it, didn't start pleading and carrying on."

"She'd show you her ta-tas?"

"I'd say it wasn't necessary, knowing she would anyway, to show her gratitude."

Kelly saw his smile, there and gone.

And now he was telling her that Montez Taylor, seventeen years old, "Was convicted of aggravated assault and sentenced as an adult to two years at Jackson and it changed his life. Montez got connected and came out to deal drugs. Now he's a baller, a ghetto star, still in his teens making six figures. Has the strut, his bling bling, has his girls iced up, big spinning rims on his car, a heavy bass in his sound box. Montez is now called Chops. He has the chops to do what he wants. He also has a criminal lawyer now who knows his stuff, a Clinton Street dealmaker, and Montez draws probation for giving them this and that instead of taking serious falls."

"Mr. Paradise," Kelly said.

"No, another lawyer before him, Avern Cohn. Montez was brought up on assault to do great bodily harm, was severely beaten by the cops, and now both Avern Cohn and Tony Paradiso want to represent him, seeing a chance to bring suit against the police. Old Tony had the reputation for winning this kind of civil action, so Montez went with him. Tony got Montez off on the assault but didn't make it suing the cops."

Kelly was nodding. "Montez said the old man put a suit on him and made him his monkey. Yeah, I can see now what he meant."

"That's high disrespect," Delsa said, "for a guy they called Chops. Tony Jr. says the old man referred to Montez as his pet nigger. Have you met him, Tony Jr.?"

"No, and from what Chloe said I hope I don't."

"What, that he's a prick?"

"Her exact word."

"Everybody calls him that. But you don't suppose she did because he kept her out of Tony's will. You mentioned that last night. But if the old man wanted to leave her something, don't you think he'd find a way?"

Kelly felt exposed standing in front of him. She sat down on the edge of the sofa, a cushion between them. She took a sip of her drink, and another and said, "I thought we were talking about Montez."

"We are," Delsa said. "What it comes down to, Montez knows what Chloe was getting and he wants it."

He was waiting for her to say something. Kelly shrugged and sat back in the cushions. "You think so?"

"The other night," Delsa said, "Jackie Michaels

and I followed a trail of blood, like arrows, from a murdered woman in a stairwell to the man who killed her, sitting in his hotel room. Jackie said, 'Do you thank God like I do they're stupid, or stoned or generally fucked up?' Here, the arrows were pointing to Montez even before he opened his mouth and said you were Chloe. He's a bad guy and he has a motive, the old man dies and he cashes in. He's not in the will, neither is Chloe, but he knows she's getting *some*-thing. I think what happened," Delsa said, "he had to change his plan in a hurry. You said he didn't know you were coming and it upset him. He tried to make a phone call. I asked you if he spoke to anyone. Have you thought about that, how he acted? Your being there blew his plan. The two white motherfuckers show up and there's company."

"But you had to let him go," Kelly said.

"The focus is still on him, you know that. He told you what she's getting, didn't he? He must have if you're playing a part in it. He tells you his plan inspired by desperation and you look at it thinking, Hmmmm, could it work? Who's out anything? Not Chloe or the old man. But if you go along with him you'd be dumber than he is, because you know he'd have to kill you. Just like the two guys had to do Chloe, because she was there."

Kelly leaned forward to pick up her glass and have a good sip from it, Sade's voice murmuring in the quiet, and sat back again before she said, "Chloe thought it might be an insurance policy, in her name."

"There's nothing like that," Delsa said, "in the old man's files."

"I think it might be stock," Kelly said. Hung that out to see what he'd say and took another sip, her confidence in pretty good shape.

"But if it's in her name," Delsa said, "she'd know what it is, she'd get a statement every month."

"I know about statements," Kelly said, "I was wiped out holding dot-com stocks three years ago. Chloe never got statements. But if it's a stock certificate, something the old man bought a long time ago and signed over to her, she wouldn't get statements."

"And he didn't give her the certificate."

"If that's what it is. I guess what I'm saying, I don't know what else it could be." She let that hang for a moment before she said, "But I might know where it is."

She placed her glass on the bamboo table, picked up her pack of Virginia Slims and lit one.

Delsa said, "You gonna tell me about it?"

"In a bank deposit box."

"Where?"

"Chloe didn't say."

"It's in her name?"

Kelly shook her head. "Montez Taylor."

Delsa took a 120 from the pack. Kelly extended her lighter and flicked it.

"Montez gets the certificate out of the bank box," Delsa said, "and brings it to you."

She sipped her drink and poured a little more, giving herself time to come up with a reason. She said, "I think the old man wanted this to be a surprise for Chloe and told Montez to give her whatever's in the box."

Delsa said, "You just thought of that?"

Kelly said, "Somebody has to get it out of the box. I know Chloe didn't have a key. The old man's dead . . ."

"So is Chloe," Delsa said. "So now Montez gets the stock certificate—"

"Or whatever it is."

"And brings it to you. You cash it in or sell it, do whatever you do, acting as Chloe, signing her name, and you give him the money. Unless you think you can get away with not giving him the money. In that case he shoots you or has the two white motherfuckers do it." He paused, said, "I bet you could pick them out of a lineup," paused again and said, "and I bet these guys are deer hunters."

Kelly, listening, going along, said, "Why?"

"The way you described them. I see the two guys in the woods with rifles, red jackets and the baseball caps. The kind of guys who walk off the job during deer season. You said they looked like workingmen."

Kelly nodded.

So did Delsa saying, "That's how I see them. Tigers fans, or they just like the caps. They wear them straight, don't they, not turned around."

Kelly nodded again. This was good.

"They might not follow the Tigers, the way they've been playing, but they're definitely hockey fans and follow the Wings, 'cause the Wings know how to win. Till last year. I could go to Joe Louis tonight, Toronto's in town, and look for two guys in Tigers road caps with the orange *D* and pick 'em up."

"You're kidding."

"Yeah, but when I do nail those guys, the first thing I'll ask is if they were at the hockey game tonight. I'll let you know what they say."

"If you find them," Kelly said.

"The past year we've had a few homicides where a witness saw two white males, ordinary-looking, working-class guys. They're pros, but not very professional. Firearms is checking the Paradiso bullets, see if they can get a match on another homicide. A couple of *white* hit men? What bothers me, why you've been holding back, not telling me everything."

"Why do you think? I'm scared to death."

"Well, a little scared," Delsa said, "that's part of the bounce you're getting. I see you playing with Montez the same way you're playing with me. Take it slow and see what happens."

Kelly said, "Really, I've told you all I know."

"But you don't know Montez," Delsa said. "What do you think he's been doing the past ten years? He was making six figures as a kid, now he's running errands for an old man? Why would he put up with being a monkey in a suit all those years? He saw a payoff, a big one. He tells himself he's comfortable in the suit, ride it out. Is he in the will? No, I checked. The old man was gonna give him the house and changed his mind. Lloyd, the houseman, said Montez had a fit. But he's a hustler, and he's given the opportunity to handle Chloe's payoff, so he'll go for that one. He doesn't know he'll fuck it up. But even if he knew the odds were against him, he'd have to do it. It's his nature to hustle."

Kelly said, "But you're not sure."

"Yeah, I am, I'm sure. But the only thing you

can be sure of, as long as Montez needs you, you're fairly safe."

"You mean," Kelly said, "Montez or the two motherfuckers won't try to shoot me?"

Delsa shook his head. "I didn't say that."

THE PHONE RANG AT ELEVEN AND KELLY JUMPED, alone now in that cushy sofa. It was Montez downstairs in his car. He said, "You don't buzz me in, babe, I'm gonna bust all the windows in your car." His voice softened to say, "Girl, there things I need to discuss with you."

Montez walked into the loft, stopped, raised his face to the hip-hop coming out of the system and said, "Missy Elliott."

" 'Get Ur Freak On,' " Kelly said.

"Shit. What else you got?"

"Da Brat, 'What Chu Like.' Lil' Kim being ultra nasty." Kelly moving now, shoulders back, hands in fists.

"Shit," Montez said.

"Gangsta Boo and some Dirty South."

"Yeah, shit, I thought you was only into collegiate riffs, doing the cheers there."

"Rah Digga," Kelly said.

"Rah Digga . . . ?"

"Used to be with Bustah Rhymes."

"Yeah, I know her. I love those ladies, 'specially that dirty mouth Lil' Kim." He saw the two glasses on the coffee table, a little something still in the pitcher, and said, "You had company, huh?"

"Frank Delsa."

She watched Montez pretend to glance around the room.

"Not still here, is he?"

"Left hours ago."

"But he had a drink."

"You want one?"

"What'd he come for, hang a wire on you? Down in those nice cargo pants?"

She wore the cargoes with a black cashmere sweater. She said, "I thought you only wore suits."

"I've been set free," Montez said. He had on cargo pants, a T-shirt underneath a sweatshirt with a hood under his cashmere topcoat that he took off now and laid over a chair. He said, "We both in style, huh?" and pulled the legs of his pants out to each side. "Diesel, one-twenty-nine."

Kelly pulled the legs of her pants to each side and said, "Catherine Malandrino, six-seventy-five. But yours aren't bad."

Montez grinned and said shit and sank into the sofa that Kelly saw now as designer quicksand. She'd had two drinks and wouldn't mind another.

"What'd that man want to know this time?"

"Same old same old, why did I tell them I was Chloe." She poured the last of the alexanders into a glass and offered it to Montez. "It's my glass, not the cop's."

"I don't drink anything looks like medicine," Montez said. "He wanted to know why you told them you was Chloe. What'd you say?"

"I told him you threatened me."

"Wait now."

"Go along or I'd be shot in the head."

"You're playing with me."

"What do you think I told them? You made me. Why else would I do it? They're not stupid. But it's your word against mine so we're both off the hook."

Montez, sitting back staring at her, said, "What else you tell him?"

"He's already figured it out. Whatever Chloe was getting, you want me to get it for you."

Montez looked like he was thinking now as he stared.

Kelly said, "I don't know what it is, do I? I'll tell you what I think it is, a stock certificate. Am I close?"

"You tell him where it is?"

"In a bank deposit box, but I don't know which bank."

"You told him that?"

"It's your box, isn't it? What's the problem?"

She got up with her pitcher and her glass and walked toward the kitchen.

"You want a beer?"

"A Henessey, a great big one."

Kelly placed the pitcher on the counter and finished the last alexander. She'd make one more. She got out the cognac, a snifter glass. She looked at Montez across the room in the sofa.

"Why don't you get whatever it is and we'll take a look at it."

She watched Montez pull himself out of the sofa and come toward the counter. She said, "Look, he knows you've got something in a deposit box. So what? Go pick it up. Maybe he can trace your name to the bank and he's there when you open the box. So what? You've got something made out to Chloe. You didn't put it there, but you were instructed to pick it up after the old man's death. Okay, you're picking it up. If no one's watching, walk out. If Frank Delsa's standing there, hand him whatever it is. You don't get your payoff, but you don't go to prison, either. It's up to you how you work it," Kelly said, pouring Montez his great big one. "But it's always been up to you, Chops. Hasn't it?"

Montez, at the counter now, stared at her.

Avern Cohn, at home in his study, was watching Jay Leno "Jaywalking," interviewing nitwits on the streets of L.A., asking one of them if he knew who was buried in Grant's Tomb. The nitwit said, "Cary Grant?" and laughed. Jay Leno said, "Yeah, Cary Grant," and the nitwit said, "Hey, I took a guess and I was right."

Was he putting Leno on? Avern decided no, the guy was a true nitwit.

His cell phone beeped, on the lamp table next to his burgundy leather chair.

Montez.

"I'm in my car coming out to see you. On 75 right now passing Hamtramck."

"Which phone are you using?"

"My own."

Avern said, "Call me back on the disposable," and laid the cell on the table again.

He wouldn't say Montez qualified as a nitwit. He was a high school graduate—not bad for a former street thug. If you asked Montez who was buried in Grant's Tomb he'd say, "Yeah, Grant's Tomb," giving himself time to decide if it was a trick question. Montez' weakness, he was too cool to be concerned with the little things that could trip him up. Lloyd said, "He knows everything so you can't tell him nothing."

Ten years ago, Avern ready to defend him on the assault with intent charge, ready to go after the cops for beating him up, Montez chose Tony Paradiso to represent him, Tony and his son, the prick, chasing any case that could become a civil action against the police. Avern had managed to put Montez out of his mind. But then recently, talking to Lloyd about dumb criminals they had known, Lloyd began filling him in on Montez' activities working for Tony Paradiso, Lloyd saying he was now trying hard to pass as a house nigger to get in the man's will. Avern said maybe he could help the boy and began hanging out at Randy's on Larned, Montez' favorite spot according to Lloyd, on account of the stylish working girls who stopped in there.

The idea: advise Montez on how to act with a gentleman racist and pay back Tony Paradiso, the guinea fuck, for stealing his client.

It wasn't long before they were meeting for drinks, Avern showing no resentment and Montez sorry he had given up on him as his lawyer to become Tony Paradiso's monkey. Well, he wasn't making it into the man's will, but was getting the house instead. Avern said, "I can get you a million and a half for it. When do you want to take possession?" In other words, when did he want the old man to die. Montez said how would that work? And Avern said, "Don't ask unless you want it to happen."

Next, Montez wasn't getting the house after all, goddamn it, and was mad enough to whack the old man himself. Ten years he put in for nothing, and the old man's ho was getting something worth as much as the house. Montez explained his part in it, the old man using him so his son the prick wouldn't know about it. A stock certificate, Montez said, worth a million six at least, according to the old man.

Avern said, "He can still be sent to his reward any time you want. You give the ho her stock and she signs it over to you. What's wrong with that?" Avern checked it out with Lloyd and Lloyd said yeah, that's how he understood it was set up. Lloyd being in the will was okay with Tony Jr. And if the man was to go ahead of his time, that was okay with Lloyd. Once the will was read he was moving to Puerto Rico.

But now with Chloe dead . . .

Jay Leno was asking another nitwit who America fought in the American Revolution to gain our independence. The nitwit this time said, "Other Americans?" and laughed. He said, "Was it the South? The South Americans?" and laughed. The nitwits knew they were wrong and thought it was funny.

Montez thought he was a genius making Kelly pose as Chloe. He got the cops on him as a suspect and Fontana and Krupa pissed off enough to want to shoot him. Which could happen.

His phone rang with an annoying sound.

Montez said, "Whereabouts in Bloomfield Hills do you live?"

"You'd never find it," Avern said. "What's up?"

"I went to see this Kelly at her place? She says get the stock certificate and bring it to her and she'll take a look at it."

"That's the idea, isn't it?"

"I don't know can I trust her. She was real friendly though, sounding like she wanted to help me out."

"She didn't act scared?"

"Not as much."

See? This is what you were up against trying to do business with felons. They tended to be—not as nitwitty as the ones Leno ran into on the streets of Los Angeles, but dumb enough, prone to blow whatever they got into. Avern wanted with all his heart to believe Fontana and Krupa were the exceptions.

"I told you," Avern said, "your false I.D. of Chloe was a bad move, done in haste and it's got them looking at you. If you'd waited until you were in the clear and *then* went after Kelly, it wouldn't be that much different than dealing with Chloe. I told you from the beginning, how you get her to sign it over to you. The means you use, is strictly up to you. Where are you?"

"Coming up on Fourteen Mile."

"Turn around and go home," Avern said. "If you want, call me at the office tomorrow. But I'll tell you right now, I don't see how I can help you."

"Man, you the one got me into this."

"And you told me you could handle it," Avern said, "so handle it." He paused and said, "She was quite friendly, uh?"

"Loose, she'd been drinking cocktails."

"How friendly was she?"

"I tried to get her on the couch, she turned me down saying it wasn't a color thing, she had a boyfriend once was African-American. Said she just wasn't in the mood. We talked about things . . . But can I trust her?"

"That's something you'll have to decide," Avern said. "I'm going to bed."

He broke the connection but held on to the phone, wondering what his boys were doing. He'd have to let them know as soon as possible, once he decided how best to explain it, Montez might have to be taken out, so be ready. They'd holler, but there was nothing he could do about it. He'd rather tell Fontana, Carl a few points smarter than Art. But if he called him he *knew* he'd have to talk to that fucking Connie. He'd lose his patience and scream at her and she'd hang up on him. So he'd call Art, first thing in the morning.

LLOYD, WEARING A STARCHED WHITE DRESS SHIRT
hanging out of his pants, opened the front door
and stood facing Jackie Michaels in her winter
coat, her patterned red scarf, her hair combed
out, no dreads this morning, Jackie looking at
peace.

"Now what you want?"

Her gaze came up from the square of cardboard taped over the broken pane of glass to
Lloyd. "You ever gonna get this fixed?"

"I had to find out who's paying for it," Lloyd
said. He stared at Jackie another few moments. "I
don't have to let you in, do I?"

"It's still considered a crime scene," Jackie
said. "I can come in if I want, but I'm leaving it
up to you."

"You have a different tone of voice this morning," Lloyd said. "Come on in and let's see if it works on me."

He brought Jackie through the dining room and pantry to the kitchen, bigger than her living room with a range made for a restaurant, every size pan hanging above the worktable, Lloyd telling her Mr. Tony Jr. was here just a while ago.

"Had his daughter with him, Allegra, nice polite girl. She stops and looks at those old paintings in the foyer. Say she wants to have somebody from DuMouchelle come and look at them. I asked her daddy who was paying to have the door fixed."

Jackie was looking at the bottle of Rémy and the teapot and cups on the plain-wood worktable.

"He said to call somebody. I said, 'I know how to do that, but what do I pay 'em with?' I said, 'Your daddy always paid the tradespeople cash.' I said, 'Let me have some money till I'm gone to Puerto Rico.' "

"You have family there, uh?"

"Yes, I do, a flock of cousins still living. Tony Jr. takes out a wad—the man has on a three-thousand-dollar suit of clothes and carries a wad. He says how much did I want, a couple hundred? I told him a couple hundred don't get the toilet fixed. I said give me fifteen hundred.

He give me a thousand. But try to get it out of his hand—"

"Hangs on to it," Jackie said, "while you're pulling on the bills. My daddy was like that."

"He still living?"

"No, he went early. He'd be your age now, about sixty?"

Lloyd smiled at her showing gold in his teeth. "You know how old I am, you been through my jacket a few times, haven't you? You wondering, could this seventy-one-year-old geezer play any part in this? I bet you think you know all about me, my scores, the falls I took—"

"Only to become, from what I hear," Jackie said, "the perfect nigga for around the house. You gonna pour the tea, or you want me to?"

"Go ahead," Lloyd said. "You want sugar in yours or just the cognac, the way 'Lizabeth Taylor use to take hers?"

"I love to learn things like that," Jackie said. "I'll go with Ms. Taylor."

"I'll tell you something else," Lloyd said. "I was only sixty, you'd of smelled my lust before we's through the dining room."

Jackie said, "Takes a little longer now?"

The second time they passed the house in Carl's Tahoe Carl said, "That's a cop car."

"Chevy Lumina," Art said, looking back as they headed up Iroquois. "It could be Lloyd's, couldn't it?"

"The help don't park in the drive," Carl said. "Cops are in there looking for clues, like we're gonna do now. Go on over to Orlando's, stick a finger up our butts and wonder what the hell we're looking for. But, shit, tell me what Avern said. He wants us to take Montez out?"

"He says we might have to. Montez gets his nuts in a crack he starts looking to make a deal."

"You ask him who pays for this one?"

"Avern says it's self-preservation. Keeps us from going back to D Block."

"Next time we talk to him," Carl said, "I'll let him know he's paying for it, twenty each to stay out of jail."

"Avern?"

"Yeah, Avern. Otherwise, we get caught we give him up. He has to know that."

"Same with the smoke this afternoon," Art said, "if he don't have the cash."

Carl said, "Yeah, if he shows up. He don't, we have to look for him. Shit, this deal is all work and no pay."

They were seated at the kitchen table now with their Elizabeth Taylor hot tea and smoking leftover Virginia Slims. Jackie said, "Tell me, Sugar, for the record, you a hostile witness or you want to help us out here?"

"Do I look hostile to you? I'm watching what happens," Lloyd said, "like I'm at the movies."

"You find it interesting, how it's going?"

"Let me say predictable."

"You'd of done it different?"

"Done what?"

"Figured out how to get Chloe's money?"

"That's what this is about? I thought it was a murder case, somebody shooting Mr. Paradise and his sweetie."

"You have a motive for that, too. You're in the old man's will."

"You getting tough with me again? Finish your tea."

"It just slipped out," Jackie said, "from habit."

"I figured from the time you was here before," Lloyd said, "you the one plays the mean cop, the one don't take any shit, huh?"

"Sometimes, yeah, I try to mess with their heads."

"That's a shame, ask a nice-looking woman to do that. Listen to me. If I'm in the man's will and he's up in his years, what's my hurry? I been living in a big, comfortable house. I got all kind of hand-me-down clothes I'm taking to Puerto Rico with me for my cousins. I got hand-me-down shoes looking good as new. Always had shoe trees in 'em."

"They fit?"

"That's the only trouble. I took a pair and cut slits in 'em?"

"On the side by the little toe," Jackie said.

"That's right, and the man got mad, said I'd ruined a nine-hundred-dollar pair of shoes. I said, 'But they hurt my feet.' Didn't matter. He made me put the shoes back in his closet. I'll take all his shoes along, too. In my youth, I would've kicked his white ass with those pointy motherfuckers. See, but now I have control of my impulses."

Jackie said, "Wisdom coming with age."

"And a nine-year stretch."

Jackie said, "Learned crime doesn't pay."

"Listen to you," Lloyd said, "you don't know shit. It paid good when I was doing stickups on my own. Not till I teamed up was I ever caught."

"And your partner finked on you."

"A young man I thought I could trust."

"They all do it now," Jackie said. "Especially the dopers, they'll give you anybody you want looking at thirty years. I was wondering," Jackie said, stirring her tea for no reason, "if you'd like to say a few words about Montez. How he was seriously pissed off over not getting the house."

"Sign a statement?"

"Would you?"

"You won't need my help," Lloyd said. "Whatever Montez is into, he'll fuck it up all by himself."

They parked the Tahoe in the lot behind the White Castle and sniffed the air crossing the street to the redbrick two-story house: Art saying they ought to pick up a sack of burgers when they were through. Jesus, smell those fuckin onions. Carl saying those bricks must've been laid a hundred years ago, that old-style duplex, bay windows up and down, the tall chimneys, oval front doors. "The one on the left," Carl said. "See how the brick above the door's all black? From the smoke. That's the one we want. Twenty-two-ten."

The door had been battered in to hang on one hinge, the living room charred and smoke damaged, water dripping from the ceiling. Carl went in the kitchen past a blackened dining table, came back and said, "The kitchen's a mess, all tore up."

Art said, "What's this room, pretty nice? Look at that TV hanging on the wall. That cost some money."

"All they do in the weed business is make

money," Carl said. "You think we ought to look into it?"

Art said, "Shit, I don't mind. This guy's out of business, we could take over his customers. You suppose there's any in the house?"

"What?"

"Weed. I think I got some Zig-Zags," Art said, getting his raincoat open to pat his jeans. "Yeah, I got a book of one and a halfs. If we get lucky."

"Cops've been through the place," Carl said.

"Avern said something like a hundred pounds were delivered by the guy got chopped up. But what'd he say to look for?"

"You was sitting there."

"He told you about it first. I'm on the phone with Smokey." He said, "Hey," looking past Carl and out the front window. "A colored guy's coming to the house. The hell's he want?"

"I doubt he's a looter," Carl said. "He ain't hesitating or looking around, is he? No, he could be coming back for something stashed—what do you think?—and knows where it is. Let's step out of the way."

Jerome already had a wanted sheet folded in a pocket of his cargoes he was wearing with a Tommy ski jacket and a black watch cap pulled down over his ears. He ripped down another sheet—Orlando's profile on it, his rows, his shitty beard with the bare spots in it—from the wall next to the bay window and went inside, into the living room and stopped.

Two white guys standing in the dining room were holding nines on him.

But not saying a word. Not telling him to freeze or do any of that shit cops told you to do. Jerome looked at their black no-style coats, at their regular shoes and said, "Don't shoot," raising his hands in the air, one hand holding the wanted sheet, "I'm on your side. I'm checking this place out for Sergeant Frank Delsa. He's on the police Homicide and my name's Jerome Jackson, I'm a C.I."

They still didn't say anything. Not telling him to go on, get outta here, nothing.

"Y'all are Homicide, too, aren't you?"

Carl said, "You know what we are, but we don't know what you are."

"Man, I told you, I'm a C.I. working for Frank Delsa, Squad Seven. I came over to have a look around."

Art said, "For what, weed?"

"There wouldn't be no dank in here now."

"What're you looking for then?"

"I'll know when I see it," Jerome said.

Art said, "You getting smart with me?"

"You never heard that? I start looking for phone numbers. You look on the wall," Jerome said, "where a phone was somebody ripped out. A man that don't mind messing up his walls."

Carl said, "What's that you got?"

He came over and Jerome handed him the sheet saying, "Twenty thousand reward, man, for Orlando Holmes, but y'all can't collect on it, can you, being with the police."

Art said, "What's he talking about?" and now both the guys were reading the sheet.

Jerome said, "Frank Delsa gave me one. Y'all haven't seen it? They some more stuck on the front of the house."

Art said, "Jesus Christ, we put him away we could score thirty each."

Jerome didn't know what he was talking about but didn't ask. The other one said to him, "See, we been on our vacation, only got back today. We're helping out here till we get, you know, assigned to some squad needs us." He said, "But you can collect this money, huh?"

"Since I ain't on the police, only working for 'em, yeah."

Carl said, "What if we help each other?"

"I don't know," Jerome said, "I guess." He wondered should he ask to see their badges. He said, "Even if you don't get any of the reward we find him?"

"It's all yours," Carl said. "As you say, we can't touch any part of it."

DELSA WASN'T WORRIED ABOUT TAKING DOWN
Montez. He believed that once he did, Montez
would see he had to deal and give up the two
white guys, the shooters. No, Delsa's problem
was Kelly Barr. He couldn't stop thinking about
her and there was nothing he could do about it,
no one he could talk to. Jackie Michaels would
roll her eyes at him. "You've known her, what,
three days and you're in love, huh? Baby, you
need to get laid's all."

It wasn't about getting laid.

It was about her.

It was the cool way she looked at him as she
smoked the Slim. It was the confidence she
showed in her underwear shots, the low-rise
thong and the low-rise v-string, the demure way
she crossed her arms to cover her breasts.

It kept getting harder to treat her like a witness. Lying in bed in the early morning, the house still, he would think of reasons to call her.

At his desk later in the morning he punched her number on his phone. He had a real question to ask and it worried him a little.

Wendell Robinson walked in the squad room, came right to Delsa's desk as Kelly's voice said hello.

"Listen, I'm gonna have to call you back. This is Frank Delsa."

She said, "I know who it is."

"I'll get right back to you."

She said fine.

He hung up and Wendell said, "The guy that was shot thirteen times . . . ? You know I gave it to Four when you started losing people. They identified the complainant as Henry Mendez. Street name, Fatboy," Wendell said, "a big P.R. kid twenty years old nobody liked much, but had a '94 Cutlass with nice rims. Last month Fatboy and three homies held up a party store on Springwells. Shots were fired, the manager and the clerk went down behind the counter, nobody was hit. Fatboy, we find out later, waited in the car. The next day he's dead, with all those bullets in him."

"I saw him," Delsa said, "lying in the weeds back of the cemetery. That was three weeks ago."

"That's right, and now just the other day," Wendell said, "three white boys are I.D.'d on the robbery and picked up. Wayne and Kenny, both twenty, and Toody, eighteen, all three on LEIN for B and E, assault, felony firearms. It's this Toody that steps up, the smartest one, and asks can he cop to something else and get a pass on the armed robbery. Toody says all he did was wait in the car with Fatboy. He said it was Wayne shot him. Fatboy was complaining about his cut and Wayne was afraid he'd give them up."

Delsa said, "Who's working it?"

"Eleanor Marsh. You know Eleanor, big, good-looking white woman. Came to Four from Vice about a year ago. She's working with you now. Jackie's got her checking with the Crime Lab on Paradiso and the girl."

"Jackie told me," Delsa said.

"Fine-looking woman," Wendell said. "I know working Vice she liked to get out on the street in a little skimpy playsuit and white boots. You'd see her over on Cass hustling the johns."

"Eleanor and Maureen were good friends," Delsa said. "She'd come over and hang out."

"Well, Eleanor took what Toody said and asked Kenny what he knew about Fatboy getting hit, waving a plea deal on the robbery at him, and Kenny jumped at it. He said they went down by the cemetery looking for a crackhead Fatboy could shoot to prove himself, get off the hook. Only Wayne tells Kenny to give Toody the gun, the Ruger. Kenny's the gun guy. He picks them up different ways, some doing burglaries and sells them. Wayne tells Toody to shoot Fatboy, but he can't do it. He hands the gun to Wayne and Wayne empties it into Fatboy, shoots him seven times in the head, six in the body. So then it's Wayne's turn to be questioned. Eleanor asks him where he was that night. Oh, he was visiting his girlfriend in Clawson. Took her to dinner at the National Coney, Fifteen and Crooks. Wayne stays with that, won't budge, even though his prints are on the Ruger and all over the car, the Cutlass."

Delsa wished Wendell would hurry up.

"Now this jailhouse lawyer named Dominic talks to Eleanor. He's on Four Northeast, same as Wayne and the boys. He says Wayne came to him for legal advice. Said he pumped thirteen bullets into Fatboy, kept shooting even though the man had to be dead. What he wanted Dominic to tell him, would it work as an insanity defense if he started acting crazy?" Wendell shook his head. "They don't think before they shoot somebody. They do all their thinking after." He turned to go and stopped. "Eleanor's coming to see you. Has something looks pretty good from Firearms."

He turned again and walked out.

And Delsa punched Kelly's number. This time he had to wait to hear her voice.

"I'm sorry I had to cut us off."

"That's okay." She said, "Listen, I'm working tomorrow night, a fashion show at the DIA, the art institute. It's black tie, if you want to come."

"I want to stop by, pick up Chloe's driver's license."

There was a pause.

"I have it?"

"I gave it to you the night we left the scene."

She said, "The scene—you mean Paradiso's?"

"You put it in your coat pocket."

She said, "I have to leave soon, drive up to Saks for fittings."

"When can I pick up her license?"

She said, "Let me see if I have it."

The squad room door opened and Wendell came in again, with Eleanor Marsh this time, Eleanor smiling at him, Wendell saying, "I meant to tell you—"

Delsa heard Kelly's voice, "Frank . . . ?"

He held up his hand to Wendell and said to Kelly, "I'm sorry, I'll have to call you back."

This time as he hung up Wendell said, "The guy shot in the SUV on St. Antoine? Remember that one?"

"Last year," Delsa said, "right before Christmas," and watched Eleanor Marsh looking around the empty squad room, Jackie and Harris both on the street. Wendell had it right about Eleanor, a tall, good-looking brunette in a black suit, the skirt fairly short.

Delsa said, "I remember we couldn't get a lead on that one, no witnesses, nothing."

"Let me tell you what happened," Wendell said. "Two boys come along, one of 'em's Maurice Miller. They see the man sitting in his vehicle making a phone call. You like irony? If he'd been talking on the phone while he's driving, he'd be alive today. The two boys go in the grocery store right there, come out, the man's still talking on the phone. They run around the corner, down the block to Maurice's house. They come back with a nine and Maurice shoots the man in the head. They gonna jack the car. But now it's all messed up inside with the man's blood, his brains, hair stuck to the windows. They don't want the car now."

Delsa hung on knowing it was about to get good.

"Yesterday, Juanita Miller comes home from

work, her brother Maurice is eating pork and beans, the can sitting on the sink. Juanita blows up. She bought that can of Van Camp's hickory-smoked pork and beans for herself, not her lazy-ass brother. She yells at him to go get her another can right this minute. Her lazy-ass brother tells her to get fucked. Instead . . ."

Eleanor was grinning, waiting for the punch line.

"Juanita calls Homicide, calls us direct. You know how she has the number?" Wendell said. "A Homicide card was left at that house one time we stopped by to ask about Maurice. She tells the desk Maurice is the one killed the man on St. Antoine last year, in his SUV. She's asked does she know where the gun is. She thinks it's in the house someplace. Does she know where Maurice is. Juanita says, 'He's in the kitchen eating my fuckin beans.' "

Eleanor laughed out loud and Delsa said, "You know what Jackie always says."

"About thanking God they're stupid? That one?"

"That one."

"I also meant to tell you," Wendell said, "I called Avern Cohn this morning. I think I've known Avern my whole adult life. You can't trust him, he talks out of both sides of his mouth at the same time, but he's good at making deals for his clients. I asked was he representing Montez Taylor. He goes, 'Oh, what did the boy do now?' Like he isn't on top of the Paradiso hits. I told him Montez pulled out your card yesterday and threatened me with it. I don't leave him alone he's gonna bring you in to defend his raggedy-ass name. I said for him to tell Montez to think up a more interesting story for us, don't make himself so lily-white. Give you a chance to come up with one of your famous plea deals. I thought he'd like that."

Delsa listened to every word. "What'd he say?"

"He played dumb, like he didn't know what I was talking about. And that's hard for Avern, considering the high opinion he has of himself. But that's the way I see it's gonna happen. Montez gives us his shooters in return for twenty-five to life. He can be out for his sixtieth birthday party." Wendell said, "Frank, I'm leaving Eleanor with you," and walked out.

Delsa looked up at her standing by his desk now holding a folder, ready.

She said, "Frank, you won't believe this."

He almost asked her to wait, let him make a phone call first. But she was eager to tell whatever it was he wouldn't believe and he said, "You tell me, Eleanor, you know I will. Have a seat."

She sat down and rolled the chair around the corner of the desk to face Delsa and tugged at her skirt without getting it down much on her thighs. She placed her folder on the desk and took out witness statements, requests for laboratory services stamped FIREARMS and Medical Examiner postmortem summaries and opinions.

"I go to Firearms to check on Paradiso and the girl, Chloe. The first thing I find out, two different guns were used, both nine-millimeter."

"How'd they treat you?"

"Firearms? They couldn't of been nicer if I'd blown them. I'm kidding. The gun they're pretty sure of is a Smith & Wesson, the one that did Paradiso. The other one, they're leaning toward a Sig Sauer. It's all, you know, lands and grooves, the way the bullet twists . . . We didn't get into any of that in Vice. So then they checked out the bullets on I-BIS, and I have no idea what that stands for."

"I think it's Something Ballistics Identification —no, Interpretation System," Delsa said. "Compare our slugs to bullets from other shootings. They found a match?"

Eleanor said, "You know the guy that was shot thirteen times?"

"If this is what I'm not gonna believe," Delsa said, "I don't. Wendell said Fatboy was shot with a Ruger."

"I know that," Eleanor said. "The reason I mention Fatboy, he was in on a robbery, a party store on Springwells, the day before he was killed. Shots were fired in the store. They dug the bullets out of the wall and put them on I-BIS, pretty sure they're from the same gun that did Fatboy." Eleanor shook her head. "The ones in the wall were from a Smith & Wesson. Then I come along and ask about the Paradiso slugs. Frank, they compare to the ones dug out of the wall. They're as close a match as you can get."

Delsa had to stop and think.

"But those guys couldn't of done Paradiso."

"No, they were already in custody. Wendell told you Kenny sold guns he managed to pick up? I went over to Four Northeast to ask him what he did with the Smith, since it wasn't in his apartment. We're in the interview room with the glass between us? Kenny goes, 'I'll tell you if you show me your tits.' I hadn't heard that since Pine Knob, Jesus, trying to get backstage."

Delsa let it pass.

"I said to Kenny, 'Shame on you, I'm old enough to be your mother, you punk. Tell me what you did with the gun or no deal on the robbery.' He said he sold it to a guy. What guy? A white guy he ran into at Paycheck's Lounge in Hamtramck. Gave Kenny four-fifty and took the gun off his hands. I said, 'This guy walks up and asks if you happen to have a gun for sale?' Well, actually the guy called and Kenny told him where to meet him. I asked how the guy knew he sold guns. He said somebody must've told him. The guy did come by Kenny's place one time before, but didn't see anything he liked."

Delsa said, "Just the one guy, nobody with him?"

Eleanor said, "Frank, I looked through your case file and read Kelly Barr's statement about seeing two white guys, so I asked Kenny if there was another guy. There was, and Kenny happened to sell him a Sig Sauer when they came to the apartment. Then, by the time the other guy called him, Kenny had the Smith and they met at Paycheck's."

Eleanor waited for Delsa to ask the key question.

But he didn't. He wanted to know about matches, if Firearms came up with any more.

"One," Eleanor said, "but it wasn't a homicide. A guy shot at in his car, on Gratiot. I had to go to the Ninth to get the report. It's in here," she said, shuffling through her papers, "somewhere. Santonio Davis, black male, forty-one, known drug dealer. He's driving north on Gratiot, mid-afternoon, and two white guys in a car start shooting at him. Santonio gets up to sixty weaving through traffic, bangs off a car, swerves over to the southbound side of Gratiot and gets hit by a semi. Santonio's okay, tells the police somebody was shooting at him. Firearms takes the bullets they dug out of the upholstery and the dash, puts them on I-BIS and comes up with a probable match to both guns used at Paradiso's, the Smith and the Sig."

"You're gonna have this case closed," Delsa said, "any minute now."

Eleanor said, "While you're still working on Kelly."

"I'm making progress."

"I'll bet you are."

"She's afraid of Montez. Kelly tells me a little bit at a time. I'm writing up a supplemental statement."

"She's teasing you, Frank."

"She thinks she's smarter than I am."

"She probably is. Did you give her that business, she's a witness and you have to keep your distance?"

"I tell her there's nothing more serious than a homicide."

"Yeah, but you wouldn't mind fooling around. I know you, Frank. How come you haven't called me?"

Giving him the look now, the one she'd been giving him since Maureen's funeral.

"You wore me out that time."

The Saturday he'd gone to Eleanor's for dinner and didn't get home until Sunday evening.

"Frank, I'm not looking to get married again, I just want to have some fun. Anyway," Eleanor said, "while you're hanging out with Kelly Barr I'm looking for two white guys who shoot people. I got three off CaseTrax. The first one a black male thirty-seven having lunch at Baby Sister's Kitchen."

"Ray Jacks," Delsa said, "last November."

"Two white guys come in. The waitress, according to the PCR, said they were middle-aged and looked like workingmen. They ask Ray if he's Ray Jacks. He says, 'What can I do for you?' They blast him, and hit his bodyguard on the way out."

"It was Four's case," Delsa said. "I remember thinking it ought to be easy, two white hitters in this town?"

"Another one, Squad Six got," Eleanor said, "was last summer. Columbus Fletcher, black male forty-two, was at his hangout, the Brass Key on Livernois, a strip club. A boy comes in and tells Columbus somebody hit his car in the parking lot, put a big ding in the rear end. Columbus runs out, the two guys are waiting and shoot him four times. White guys who look like workingmen." Eleanor said, "You remember that one?"

"Columbus Fletcher? I remember all of them."

"But you haven't looked them up."

"Isn't that what you're doing?"

She told him about a black male forty-one, Andre Perry, who opened the front door of his home on Bethune, behind the Fisher Building, to two white guys who asked his name. He told them and they shot him. Andre's wife described them as middle-aged and "ordinary-looking."

Eleanor said, "You remember Andre?"

Delsa nodded.

"He was a drug dealer. All of them were, except Mr. Paradiso."

Delsa nodded again.

"The last one and the oldest, I got from Cold Case. It was the year before last. Sahir Nasiriyah, a Chaldean, ran a BP station on West Grand just off the Jeffries. He sold gas and oil, sandwiches, potato chips, pop, toys, weed and cocaine. Two guys walk in pulling ski masks over their face, ask if he's Sahir, shoot him and rob the place. The Chaldean's son, George, making subs, assumed they were black guys, until one of them cleaned out his register with, quote, 'the hands of an older white guy who had worked with those hands all his life.' George said they were of average height, nothing unusual about them or their clothes. If they're the same guys," Eleanor said, "this was the only time they wore masks or robbed the place."

"But what did all of them," Delsa said, "have in common? They asked the guy his name before they shot him. Made sure they had the right one each time. They were hits. Somebody paid these two guys."

Eleanor was nodding. "And used the same guns only twice. There were no other matches. The Smith and the Sig."

Delsa said, "That takes us back to Kenny. There was something I wanted to know. You said the guy who bought the Smith phoned Kenny—"

"I've been waiting for you to ask. Kenny has Caller ID and we have a warrant to search his place. All the notes, everything is in Fatboy's case file." Eleanor said, "You want to know who called him three weeks ago?"

"I wouldn't mind," Delsa said.

He liked the way she was doing it, watching her leaf through her papers. She lifted out a sheet of names and phone numbers and handed it to him saying, "All the ones checked are buddies and girlfriends."

Delsa looked at the list in sunlight coming

through the dirty window, forty-seven degrees out, a high of fifty expected by this afternoon, spring beginning to show itself.

"Who's the one with the question mark, Connie Fontana?"

"Some woman. I called her. I said, 'Hi, is this Connie? I'm calling for Kenny, returning your call.' Connie says, 'Carl isn't home,' and hangs up on me."

Delsa said, "Carl Fontana."

"You know who he is?"

Delsa said, "No, but I bet he's on LEIN," and smiled at Eleanor. "You did all this in two days?"

She said, "Why, is it supposed to be hard?"

He dialed Kelly's number as soon as Eleanor was out the door. This time Kelly's voice said, "Leave a message." He asked her to call him, he still needed that driver's license.

Richard Harris came in saying, "Montez has a checking account at Comerica, the one on East Jefferson. This morning he closed out his deposit box. I just missed him. I went to the house, he wasn't there. Lloyd was packing, putting clothes in boxes, didn't know where Montez was." Harris said, "We need Lloyd?"

"Jackie says he's clean. She might go to Puerto Rico with him."

"You're kidding me."

"It's what she said."

"Who you running off with, Kelly Barr?"

"I'm thinking about it."

"Dreaming," Harris said.

Eleanor Marsh came back with a LEIN print-out for Carl Fontana, his home address and phone number. "It's the one I called," Eleanor said. "You want me to follow up?"

Delsa looked at the sheet. County time for assault, sixty days, ninety days, several warnings for Domestic Disturbance; forty-two months state time in Jackson for Man One with a deer rifle. Released almost two years ago. Time enough to get ready to shoot black drug dealers and Mr. Paradiso.

He said to Eleanor, "No, what I'd like you to do, find out who represented him on the manslaughter."

She surprised him. She said, "Why?"

And he had to stop and think.

He said, "I don't know, but I'm curious." He said, "Would you find that out for me, please?" and handed her Fontana's printout.

Eleanor left and a few minutes later Manny Reyes, with Violent Crimes, came in. Manny spent a few minutes talking to Harris, and brought Harris with him when he stepped over to see Delsa, Manny saying, "Hey, is nice out, I think winter's over, man."

Saying, "You right about the triple at Orlando's. The guy chainsawed is called Zorro, all three of them with the Cash Flow Posse. Orlando's girlfriend Tenisha tole you it was a Mexican came to the motel that night? It was a guy from a different posse called Dorados. They want to put Cash Flow out of business but, man, that wasn' the way to do it."

Manny saying, "I spoke to Chino, the boss of the guys that were killed. I tole him, 'You don't want to do nothing dumb, man. There're boosters driving around watching you.' He says don't worry about it, is taken care of. See, I already talked to some of his guys at different places in the neighborhood drinking. Nobody wants to tell me anything, they scared of Chino. This guy I went to Holy Redeemer with is shaking his head and drinking, man, getting drunk. So when the place closes I say, 'Lemme take you home.' I get the guy in the car, start asking him questions about Chino, what he's up to. He tells me Chino took two guys from the Dorados, this small posse that wants to get bigger? Has the two guys held down with their heads sticking out over the curb, face up looking at Chino, as he asks the first one who it was cut up Zorro and killed his three guys. The guy says he doesn't know. Chino stomps down on the guy's face with his foot, once. The guy telling me says you hear this *crack*. The other guy said the Dorados made Orlando do it, saying they'd give him a good price on the weed. Orlando didn't want to, but they made him."

Delsa said, "What happened to this guy, who told him?"

"Chino stomped on his face."

"They're both dead?"

Manny shrugged. "They're disappeared."

Harris said, "No body, no case."

Manny said, "I talk to Chino again. I said, 'Man, you don't want to go after Orlando.' He said what he tole me before, 'Is already taken care of.' "

"Meaning . . . ?" Harris said.

"He has somebody to take out Orlando."

"Hired somebody?" Delsa said.

"That could be, sure, why not? There's also that reward."

"You want to get some guys?" Delsa said. "We're gonna need backup."

"Sure, where you going?"

"See if we can pick up Carl Fontana."

CARL ASKED FOR MONTEZ TAYLOR'S ROOM NUM-
ber. The clerk behind the sheet of bulletproof
glass checked and said there didn't seem to be no
one of that name staying with them. Carl said to
Art, "You hear that?"

Art was facing the University Inn's L-shaped
area in front, Carl's Tahoe and a few cars parked
out there. Art turned saying, "Fuckin smoke."
The clerk, a black guy with size, asked if he was
speaking to him. Art said, "No, Sambo, I wasn't
talking to you, I was talking to my partner."

The two walked out, drove up Woodward
Avenue to the river and over Jefferson east to the
Paradiso residence on Iroquois. Carl pulled into
the drive and stopped by the front doors.

"They haven't replaced the glass yet," Art said.
"Take 'em five fuckin minutes."

"Maybe that color glass," Carl said, "is hard to get and they have to order it. You know, that shade of pink." He said, "You feel funny about going in there?"

"In the house?" Art said. "I don't feel one way or the other."

Lloyd opened the door wearing the white dress shirt that was a couple of sizes too large, space showing around the collar. He knew right away who these two mutts were and it surprised him, the shooters coming back to the scene? He said, "Yes . . . ?"

The one he believed was Carl Fontana, the short one, said, "Where's Montez?"

"He could be in his room," Lloyd said, "you want me to see?" Stepping aside and they came in. The other one, with the grayish hair slicked back, would be Art Krupa. Lloyd had known all kinds of guys like these two at Jackson, where they learned to be criminals if they weren't already. Avern, drinking martinis, had told him about these two, his guinea and his polack; and Montez, drinking Rémy and doing lines, had told him their names. It was amazing what criminals talked about and then were surprised when they got busted.

Carl Fontana said, "Yeah, get him," and they

followed Lloyd out to the kitchen where he used
the wall phone to call. Lloyd saying to Montez,
"They's two gentlemen here to see you."

Montez said shit, and wanted to know if they
were cops. Lloyd put his hand over the phone and
said to Carl, "He wants to know are you the police."

"Tell him," Carl said, "we're the pissed-off
guys he was supposed to meet, at the motel."

Lloyd said into the phone, "No, they the guys
you was suppose to meet. Now they angry."
Lloyd heard Montez say shit, tell 'em I'll be right
there. Lloyd replaced the phone on the wall saying, "He's coming. He's sorry he missed you, he
fell asleep." Lloyd frowning now, saying, "He's
taking it hard, what happened to Mr. Paradise. I
'magine you saw it on the news?"

Art Krupa said, "Where is he?" sounding impatient.

"At his place, over the garage."

Art turned to the table in the alcove of windows that showed the garage in the backyard,
three doors on it.

Lloyd said, "It's finally turning nice out, huh?"

Carl said, "You know who we are?"

"I guess you friends of Montez."

"And you're a friend of Avern Cohn."

"The lawyer? Yeah, I know him."

"You took some falls he defended?"

"A long time ago."

"What'd you do?"

"Jes some stickups."

"You ever shoot anybody?"

Look at him sneaking up on it, dying to tell who he was. The man sounding like he had something in mind.

Lloyd said, "No, I never had the opportunity. I guess there was nobody I wanted to shoot bad enough. Except one."

"But you did time."

"Nine years straight up."

Art, at the alcove of windows, said, "Is he coming or not, goddamn it."

Carl said, "Avern had you watching Montez, huh?"

"Watching him?"

"Telling Avern what he's up to."

"Mr. Cohn told you that?"

Art said, "Well, he's finally decided to come," and went over to open the door.

Carl said to Lloyd, "I wouldn't be surprised we aren't both on the same side."

Montez came in the kitchen wearing a heavy white designer turtleneck that came down over his butt, some of Montez' new look, getting away from the business suit image. Came in and the first thing he said was, "Lloyd, leave us, man."

That was the last thing he heard from the room. Montez shut the door and got ready to do his act. Lloyd believed nothing would happen. They wanted to be paid. Montez didn't have it, but had the thing that could get it for him. Picked it up this morning, the stock certificate. Getting Kelly to sell it would be the trick.

But what was Carl Fontana talking about, their being on the same side? He imagined Carl's daddy had come up from Tennessee or someplace with all the ofays to work in a car factory and make a living. He had thought the kid who finked him out and got him the nine years was smart, but didn't think Carl Fontana was. Oh yeah? He was smart enough to listen to Avern drinking martinis tell about the situation here. Avern had even said one time he hoped these two didn't fuck up and make the Dumbest Criminals I Have Known list. He'd almost said to Avern, "What happens to you if they do, they get busted?" But he didn't, because he didn't think Avern had ever asked himself that. It made him wonder if maybe Avern ought to be on the Dumb list.

Lloyd hung out in the pantry where they kept

the good glasses and china, sixteen place settings he wouldn't mind taking downtown to Du-Mouchelle's and sell it off. What else? Not the paintings. Allegra liked the paintings and he liked Allegra. She said to him John wanted to move to California and make wine, but it was awful risky. He told her, "Honey, go with your husband." Thinking, any man can make a bull come and then sell it, can do anything he wants.

The door opened. Art came out and stood there staring at him. Lloyd heard Montez in the kitchen say, "You don't worry about police coming by, stay as long as you want. I'll put on some doo-wop for y'all."

Now the other one, Carl Fontana, put his hand on Art's and got him going again. Montez came out and stopped next to Lloyd.

"You hear any of that?"

"Not a word."

"You never hear anything, you never talk about what you don't hear, either, do you?"

Lloyd said, "All you got on your plate, you want to worry about me?"

DELSA AND HARRIS PICKED UP A WARRANT AT
Thirty-sixth District Court that would allow
them to enter Carl Fontana's residence, then
waited for Jackie to come out of a pretrial exam.
In the car Jackie couldn't get over the defense
lawyer describing Ardis Nichols, the defendant,
as this sweet guy who loved Snowflake, the
hooker who lived upstairs and had died of blunt-
force injuries, hit repeatedly with a piece of pipe.

"You know why I didn't believe Ardis?" Jackie
said. "I'm talking to him in the basement where
he lives. Has his TV, his medicine and shit on a
little table by his bed, his clothes hanging from
pipes. Ardis's wearing a wife beater like Kid
Rock. We're talking, I notice a huge rat lying on
the floor by the furnace. I say to Ardis, 'Isn't that
a rat over there?' He says no, it ain't a rat. I say

yes, it is, it's a huge fuckin rat. He walks over and steps on the rat and you hear like air come out of it. See, what he might've meant was no, it wasn't a *live* rat. But the man had lost his credibility with me saying no, it wasn't a rat."

Delsa said, "Just having a rat in his room."

"That was enough," Jackie said.

"Is he going to trial?"

" 'Less they agree on a deal."

"There you are," Delsa said.

They took the Fisher west—Manny Reyes and Violent Crimes behind them—and found the house on Cadet, a few blocks beyond Holy Redeemer, a frame house with green paint fading, eight steps to the porch, Manny and his guys going around back.

The door opened and here was Connie Fontana in a housecoat in the afternoon, a big redheaded woman scowling at them, TV voices coming from the living room.

Jackie said, "Mrs. Fontana . . . ?" pausing in case it wasn't. "Is your husband at home? We'd like to speak to him."

Connie said, "What about?"

"It's a police matter," Delsa said. They all had badges showing. "Is Carl home?"

The woman's hair was big and, Delsa thought, involved. He couldn't understand the reason for it. She shook her head and her hair seemed to sparkle.

She said he wasn't there. Delsa asked if she knew where he was and Connie said, "Who knows where that shitbird is. What'd he do now?"

"We'd like to come in if it's okay," Jackie said, pushing the door, forcing Connie to step back, Delsa and Harris following as Jackie said, "Thank you," to Connie and kept going, through the living room—past Dr. Phil on TV saying, "Does that make you feel good? Talking to your sister that way?"—and down a narrow hall to the kitchen. Delsa could see her unlocking the back door and Manny and Violent Crimes coming in, three of them, wearing vests under their jackets. They came through to the stairway with Glocks and a shotgun. Delsa nodded and they went up the stairs.

"Jesus Christ," Connie said, "what in the world did he do? He got in another fight, didn't he?"

Dr. Phil was saying, "You mean this whole thing is about her *nose*?"

As Connie was saying, "It's his buddy gets in the fights with his ugly mouth. He's an ugly man, his whole disposition. He's always looking to be insulted. Carl tries to stop the fight and he gets in it. He's short, but, boy, is he scrappy. It's been a while—I'm surprised he's fighting again."

Delsa was trying to follow Connie and Dr. Phil at the same time. It seemed the girl with their dad's nose, it was a honker, was jealous of her sister who had their mother's cute nose. He said to Connie, "It's not about a fight. What's his friend's name?"

"Gene Krupa."

"Wasn't he a drummer?"

"I mean Art Krupa. He thinks he's hot shit 'cause he use to be with the Detroit Mafia."

"They hang out together?"

"Carl spends more time over there, at Art's, than he does here. I told him, you don't come home, I ain't cooking for you no more."

The TV audience was applauding Dr. Phil as the Violent Crimes guys came down the stairs, Manny shaking his head, and went out the front.

Delsa said to Connie, "Can you tell me where this Art Krupa lives?"

"Hamtramck. I think on Yemans."

"What's Carl do for a living?"

"Lays bricks. Does pretty good, too."

"This time of year?"

"He started before it turned cold and snowed."

"When's the last time you saw him?"

"Yesterday he come by, brought me a fifth of

vodka, real expensive stuff. I said Jesus Christ, you could've bought me two gallons of Popov for what you paid for it."

Delsa looked past Connie to see Jackie coming out of the hall. She held an empty Christiania bottle by one finger in the neck. Now Connie glanced around. She said, "What're you doing with that?" her voice rising. "There was still some *in* there."

The poor woman sounding desperate.

"No, I put it in a glass," Jackie said. "I saw this beautiful bottle—you mind if I take it?"

Delsa said, "She collects bottles, ones with unusual designs on them." He handed Connie one of his cards. "If you hear from Carl, would you mind giving me a call? I'd appreciate it." He put his hand on hers as she took the card and looked down to read it. "I'm Frank Delsa."

"She could've asked me first," Connie said.

Delsa patted her hand and said it was nice talking to her.

Manny was outside by the cars.

Walking up to him Delsa said, "Anything good?"

"Here," Manny said, handing Delsa a leather-bound address book, a small one. "Guy lives like a fuckin monk."

"He's never there," Delsa said, skimming through the book, stopping now and then.

"No guns, but a box of forty caliber."

"Here's Art Krupa's number, and address."

"I'll call the Fourth," Manny said. "Get the precinct to watch the house till we put a crew on it."

"And Avern Cohn's number," Delsa said.

They parked down the street from where Art Krupa was living on Yemans in a neat little two-story house on a thirty-foot lot, no driveway, green and white metal awnings over the windows, a statue of the Virgin Mary holding a dish, a birdbath, in the front yard.

"This Art Krupa," Jackie said, "what's he, a religious hit man?"

She called Communications and had the address checked. It was listed in the name of a Virginia Novak. Jackie called the house and asked for Art. She was told he wasn't home.

"Is this Virginia?"

The woman said, "Yes, it is," in a tiny voice.

"Can you help me out, Virginia? Tell me where I can get in touch with Art?"

"Who is this calling, please?"

"I'm in his lawyer's office," Jackie said. "Will Art be back soon?"

"I have no way of knowing," Virginia said. "I'm sorry."

Jackie told her she'd try again later and said to Harris, behind the wheel of the Lumina, and Delsa in back, "The Blessed Virgin must belong to her. She sounds like a timid little thing."

"Live with a man shoots people," Harris said, "I would be, too." He turned his head toward Delsa. "How long you want to wait?"

"We're here," Delsa said, "we might as well hang for a while."

"Art could be in the house," Jackie said. "Carl, too."

"Let's wait and see if anything happens," Delsa said. He got out his cell to call Kelly, anxious to hear her voice.

She said, "I've been trying to get you."

"I felt my phone vibrate, but couldn't answer. We're on a stakeout, looking for the shooters."

"You know who they are?"

"We're pretty sure. How'd you do?"

He didn't care if Jackie and Harris listened.

"I told you it was a fitting? At Saks. They've already shown the collection a few times, so they have to make adjustments, make sure they have all the buttons and the zippers work. We have to try on shoes and boots—they bring dozens of eights, nines and tens. I'm usually a nine." Kelly talking fast. "A rep for the collection was there, and thirty girls for twenty spots, all from Detroit.

Sometimes, if the rep wants a certain type, like a predominant hair color, he might bring a girl or two from New York. It's Chanel's Fall Collection. They decide who wears what for about eighty different looks coming down the runway—and that's in just twenty-five minutes—so most of the girls will have four changes. I'll have five tomorrow."

Delsa said, "Yeah?"

"You know why?"

"Why?"

"I look great in Chanel."

"Is that right?"

"My favorite that I wear in the show, I think of as kind of a biker look, a nubby burgundy suit that barely covers my butt, silver chains around my neck and my hips and these cool velvety boots. My Harley look, I think it'll stop the show. They'll start with suits and dresses, get the audience sitting up, and then swing into activewear, ski and après-ski this year. They'll show little black dresses for the cocktail look, and finish big with evening wear, opulent dresses. That's four or five segments, with different lighting and music for different moods."

"Do you walk funny?"

"Do the crossover? That keeps you walking straight, but I just walk. I hear the beat and I'm on it, I just try to act natural. If you're in the audience I'll find you and give you a smile. People will look around at you, wondering who you are, if you're my lover."

He said, "Yeah, right."

And heard Jackie say to Harris, "You hear him, the conversationalist?"

"I'll call you later."

She said, "I'm going out tonight."

It stopped him. He didn't know what to say.

"I've got a date. But if your pants vibrate, Frank, pick up. I might have to call you."

For the next ten or fifteen minutes he wondered what she meant—*she might have to call him.* He had always pictured her alone. He had to stop and realize she knew people, she had friends, a life he knew very little about. He wondered if she meant she had a real date, some guy had called her, asked her to go out. Not the guy she'd called a mama's boy who left his clothes lying around. He wondered if she had lived with him. He could ask her if she was a prostitute, but not if she had lived with the guy who left his clothes lying around. Why would she need him if she was on a date with someone she knew? No, what she said was, "I might have to call you."

His phone rang. It was Jerome.

"I'm waiting to be picked up. We going to Pontiac, gonna check out a place Tenisha's mom told us he might be at. I get close enough and see Orlando's there, I'll call you. I been trying two hours to get hold of you, man."

Delsa said, "Who's *we*?"

"I didn't tell you? Shit, I got two policemen working with me case it gets rough on the street. They say they been away, on vacation. Come back, they waiting to be put to work. Couple of middle-aged detectives, out of shape."

"They show you their badges?"

"Didn't have to. They got cop written all over 'em. Know what I'm saying? The way they dress, the way they talk. But, man, they ask a question they get an answer. The one puts his piece in Jo-Jo's face?"

Delsa stopped him. "These guys are armed? What kind of guns?"

"Nines, like Berettas. The one ask this dude Jo-Jo where's Orlando at? The dude say he don't know and the one busts a cap next to the dude's ear, *bam,* the dude screams but can't hear hisself."

"They're not cops," Delsa said. "Jerome, these guys're gonna get you in trouble. Get away from them."

"Jo-Jo say he thinks Orlando went to Mississippi, someplace down there. Was Tenisha's mama gave us the dude. The woman is hot for her age, man, going on to be forty. I feel myself starting to crave her panties."

"Jerome," Delsa said, "they're not cops, they sound like bounty hunters, using you to get next to the reward."

Jerome said, "I know that. I wondered did you."

"Give me their names," Delsa said, "what they look like, what kind of car they drive and I'll have them picked up . . . Jerome?"

He was gone.

22

SO FAR THIS BOY THREE-J WASN'T DOING THEM much good. He took them out to Pontiac, way past the GMC Truck plant to an old rundown property where they used to have pit bull fights and all they did was shoot a dog.

Art did. The man holding it on a leash. Art pointed his gun at the pit bull and asked the old colored man with gray hair, was Orlando hiding out here? The man said, "Don't shoot my dog." And Art shot it. The dog's name was Sonny. Art said, "I shot him 'cause you didn't answer my question." Carl said, "Couldn't you think of a better name for a vicious fighting dog?" The man said that was its name.

The old man turned out to be Orlando's granddaddy. Art asked him where Orlando was. Art said he'd count to three and the old man said,

"He's staying in Detroit on Pingree, 700 Pingree between Second and Third. Now get outta here."

Art said he almost blew him away to teach him a lesson.

Three-J didn't say much. Carl was sure he didn't believe they were cops and didn't care. Art told him their names. It meant Art would shoot him before they were through and they'd put in for the reward. It didn't bother Carl, he didn't see Three-J as much of an asset. Three-J liked Tenisha's mama and she wasn't bad. Carl asked Art, surprised he hadn't asked him before, if he'd ever fucked a colored girl. Art said, "Sure, haven't you? Don't tell me you never had any colored poon." So they talked about different colored girls they'd had until Jerome said wait, was these regular bitches or ho's? It turned out they were whores. Three-J asked what was a ho like, since he never had one. Carl saw the boy thinking he was smarter than they were. If he didn't care they weren't cops but carried guns, he knew they'd try to get rid of him once they found Orlando. He didn't say much, no, but the colored boy was ready, keeping his eyes open, wasn't he?

They were coming back now in the Tahoe, on Woodward out in Oakland County, twenty miles from downtown Detroit.

Art said, "There's an OPEN HOUSE sign. Carl? The next right."

These two white guys were cuckoo.

They turned down a street of fairly new homes, big ones with lawns and young trees, down to a house that was open for inspection. Art took the OPEN sign hanging from the regular FOR SALE sign in the yard and brought it inside with them and handed it to the real estate man in his suit and tie grinning at them, the man saying, "Well, thank you. How did you know I was just about to close?"

"You see us come along," Carl said, "you'd be closing if you just opened."

It was going on seven, becoming dusky out.

Carl put his hand on Jerome's shoulder saying to the real estate man, "This boy wants to buy a house out here. You got anything against selling to coloreds?"

The real estate man frowned like he's never heard of such a thing, telling them no, of course not. He said the house was listed at a million one-ninety-nine. Carl asked what he would take and the real estate man said well, the people were in Florida, anxious to sell, he believed they might go as low as nine-fifty.

Art said, "You got any tape?"

The real estate man said, "I think I saw some in the kitchen," went out there and came back with a roll of silver duct tape saying, "Can I ask what you need it for?"

Art said, "To tape your mouth shut."

Jerome watched them sit the real estate man in a dining room chair and tape his arms to the arms and legs to the legs of the chair, the man not saying shit, but his eyes open wide watching them. As Art was about to tape his mouth shut, the man said, "Please be careful you don't cover my nose, too, okay?"

He should never've said it.

Art covered his nose and Jerome could see the man couldn't breathe, his face turning red as he pulled against the tape holding him to the chair.

Jerome watched Carl shake his head. Carl said, "Goddamn it, Art, the man can't fuckin breathe." Taking his time, cool about it.

Art said, "Fuck him."

Carl pulled the tape off the man's nose and mouth, let him suck in air a few times and put the tape back on over his mouth.

"Look around," Carl said to Jerome, "see if there's anything you like."

The two went upstairs.

Jerome went to the kitchen and looked in the fridge and took out a can of beer and sat down to drink it with a good-size roach he had on him and lit with a kitchen match, Jerome pretty sure these guys were crazy. They didn't care who saw them or who might come to the house. They were cool, though. Walk in a house and take it over. Jerome wondered why he hadn't heard of doing this. Drive around looking for OPEN signs.

Jerome took out his cell and phoned Frank Delsa.

"Hey, man, how you doing?"

"Where are you?"

"Out in the suburbs. Orlando wasn't in Pontiac. His granddaddy say he's in Detroit and told us where, but I don't believe him. Would you? His granddaddy saying it?"

Delsa said, "You still with the two guys?"

"On and off. They cuckoo. Next time I see you I'll tell you what we doing at this house the real estate man say he's gonna sell for a million one-ninety-nine—give you an idea where we at. I never been in a house cost this much, even when I was busting into places. I see you I'll tell you about it."

"You know their names?"

"I ain't telling you. You might know these motherfuckers, man, they outrageous. I don't know why you don't have 'em locked up somewhere. The granddaddy goes, 'Don't shoot my dog.' The one shoots his dog. You know why? 'Cause the old man say don't do it. They been to Jackson. One of 'em mentioned something about when they was there about the noise in the cell block. Bunch of retards in there making noise. Frank, these guys want the money."

"I told you that," Delsa said. "And they'll kill you for it."

"I know. It's why we do see Orlando—go in someplace and there he is? I say it ain't him."

"He won't look like his picture."

"Or somebody could point him out to me? I say no, that ain't Orlando. Then soon as I get away from these motherfuckers I give you a call."

"Where are they?"

"Looking around upstairs."

"You said before they're middle-aged—"

"They coming down. I got to go," Jerome said. He put away his cell and picked up his beer.

They came in the kitchen with men's and women's watches, some jewelry, and laid them on the counter where Jerome was sitting. Art got beers from the fridge saying he thought Virginia would go for that Lady Bulova. Carl got a fifth of Canadian Club from the liquor cabinet and poured a couple, not asking Jerome if he wanted one. It was okay, he'd rather watch these two than get high. He said, "What would you do if the people that live here walked in the door?"

"It's like a home invasion then," Art said. "What you do is strip 'em and tie 'em up." He sniffed the air, looked at Jerome and said, "Somebody's smoking a joint," sounding eager.

Jerome offered the roach.

Art seemed about to take it, but said, "Shit, not after you nigger-lipped it."

Jerome let it pass for the time being. He said, "How come you guys never get caught? You don't seem to care who sees you. You leave tracks every place you go. How come you don't get picked up?"

"We could get caught," Carl said, "but we don't."

"We work under contract," Art said. "So far we've whacked six people."

"Eight," Carl said, "the two before we teamed up."

"You count those?"

"Why not?"

"How many's that?"

"I just told you, eight."

"You count the bodyguard?"

"No, I didn't. That's nine."

"Nine we've whacked," Art said, "without getting caught."

"Except the first two," Carl said.

Jerome watched them throw down their shots of Club and make faces.

"We use semi-automatics," Art said. "Use 'em one time only. Throw 'em away and get new ones for the next job. All the contracts are drug dealers."

"A couple weren't," Carl said.

"No, but all the rest were," Art said. "We don't give a shit what they do. It just happens they deal drugs."

Jerome said, "You do this for money, huh?"

"Fifty gees a pop," Art said.

"Man, that sounds high. How you get jobs like that?"

"Drink up," Carl said, "we're outta here."

Art wanted to take some of the booze and Jerome said he'd like to run upstairs, have a quick look around. Carl gave him five minutes.

Jerome went straight to the master bedroom hoping, looked in the drawers of the night tables on both sides of the bed, nothing, then under the king-size mattress along the edge and found a pistol: Sig Sauer three-eighty, loaded, seven in the magazine. He wrapped it in a dark red scarf he got from the bureau he could use as a do-rag and shoved it in the back pocket of the cargo pants falling off his ass.

*   *   *

Driving south on Woodward again toward Eight Mile and Detroit, Art called home.

He listened to Virginia and said, "Honey, nobody from the lawyer's office calls me on the house phone, I never gave 'em the number. If the woman called ain't selling something she's likely the police." He said, "Now don't get nervous on me—Jesus. What you do is walk up to Rite Aid on Campau and buy a pack of cigarettes. See if there's anybody sitting around in a car. Virginia? Look without them noticing you're looking. I'll call you later."

Jerome, sitting behind them, listened to Art and heard Carl say, "Shit," and Art say, "I'll check on Connie, see if anybody's been there."

He said, "Hey, Con, how you doing? It's Art." He listened and said, "Yeah, the old man's busy driving. We got you another couple bottles of vodka." He said, "Oh, is that right?" and listened for a couple of minutes before saying, "Here, I'll let you tell Carl."

Jerome watched him hand Carl the phone.

Carl said, "Hi, sweetheart, what's going on?"

Jerome heard him say yeah and uh-huh a few times as Carl listened to Connie, Carl finally saying, "They come by again, tell 'em you have no idea where I'm at, 'cause I sure as hell don't know where I'll be. I'll call you later on, let you know."

He said to Art, "They took the vodka bottle, the one from the old man's house. These others come in the back with their guns out. She tell you that?"

Art said, "There's no fuckin way they could be on us."

Jerome watched Carl turn his head to look at Art and say to him, "That fuckin Montez. He gave us up."

They were both quiet now staring at the road, coming up on Eight Mile, the city limits.

Jerome said, "Now where we going?"

Neither one answered him.

THE SOUND WAS DETROIT HIP-HOP, A GRITTY
energy that wrapped itself around Kelly walking
into Alvin's, the crowd wall-to-wall waving,
bobbing their heads in that funky way as if they
were plugged in, wired to the hypnotic beats
coming out of a white emcee called Hush, guys
prowling the stage in wife beaters and sock hats
delivering their message, in-your-face lyrics that
got Kelly's attention. Big security hunks in black
T-shirts faced the crowd looking mean, daring
anybody to get out of line. The scene made her
think of *Fat black bucks in a wine-barrel room*,
from a poem in a schoolbook her dad had kept,
Boomlay, boomlay, boomlay, boom, but couldn't
think of what the poem was called. She moved
through the pack to stand behind two young
guys at the bar in caps turned backwards, Kelly

waiting for the bartender to see her. The young
guy on her left pressed his chin against his shoulder and asked how she was doing. Kelly raised
her voice to ask him what they were playing. He
said, " 'Get Down,' from Hush's album *Roses
and Razorblades*." Kelly shrugged. "He's okay."
The other guy put his chin on his shoulder and
said, "You like to come here?" Kelly said, "I'm
here, aren't I?" He asked if he could buy her a
drink. Kelly said, "Scotch with a splash would be
nice." The first guy turned on his stool to ask if
she knew Hush's dad was a homicide cop. She
said, "Really?" He told her the other emcee up
there was Shane Capone, does the track with
Hush on *Detroit Players*. And asked if she'd seen
Bantam Rooster here. Kelly said one of the guys
in that band worked at Car City Records, where
she bought her tunes, but the only punk in her
book was Iggy. The other guy at the bar handed
Kelly her scotch. She thanked him. The first guy
offered her his seat. Kelly thanked him too and
that was the end of the bar conversation. She
said, "I'm meeting someone," and left them,
moving into the crowd.

She found Montez on the other side of the stage
from the entrance, came up behind him, stuck her
finger in the small of his back and said, "Stick

'em up." Montez came around and Kelly was looking at herself in his sunglasses.

He said, "Don't ever do that to me, girl." And said, "Why you want to meet here? Watch these white boys trying hard to be black."

She said, "Did you get it?"

"This morning soon as they opened the bank. It's a stock certificate."

Shouting at each other, frowning to hear in the heavy beat pumping out of the stack of woofers.

"For what?"

"I just told you, a stock certificate."

"What's the company?"

"Out in Texas, I think it's oil."

"How many shares?"

"Twenty thousand. It says it in statements the old man put in with the certificate."

She shook her head. "I didn't hear what you said."

"Come on," Montez said, taking her by the arm away from the stage to the wall along the side. "We can't talk in here. Let's go to your place. Hear some of those dirty girls doing their rap? Have us a beverage?"

Kelly saw one of the security guards, his back to the stage, watching them. A big white guy with a beard.

She said, "I worked all afternoon getting ready

for a fashion show, I'm too tired to party. All I want to do is go home—" She stopped. "You brought it, didn't you?"

Montez, still holding her arm, put his free hand on his cashmere coat. "Got it right here."

"Let me have it," Kelly said. "I'll check it out and give you a call tomorrow."

Montez made a face, frowning, straining to hear over Hush.

Kelly leaned close to him. "I said I'll find out what it's worth and give you a call."

The bouncer, the security guy, was still watching them, staring hard.

Montez brought a manila envelope folded in half out of his coat. He held on to it as Kelly tried to take it from him, Kelly saying, "Just let me see what it is."

"I told you, I think it's a big oil company out in Texas. Has DRP in a fancy style on the folder."

She saw the security guy coming toward them and tugged at the envelope and gave Montez a shove and stepped back as the security guy caught Montez, took the envelope from him and gave it to Kelly, Montez trying to twist out of the guy's tattooed arms, yelling at him in the band racket, wanting to know what the fuck he was doing—Kelly pretty sure that's what he was saying.

She edged along in front of the stage past the pack waving, moving, Kelly moving toward the entrance on the other side, looking up at Hush in his sock hat, close enough to hear lyrics about sticking a condom in your ear to fuck what you heard, Kelly thinking it almost made sense, thinking that *Fat black bucks in a wine-barrel room* would work in here, the first rap, and remembered part of another couple of lines from the poem, something about the crowd—that was it— *gave a whoop and a call and danced the juba from wall to wall,* and walked out of Alvin's.

A lot of the time she was restless. She liked to take chances and liked to bet on things and drive fast, run through red lights late at night on the way home. There was always a carton of Slims in the loft. She'd look at Chloe's pack on the coffee table and bet her ten bucks there were exactly ten cigarettes in it. Chloe said okay that time and shook out eleven. Kelly loved to drink cocktails, almost any kind, and talk, alexanders, Sazeracs, daiquiris in different flavors she had in the liquor cabinet. She brought home a pair of sealskin mukluks from a shoot in Iceland, seeing herself posing in them for a panties shot, but none of the catalogs went for the idea.

Driving home she thought of her dad, wonder-

ing what he would do in this situation: if he were
a girl and had a stock certificate in Chloe Robinette's name, could fake her signature and had
her driver's license. He asks how much the stock
is worth and she tells him possibly a million six
hundred thousand. He'd clear his throat and say:

"Or more if the value went up?"

Her dad was a gambler who always had his
trade, scissors and a comb. When she was sixteen,
talking about getting into modeling, he'd said,
"Sweetheart, go to barber college and get a trade
first. You ever see me I don't have money in my
pocket?"

Tonight he'd say, "What's the stock?"

"Del Rio Power."

"Never heard of it."

"But you're not in the market."

"Not as long as you can bet at a casino."

"I'm about to look it up. But tell me what
you'd do."

"I'd check to see what it's actually worth. See,
then you have to decide what your price is. If you
get caught for stock fraud or forgery, I doubt
you'd do more than a year, if that. Get a dress at
St. Vincent de Paul to wear to court. What's the
risk of having a sheet worth to you? Assuming
you can handle your conscience okay. Think of it

as nobody's money. What's wrong with putting it
in the economy?"

She'd lay it out before him to see what he'd
say, not to take his advice.

"Okay, what's your price?"

Her dad would say, "You kidding? At a million
six I'd go for it. Wouldn't you?"

Kelly sat at the computer in the study with a Slim
and a scotch. The stock certificate and statements
from Del Rio Power came in a green folder with
DRP in an elaborate design on the cover, the
folder open now next to the computer. The statements told that the original 5,000 shares of stock
were purchased in 1958 at eight dollars a share.
Since then the stock had split twice, making Anthony Paradiso the owner of 20,000 shares. A
form, signed by Paradiso, would transfer the
stock to Chloe Robinette once she added her signature.

Okay, he'd paid forty thousand for the stock
forty-five years ago, no doubt on an inside tip.
Let's see what it was worth now.

Kelly keyed in the Web address for the New
York Stock Exchange, got the home page, and in
the SYMBOL LOOKUP window entered DRP and
clicked the QUICK QUOTE button.

It came back with "Error: Symbol Not Found."

She said, Uh-oh, entered "Del Rio Power" into another window and clicked SEARCH. Now she got a headline that read "NYSE to suspend, apply to delist Del Rio Power, Inc."

Shit.

She got out of the Stock Exchange and found Del Rio's Web page through Google. It told her the company was a North American provider of natural gas . . . has a core business in the production, gathering, processing . . . and was committed to developing new supplies and blah, blah, blah . . . Kelly clicked on MARKET DATA and got the company's fifty-two-week history, the price of Del Rio stock one year ago was $81.40 a share, making the whole load worth $1,628,000. She clicked on CURRENT VALUE and looked at it, sat back in her chair and said, "Shit," feeling let down, even though she wasn't that surprised.

The current price of Del Rio stock was 53 cents a share.

She heard her dad say, "Yeah? What's wrong with ten thousand six hundred?"

Kelly went back to the Google search list and clicked on a *Business Week* story about "Fraudulent energy trading . . . Could be looking at bankruptcy proceedings . . . Trying to work out a settlement with states where they owe money . . ." and heard her dad calling them a bunch of crooks.

Now she tried to imagine what Chloe would say, hanging in as the old guy's mistress for almost a year, for what she made in two weeks. She wouldn't throw a fit. She'd say, "Fuck," and let it go. But then she might play with it, say something like, "Maybe it'll come back," in an innocent tone of voice. Or, "Maybe I should sell before it goes any lower." Kelly loved her, loved to sit with Chloe, both sunk in the sofa with drinks and Slims, talking about movie stars, about Iraq, Chloe saying, "Throw out Saddam, you get one of those guys wears his turban on the back of his head." Or she'd say, "It takes a heartless dictator to handle those nuts over there."

She missed Chloe and her stories about guys trying to act cool and did everything she could not to see her sitting in the chair in her blood. She would think of Chloe, feel herself moments from tears, and would think of Frank Delsa and the way he looked at her. He was almost always on her mind.

She knew Montez would phone from downstairs on his cell, wanting to come up. When he called, he had to first tell her what the bouncer did. "The man threw me out on the street in my good coat."

"You sound like it's my fault."

"What'd you say to him? Nothing, not a word."

"You mean I should've explained we're friends, working on a fraud scheme? Getting thrown out of Alvin's isn't your problem. You want to know what the stock's worth?"

He paused before saying, "All right, how much?"

"As of the closing bell today, fifty-three cents a share."

"Hey, come on—I don't believe you."

"Down from eighty-one forty a year ago."

"You're playing with me, aren't you?"

"It comes to ten thousand six hundred. Not worth your time, Chops. You want the stock certificate? I'll mail it to you."

Montez said, "Now wait a minute, hold on. I want to talk to you."

"Go ahead."

"Come on, babe, buzz the door for me."

"I would," Kelly said, "but there's nothing you can say that I want to hear."

Now a pause before Montez said, "Turning on me, huh? The money ain't what you expected."

"I told you from the start I wouldn't help you," Kelly said. "Why can't you understand that?" She said, "Listen, Frank Delsa's on his way over. You want the certificate or should I give it to him?"

"How you explain you have it?"

"I tell him you gave it to me. I've told him everything else. What's the difference?"

Montez said, "You're fuckin with me, aren't you?"

"You don't believe me, look it up. Or I can e-mail you the story, if you want—why Del Rio Power, already in the toilet, is about to go down the drain."

Montez said, "You gonna hear glass breaking out here, you don't open the door."

Kelly reached in her bag for her cell and said to Montez, "And you'll hear the nine-eleven operator on my cell ask what's going on." She said, "I forgot to mention, Delsa has the two white guys staked out. If I were you, Chops, I'd get out of town."

Kelly heard him say, "You think you done with me?"

She hung up the phone, got Delsa's card out of her bag and called his cell number and heard his voice say, "Frank Delsa," in that quiet way of his.

Kelly said, "I'm home and Montez is downstairs."

Delsa stepped inside the loft and turned to Kelly, her back to the door. He said, "He wasn't outside," and hesitated, barely, before she was in his arms and they were kissing in that dark hallway like they would never get enough of each other, her hands slipping inside his jacket, sliding over his ribs. They kissed and held each other and he told her, "I've been wanting to do this since the other night."

She said, "Love at first sight?"

He said, "Almost. It was when you came out of the bathroom with your face washed."

"It's working out," Kelly said. "I planned to jump you if you came over tonight. I'm not a witness anymore, I'm out of it," and told him about getting the stock certificate while a homicide cop's son was rapping—Delsa saying, "Hush"— and about looking up the stock and telling Montez the million six was now ten six and going fast. "You want the certificate?" She said, "I have it," leading him to the counter in front of the kitchen where the papers were lying.

She asked him what he wanted to drink. He said anything and she poured them each a scotch. They touched glasses eye to eye, put the glasses on the counter and took hold of each other and got into more of that first-time kissing, neither of them getting enough of the other until he whispered to her, "You're no longer a suspect. But you're still a witness."

She stood in her wool socks looking up at him.

"But you don't care."

"This is bigger."

She was nodding. "You're sure I'm not a suspect?"

"I think you were tempted, so you played it out."

Still looking up at him she said, " 'If you want me to, I'll love you. I know you better now.' "

He remembered the key word but not the line he'd have to make positive. He said, "And I'll be glad to reciprocate," and had to smile. "Who wrote that?"

"John O'Hara."

"I thought he was supposed to be good."

"He was. I love his short stories, especially the ones set in Hollywood. O'Hara drank a lot and was near the end when he wrote this one. It's called *The Instrument*. But he also wrote *Appointment in Samarra,* about not being able to escape your fate."

"Like Montez," Delsa said. "No matter what he does to slip out of this one, he's going down."

She said, "I was thinking more of us."

"I know what you mean. There's a lot we haven't said."

"We've barely said anything."

"See, but Montez still might want the ten six. Try to get you to sign the paper."

"I'm giving it to you," Kelly said, "and the driver's license. There won't be any way I can help him. But you're probably right. The last thing he said to me, on the phone, 'You think you're done with me?' "

"That's all?"

"I hung up on him."

"That's why you're still a witness, I don't have him yet. Or the two guys. We've got the prints of one of them on the same vodka bottle with Montez'. It could put them together at the house—if you'll testify that's what the old man was drinking, the Christiania. And I'd like you to look at the two guys in a lineup. If you can put them at the scene that night, they're done. We'll pick 'em up if they ever come home. Carl's wife Connie says he stays with Art a lot of the time. Art lives in Hamtramck with Virginia Novak. We checked, they're not married, but have a statue of the Virgin Mary in the front yard holding a birdbath. I'm hoping it was Art's idea. I didn't tell you their names, did I? Art Krupa and Carl Fontana. They could've met at Jackson, they were both there at the same time. They come out and for the past year and a half they've been shooting drug dealers, and then Paradiso."

"And Chloe," Kelly said.

"And Chloe. Montez hired them to do the old

man. But how did he find out about them? Look at it another way. How did they get the contracts to take out the drug dealers? These two guys wouldn't ordinarily have much to do with African-Americans. It's like they have someone who arranges the hits. Like a manager."

"Or an agent," Kelly said. "Have you ever heard of that?"

Delsa shook his head. "No."

"You want to spend the night?"

"Yeah, if I can take a shower first."

She said, "We can do that."

THE COUNTER GIRL TOLD DELSA IT HAPPENED
during the break time, going on eleven, between
the Egg McMuffins and the Big Macs, "The three
dudes come in—I look at the one and think I
know him. Yeah, it's Big Baby, still with the puffy
cheeks. He lived down the street from us on
Edison. I'm about to call to him, Hey, Big Baby,
and surprise him 'cause he won't remember me
from living on Edison. But then I see all three
dudes pulling guns, Big Baby taking a sawed-off
shotgun from outta his clothes, the two dudes
with nines they hold sideways—know what I'm
saying?—like they can shoot these guns any way
they want. The one dude goes to the back, the
other dude has his gun on Mr. Crowley by the
french fry station, telling him he wants the
money he knows is put somewhere. Big Baby tells

us in front—they's three of us—get down on the floor and don't move. Right then the one yelling at Mr. Crowley, the manager, shoots him and Big Baby says, 'What you shoot him for?' like he can't believe it. But see, he only shot him in the leg, up here, and the dude shot him is still yelling for the money. See, then Big Baby gets me up from the floor account he's swearing, he can't open the fuckin register. I open it and he say to me open the other two while he's cleaning out the first one. Right then they's two shots and I see Mr. Crowley fall by the carry-out window and I see the dude aim his nine at Mr. Crowley lying on the floor and shoot him two more times. Now the three dudes are yelling at each other, 'What you shoot him for?' 'You didn't have to shoot him.' The dude that killed him saying he wouldn't give him the fuckin money, and saying they got to get out of here. Big Baby and the other dude follow the first dude out and get in a '96 Grand Marquis that's a dark color, but I didn't see the license good."

Delsa was listening but thinking of last night, looking through scenes in his head, stepping into the shower and Kelly turning to him, water streaming over her naked body, her perfect breasts, her navel, Kelly smiling at him and laughing out loud as he said, "Heil Hitler," and to the counter girl, "Do you know Big Baby's real name?"

She said, "No, I only heard people speak of him as Big Baby, but I never knew why."

Delsa, seeing Kelly on the bed in lamplight, her arms reaching for him, said, "You didn't know the other two?"

She said, "No, I didn't," and said, "I told you I lived on Edison? The house was on the corner of Rosa Parks Boulevard and my name is Rosa account of I was named for her? I thought I would live there the rest of my life. But what happen when I was twelve, my daddy lost his job at Wonder Bread and we were evicted for not paying the rent."

Delsa said, "That's a shame," remembering them in bed barely dry after the hurried shower but not caring.

"My mama and daddy's living on LaSalle Gardens now. It's nice there, they gentrified it. I live in Highland Park with my boyfriend Cedric, on Winona? He's valet at the MGM Grand."

"Later on today," Delsa said, handing her his card, "come down to police headquarters and we'll write up your statement. But give me a call first, we might have to do it tomorrow. Is that okay, Rosa?"

She said she guessed she could.

Delsa looked at the manager on the floor thinking there would always be this kind of work. The middle of April the manager would be, what, the one hundredth homicide? About that. Business would pick up in the summer maybe enough to match last year's four hundred homicides. Delsa had been at it eight years out of seventeen with the Detroit Police, started at the Seventh Precinct in radio cars, went to Violent Crimes and now Homicide. In less than eight more years he could retire on half pay. He'd be forty-five. Then what? Corporate security. He had taken prelaw at Wayne, kept putting off going to law school and now he didn't care much for lawyers. What he knew was how to investigate a homicide, how to peel open a case and find out who was who, the ones lying to him and the ones telling him things he could use, until finally meeting the suspect and knowing he had him by the nuts, this arrogant guy who could not believe you'd ever take him down, and you present the evidence and watch his face, watch his fuck-you expression fade looking at twenty-five to life or life without parole. There was nothing like that moment. No guns, no need for them. Just that one time he'd fired his Glock intending to do great bodily harm if not to kill. Maybe he should've told the second guy to put it down, the guy with Maureen's gun, but he didn't and wasn't sorry. He said to himself in the McDonald's on West Chicago, This is what you do. Stick around and you'll make inspector. The section was due for a white guy running the squads. But now he went back to cutting through scenes in his mind from last night to making love in the first light of morning. Now he was having breakfast in Kelly's terrycloth robe that was tight on him but felt good. Each time she brought something to the table, the paper, the coffee, the toast, she would touch his face and kiss him on the mouth. He would watch her walk to the kitchen in a heavy wool sweater that covered her black panties and wool socks sagging around her legs and would wait to see her face coming back, looking at him.

She said, "Do you know it's Saturday? I have to be at the DIA at two for rehearsal, hair, makeup. We have dinner at five in a cozy room and the show, I think, is at seven. Five changes in twenty-five minutes and it's over. Are you coming?"

She was not like any cop's wife he had ever known.

"I'll be there," Delsa said.

"You have a tux?"

"They'll let me in."

"I'll have to drive," Kelly said.

"I could maybe drop you off at two."

"But what if something comes up and you can't make the show?"

He said, "Yeah, you'd better drive."

They were both at the table with the paper and their breakfast. He said, "You know I'm ten years older than you are?"

She was biting into a piece of toast, looking at the front page of the paper. She said, "Good for you," still looking at the paper.

He said, "We're on different schedules, aren't we?"

She put the paper down.

"I lived with a call girl for two years," Kelly said, "on quite different schedules. If we want to see each other, Frank, we'll work it out." She said, "Won't we?"

There were evidence techs on the scene, Jackie Michaels talking to the help, and the death investigator from the Medical Examiner's office, Val Trabucci, taking pictures. Delsa approached him and Val took a break. He said, "Frank, this guy got out of bed this morning—if somebody told him he'd be dead before noon, he'd say they're full of shit."

"You think about things like that?"

"All the help here liked him, a nice young guy, married. But what's his wife doing right now while he's dead and she doesn't know it? That's what I think about."

There was a silence before Delsa said, "I've got a question for you. You ever hear of a couple of guys named Fontana and Krupa?"

"Gene Krupa?"

"This one's Art."

Val said to the girl standing there watching, "Sweetheart, give me a big scoop of those fries, will you, please?" He said to Delsa, "Art Krupa. He shot a guy in a bar on Martin Luther King Day and copped to first-degree manslaughter."

"I read both their sheets," Delsa said. "I'm looking for something else."

Val was watching the girl lift the basket of french fries out of the hot oil. He had to swallow before he said, "Fontana shot a guy with a deer rifle, hunting out of season, and copped to Man One about the same time as Krupa. I remember I kept calling him Gene."

"It looks like they're doing hits now."

"Paradiso and who else?"

"Five dealers and one attempted."

"Carl and Art? Where they get the guys they hit?"

"That's what I'm looking at. I told Eleanor to find out who represented them, but she's in court this morning."

Val said, "That Eleanor's got a body on her, you know it?" He said, "You should've asked me. It was Avern Cohn got 'em both reduced to manslaughter. It was using guns got 'em the time."

"They could've met at Jackson."

"Or they came out and Avern put 'em together."

"You ever hear of a hit man service?"

"Not any that made it."

"A guy runs it and gets them the jobs?"

Val said, "Uh-unh, but that could be Avern. He'd know anybody who wanted it done. But I'll tell you, you aren't gonna make a living in this town as a contract hitter, there too many amateurs who like to shoot people. The guy that shot this man came in knowing he was gonna kill somebody in here. He was nervous about it, but dying to see what it was like. The knuckleheads that robbed this place, what was their take, a couple hundred?"

"What they got was one register."

"Offer them a grand to hit somebody you'd have a deal. All these assholes and their guns, man, their nines . . . No, you want to be a hit man in Detroit you'd have to have a sideline, like home invasions. Bust in and develop a personal relationship with the family. Beat the shit out of the guy and fuck his wife." Val turned to the girl waiting to give him his fries. He said, "Excuse my language, we're talking business here."

The girl said that would be a dollar sixty-one for the fries.

Val said, "That's all right, forget it. Your manager was alive he'd tell you it was okay." He turned to Delsa with the fries, offering them.

Delsa shook his head, but then caught the aroma and took a few.

So did Val Trabucci saying, "But how did this Montez get hold of the two guys? They're from different walks of life, you might say. Unless—"

Delsa said, "Avern Cohn. He had Montez, lost him to Anthony Paradiso and got him back again. Wendell said, 'Avern Cohn? I thought he'd been disbarred by now.' "

Val said, "Well, shit, there you are, Avern's their manager. What else you need while I'm here?"

"Avern's name keeps coming up," Delsa said. "I'm thinking I ought to talk to him."

"I would."

"See if I can make him nervous."

"Scare the shit out of him," Val said, "and see what he does."

"Let me ask you something else. I got a C.I. working his ass off for the twenty grand on Orlando."

"Who put it up?"

"Harris says the sister of one of the dead Mexicans. I gave the reward sheet to my C.I. and he got excited. But now he's got a couple of guys with him who say they're cops, but didn't know about the reward, they're just back from their vacations."

"They're not cops."

"That's what I told him."

"They let this kid tag along?"

"He says they're working together on it."

Val shook his head. "They're not cops."

Delsa said, "Here's the thing. Manny Reyes talked to a guy named Chino who runs the posse the three guys were in. The one dismembered Harris said you put back together?"

"Yeah, see if the parts matched."

"Manny warns Chino not to go after Orlando. Chino tells Manny it's being taken care of, sounding to Manny like he took out a contract on Orlando. Then Jerome tells me about these two guys looking for Orlando for the twenty grand."

Val said, "And you're on to two guys who shoot drug dealers."

"White guys. Jerome tells me about the guys he's with and I picture white guys."

"Yeah . . . ?"

"But he never said they were white."

"Why don't you ask him?"

Delsa was nodding. "The next time he calls."

If he calls.

LLOYD LOOKED THROUGH A ROSE-COLORED PANE
in the door, the broken one below it finally
replaced, and saw two figures on the stoop, one
behind the other, but no red truck in the driveway. The mutts back. But then got a surprise
when he opened the door. Was only one of the
mutts, Art, and a black kid taller than Art. Lloyd
said, "Montez ain't here."

Didn't matter, they were coming in.

Art, not looking at Lloyd or saying a word,
came in past him. The kid slouching into the
foyer, his clothes hanging on him, a red-
patterned do-rag that wasn't bad, the kid looking
up at the high ceiling and the bannister along the
second floor. Art was in the dining room now,
about to shove through the swing door to the
pantry. Like it was his house. The kid started

after Art and Lloyd said, "Wait, I want to ask you something."

The kid looked around at him.

"What's your name?"

"Three-J."

"What's your real name?"

He hesitated before saying, "Jerome Jackson."

"That's only two *J*s."

"Jerome Juwan Jackson."

Lloyd said, "Jerome, what are you doing with this ofay motherfucker? Tell me what's going on here."

Lloyd was cool, the way he said it, and Jerome was cool behind his shades, but showed some surprise the way he hesitated and stared at Lloyd.

Jerome said, "Ask them, Uncle. They don't tell me shit."

"I'm not your uncle, I'm Lloyd. They tell you who they are?"

"They say they cops, but they ain't. They looking for Orlando same as me, for the reward."

"But why they here?"

"They need to hide out a while."

"From the police and they come *here*?"

Lloyd smiled, shaking his head, Jerome staring at him.

"Why you think that's funny?"

"You don't know who these mangy cats are, do you?"

"They contract hit men," Jerome said. "They mean and they cuckoo, they kill nine people and a dog. I was you I wouldn't fuck with them."

Lloyd said, "They killed a dog, huh?"

"Art did, I saw him. Man says, 'Don't shoot my dog,' and Art shoots it, a pit bull."

"That what you want to do, shoot dogs?"

"You think I like being with them? I want the reward's all. Man, twenty grand."

"What'd this Orlando do?"

"Kill three Mexicans and cut one up. Was a drug thing, a disagreement."

"Yeah, I read about it," Lloyd said. "Who's putting up the money?"

Jerome looked surprised.

"The cops."

"You think they gonna pay twenty-K for a tip?"

Jerome brought the reward notice from a pocket in his pants and handed it to Lloyd. Lloyd unfolded the sheet and read it.

"Must be some Mexican putting it up, some relative of one of the deceased." Lloyd handed the sheet back to Jerome and said, "Where's Carl? Hiding the truck?"

"Seeing can he put it in the garage."

"These guys strapped?"

"Each have a nine stuck in their pants."

"How about you?"

"I'm fixed."

"Where you keep it?"

"Here." Jerome patted his butt.

"Must be a weapon with size, it's pulling your pants off. You ever shoot anybody?"

"Not yet I haven't."

"You do any time?"

"Thirty months federal."

"Possession, huh? Boy, I did a hundred and eight months straight up, no time off for being good. Was for armed robbery, no pussy narcotics. It means I'm in charge here. Understand? You don't do nothing but what I tell you. Otherwise keep your mouth shut. Does that suit you?"

Jerome shrugged.

"Take off your glasses and look at me."

Jerome pulled off his shades and they stared at each other, Lloyd saying, "I asked does that suit you. I'm in charge in this house. That make sense to you?"

"Yeah, but you don't know who you fuckin with here."

"I know them better than you," Lloyd said. "I never saw 'em shoot a dog, but the other night I heard 'em shoot Mr. Paradise and his girlfriend.

Right there in the living room, they watching TV."

Jerome said, "Wait now. And they come here to *hide*?"

"It's what I'm saying." Lloyd motioned to him. "Let's go see what they up to."

Carl put the Tahoe in the garage and came in with the carton of liquor from the open house. He said to Lloyd, "Art's checking Montez' place, see if he's hiding under the bed. That your Toyota in the garage?"

Lloyd said it was and asked, "How long you gonna be here?"

"That's up to Montez. You know where he's at?"

"He don't tell me and I don't ask."

Carl said, "This boy here's Jerome. He's helping us out." And said, "Listen, we'll use your car we go anywhere. That okay with you, Chief?"

Lloyd said, "Use it all you want."

Sounding helpful, and Jerome looked at him.

Art came in the back door.

He said to Lloyd, "Is Montez a faggot? He's got that place dolled up like a woman did it. No colors like you see on sports teams. You know what I mean? They're queer colors. Carl, like Connie—all those colors going on in your house." Looking at Lloyd again, "Where's Montez at, Chief?"

Lloyd said, "How'd you know I was called that?"

"All colored guys are, aren't they? Being polite?"

"You mean politically correct," Carl said.

"Yeah, being like equals."

"He don't know when he's coming back or where he is," Carl said. "You ready for a drink?" He turned to Lloyd. "Chief, why don't you have one with us?"

Jerome began sorting through all he'd just heard.

Avern sat looking across his clean desk at Montez in black leather today, the coat open enough to show his gold chains against his black T-shirt. He wore gold studs on his earlobes, something Anthony Paradiso never allowed, Anthony puzzled why any man would want to look like a girl.

"I've got some not so good news," Avern said, "that could turn into some news you're gonna like."

Montez said, "So you have to give me the not so good news first?"

"That's right," Avern said, his hands folded on his clean desk. "Carl Fontana called last night.

Both of their houses, his and Krupa's, are under police surveillance, Detroit and Hamtramck."

Montez sat in his black leather and sunglasses staring at him, waiting, showing he was cool. Good.

"It doesn't surprise me," Avern said, "the cops are aware of them. But I'm sure it's not for Paradiso, and I'll tell you why. Every gun they used on a contract went in the river, and I witnessed it. I took a risk going with them, but it was that important to me. But, they stay busy. They've pulled a few home invasions between contracts, and they could've left prints, especially Art. I told Carl he and his buddy ought to split up, get out of the state for a while, go to Florida and take it easy."

Montez said, "What's the good news?"

"They go down for home invasion, you won't have to pay them. Of course you'd still owe me."

"Wait now," Montez said. "If they go down . . ." and looked at the etching on the wall behind Avern, the white guys in robes and half-ass wigs that was supposed to be funny—Montez seeing the situation and Avern as one of the wiggy characters before looking at him again.

"They get picked up for busting into homes—"

"You have nothing to worry about."

"But they get brought up on the Paradiso gig—"

"How? If there no witnesses?"

Montez said, "Kelly saw them."

Now he tells me, Avern thought, maintaining his pose, hands folded in front of him. He said, "From where?"

"Upstairs, where you can look down."

"They're in the foyer?"

"Yeah, they leaving."

"I can see it," Avern said, "I've been to parties there when Tony's wife was alive. Look straight ahead, there's the living room. Look up, there's the second floor. But looking down from up there? I wouldn't recognize my own wife—and not because she's always changing her hairdo. That's the only time Kelly saw them?"

"What she told me."

Avern shook his head. "I'm not gonna worry about her."

"I am," Montez said, "there's any possibility she can I.D. them. Lemme point something out to you. They get charged for doing Paradiso and Chloe and go down, you think they going without me? And you? Man, you they lawyer, isn't that what you do? Play Let's Make a Deal? But who you gonna give up to help the boys out, me and you or just me? Then who's left, Avern, for me to give up? Outside of you?"

Avern gave Montez his condescending smile,

letting him know he didn't know shit about what he was getting into, and said, "You trying the case now? You have Kelly Barr on the stand? But did she pick Carl and Art out of a lineup as the two she saw in a foyer from upstairs? Twenty feet above them, looking down at the tops of their heads? My man, give me a break. There's no way in the world she could positively identify them."

Montez looked like he was thinking about it before he said, "You sure?"

"Take my word."

Montez said, "I'm gonna ask her. She says no, she didn't see 'em good, we all still friends. She says yeah, she can pick 'em out, then you tell me what should become of her."

Montez left and Avern brought a framed photo of his wife Lois, in color—taken in the backyard, bright green leaves behind her—from a desk drawer and placed it to one side on the clean surface. Lois was never on the desk when he was dealing with criminals and ex-cons. Sometimes he would smile at her carefree expression and wish he could tell her he was an agent for a couple of hit men who specialized in drug dealers. "Honey, I'm using felons to stop the traffic of controlled substances. Like Batman, they're caped crusaders." What would she say? "You charge ten or fifteen percent?" Tell her twenty off the top, get her to laugh. It would be great if she could have fun with it. No, Lois would say, "Avern," in her cool way, "you're looking at mandatory life." She'd say it knowing she was wrong to make the point, knowing he could trade down to eight to fifteen, something around there. See? He couldn't tell Lois. He couldn't tell anybody, and it was a hell of a story.

Delsa arrived at Avern Cohn Associates a little later.

He knew Sheila, Avern's assistant, from being deposed here, answering Avern's questions that went on forever. He said to her, "You watching the job market?"

This went back to when he first met Sheila Ryan and he'd kid her about Avern getting disbarred. Sheila was forty with streaked blond hair, divorced, good-looking, a downtown girl. She said, "They'll never get Avern, he's too slippery. He's an eel with a human brain."

"I'll bet you five bucks," Delsa said, "he's up for arraignment within a week. Make it ten."

"After you leave," Sheila said, "you want me to tell him how confident you are, willing to risk ten bucks?"

Sheila had been another possibility, along with

Eleanor. But not anymore. He said, "Make it twenty."

She said, "Make it dinner."

And he said something she didn't hear, went in and sat down opposite Avern at his desk, a phone and a photograph on the clean surface.

"You don't have any work?"

"All I need is the back of an envelope," Avern said, "outside the courtroom or in a holding cell. I'm glad you condemned that ninth-floor lockup. My God, it stunk up there. Tell me what I can do for you."

Delsa said, "If you represented Fontana and Krupa—"

"You telling me you have them?"

"I'm asking if you represented them for the willful murder of Anthony Paradiso and Chloe Robinette . . ."

Delsa paused.

Avern waited now.

"And you were to represent Montez Taylor for hiring these goons to kill his boss, so he could go after the money Chloe was getting, since Montez wasn't getting shit . . ."

Delsa paused again.

Avern said, "What's the question?"

"If you ·represented Fontana and Krupa, and

also Montez, who do you give up? Whoever's arraigned first gets to make the deal?"

"That's your question?"

"What if we get 'em all at the same time?"

"Tell me what you've got on this Carl and Art."

"You first," Delsa said. "What can you give me to save your own ass? That's my question."

There wasn't any more Delsa would tell him or anything Avern was ready to discuss or deny. Delsa left and Avern looked at his wife's picture, still on the clean desk.

He said, "Lois, you try to use a little ingenuity in your practice . . . you never know what might happen."

MONTEZ WAS SITTING IN THE LEXUS WITH A KID
named Ricky, fourteen, tall with big hands,
Baggies hanging on him. They were parked
across the street from Kelly's building and
Montez was showing Ricky signed pictures of
Kelly in panties and thongs.

"You know what a small world it is?" Montez
said. "I'm thinking of how I can show you Kelly
so you know what she looks like, and I remember
this girl Emily works at the Rattlesnake. I'd see
her when I felt like some white pussy. Know what
I'm saying? Something different, change my luck.
I remember Emily collects autographs of celebri-
ties come in the Snake. She ask can she shoot
them with her Polaroid. They most all say yeah,
smile at her and sign the picture. Now here's
Kelly living a few blocks from the Snake. I'm

thinking she must go there sometimes. So I call my friend Emily this morning, ask her does she know Kelly Barr. Emily says she's got more pictures of Kelly than anybody as Kelly's her favorite celebrity. She even got the latest pictures of her signed just the other day. So I go over and borrow her Victoria's Secret," Montez said, "so you know what she looks like she comes out of the building."

Fourteen-year-old Ricky said these were fine-looking bitches in here. He wouldn't mind having him some of 'em.

"Her car's over here in the lot," Montez said, "the black VW. See it? She come out and heads for the car, you get over there, start wiping off her windshield. There's a hand towel on the backseat here. You a talker, dog, turn on the personality. See can you find out where she's going and when she's coming back."

Ricky said, "What if she walks someplace?"

"Follow her."

"What if she don't come out?"

"She still at home by dark, call and tell me."

"I could be hanging here all day?"

"As long as it takes," Montez said. "Look at all the cars around here. Open one up and sit in it till she comes. You have my number—right?"

"I got it somewhere."

Montez said, "Ricky, don't lose that number. I want to hear from you, man."

This was earlier in the day, before Montez got the call from Avern and went to see him.

It was noon by the time Delsa was ready to leave the McDonald's on West Chicago. They had put out a BOLO on Gregory Coleman, also known as Big Baby, *be on the lookout* for this kid with a sawed-off shotgun and his buddies in a dark-colored Grand Marquis.

Now he called Kelly.

"What time will you leave?"

"By one-thirty the latest. I'm about to get in the shower."

"You can't wait till tonight?"

"We'll take another one. We can take all the showers we want, Frank."

"I'm coming to the show."

"I'll look for you, the only guy in a suit."

"I'm sorry I can't take you."

"Even if you have to miss the show, you'll come by later?"

He said, "I can't wait to see you."

She said, "I can't either, I'm dying."

"You know I forgot to pick up Chloe's license?"

"And the stock papers. They're right here."

"Why don't you put them in your bag? Give them to me tonight and I'll know I have them. Did Montez call, or stop by?"

"He didn't and I'm surprised."

"Keep your eyes open."

"Don't worry."

"He'll know by now we've identified the two guys. I told his lawyer, who's also the lawyer for the two guys, or was. I think he's in the middle of it, the lawyer, and I'm hoping he's started to think about making a deal, for himself."

"What if he doesn't?"

"It'll take a little longer."

Kelly said, "Well . . . maybe I should tell you what I'll be wearing tonight, so you'll know me."

He said, "I'll know you."

Montez left the car in the driveway, so he didn't see Carl and Art, and Lloyd and some gangbanger kid he'd never seen before, until he was through the swing door and in the kitchen.

This big kitchen, the commercial range and refrigerator, the long worktable in the middle of the room, another round table in the alcove of windows where Carl and Art were sitting with drinks. A bottle of Club on the worktable, an ice tray open, where Lloyd was slicing a leftover beef roast and the young gangbanger he'd never seen before, wearing a reddish do-rag that showed some style, was opening a loaf of bread, Lloyd saying to the kid as Montez walked in, "Wash your hands first."

Montez said, "Before anybody says anything," raising his hands to hold off whatever he thought might be coming, "let me tell you what Avern said to me just a little while ago. One, there is no way their witness, Kelly Barr, can identify you," wanting to call them "assholes," but keeping it simple. "And two, Avern thinks you should leave town, go to Florida or someplace, get lost in a crowd of people." He said, "Now let me tell you what I think, being closer to the situation," and paused looking at Lloyd. "Who's this gang-banger, your grandson come to visit? Y'all best get out of here."

Lloyd waved the carving knife toward Carl and Art at the breakfast table. "Your friends say they hungry. Want something to eat."

Art said to Montez, "You want to tell us what you think, go ahead. Or save it till Lloyd makes us some sandwiches. That boy there is Three-J. He's with us, so don't fuck with him."

"Wait a minute," Montez said. "You two are hiding out? *Here?*"

"We was at a Ramada last night," Carl said. "I could see staying at motels wasn't gonna work out. We want to talk to you anyway, so we thought, hell, come here. Art and I want to know did you make some kind of deal with them."

Montez knew they were dumb, but not this dumb. How could they believe . . . "You think I gave you up? Tell me how I can do that without giving myself up? Was me hired you. You think they gonna let me out on the street?" He said, "Listen to me. You swear your nines are clean, can't be traced to some other deed, they's only one way the police could get after you. Kelly Barr, man. She told me she didn't see you good, but she must've and they showed her pictures. Saw you by the front door, Art with a nine—you'd of shot me you'd been paid. And Carl with the bottle of vodka."

Art said to Carl, "Connie told you they took the bottle, the same one? With your prints on it?"

Montez said, "You gave it to Connie? Man, it's got my prints on it, too. I poured the old man his drinks. Kelly Barr saw me doing it. Understand what I'm saying? And she saw you walk out of the house with the bottle."

Art said to Carl, "The fuck you take it for?"

"You said there's some vodka for Connie—in an ice bucket."

"You're crazy, I never fuckin said that."

"I was there," Montez said to Art. "You told

him to take the bottle, and he did. And Kelly can say yeah, that's the bottle the old man was drinking from. Before you shot him and she sees you two leaving the house. You want to hear her tell about it in court?"

Lloyd listened to them getting to it as he carved the leftover roast beef he'd served last night to his friend Serita Reese. She was somewhere in her fifties, worked in the Blue Cross office and wore big pearl earrings with her satin dress, always satin when she went out. Last evening an aqua color. Lloyd called her his Satin Doll. He asked Serita did she want to go to Puerto Rico. "Oh, would I." But wouldn't dare leave her job at Blue Cross. He asked Jackie Michaels did she want to go. She was hipper than Serita, younger, and said, "You mean it?" He said why would he ask her if he didn't mean it? "An old broad like me?" Fishing. He told Jackie Michaels she stirred him, got him thinking about living with a woman again. The only reason he hadn't jumped her, he had trouble working up intimate feelings about a woman on the police. Jackie Michaels said, "But you're thirty years older than I am."

He said, "Who told you that?"

Last night he and Serita were having their coffee and Rémy, chocolate sauce on raspberry sorbet, and Allegra, the old man's granddaughter, stopped by from the funeral home with her husband, the one sold bull come, to show him the old paintings in the foyer. She kept apologizing for interrupting their evening till Serita, good at talking to white people, invited them to sit down and have some dessert. It was all right, but you had to talk on their level and laugh at things that weren't funny. Jesus, but he was tired of doing that.

Jerome turned from washing his hands at the sink and started making ugly sandwiches with the meat hanging out. Lloyd said, "Here," and took over the job. He said to Jerome, aside, "Listen to some of the Dumbest Criminals I Have Ever Known, and learn something."

All three of them sitting now at the round table by the windows.

The cheap phone inside Montez' leather coat came on playing "How High the Moon" and he brought it out and walked through the swing door into the pantry saying, "Ricky? . . . Yeah? Tell me." He came back after a few minutes and sat down at the table again with Carl and Art.

"She's in a fashion show tonight at the Detroit Institute of Arts. I told you about my man Ricky, fourteen years old? Sweet boy, can talk about fashion. He got that for me wiping off her wind-shield and made a buck."

Art said, "That's all you pay the kid?"

"What Kelly gave him. I owe Ricky another twenty's all. She told him she be home about nine-thirty. We get over there around nine, wait till she gets out of the car . . . I think as she's crossing the street to her building we roll up and snatch her, put her in the Tahoe."

Carl said, "We use your car."

"Man, you got more room."

"You got a trunk, don't you?" Carl said. "The Tahoe stays in the garage."

Art said, "We gonna shoot her?"

Montez said, "If that's how you want to do it. You the pros."

"Well, shit," Art said. "She gets back, walk up to her car and pop her."

"She has to disappear," Montez said. "Like she left town and didn't tell nobody."

"Take her out'n the woods?"

"I was thinking bring her back here," Montez said, "till we work out what to do with her. You know you could stick her head in a plastic bag. That way there won't be no blood."

Art said, "Shit, drop her in the river."

"You have a boat?"

"Off the Belle Isle bridge. Weight her down."

Carl said to Montez, "You ever kill anybody?"

Montez said, "I'm gonna talk to you about it?"

Art said, "I think he's cherry, never done it in his life."

"I doubt he has," Carl said. "Tells us we're the pros and stays out of it. Tells us, stick her head in a plastic bag, like he knows these different ways he saw in the movies, but won't do it himself." He said to Montez, "How come you didn't take the bag off your suit from the cleaners and suffocate the old man with it? He's sleeping, nobody around. We walk in the other night, a party's going on."

"I tried to call you," Montez said. "Ask Connie."

Carl said to Art, "You think he should do the girl? Since he's the one fucked up the deal, bringing her in?"

Art said, "We do it, he'll have to pay us."

"He already owes for the old man," and looked toward the worktable. "Lloyd, you getting all this?"

Lloyd turned his head to one side. "I didn't hear you. What'd you say?"

Now Montez looked over at him. "You don't hear these guys fuckin with me?"

"I'm making y'all sandwiches," Lloyd said,

finishing up the last one. "Anything you want to put on them's in the refrigerator. Horseradish, pickles, chili sauce, ketchup, mayonnaise—"

Art said, "You got any mustard?"

"We have yella mustard, Poupon mustard, whatever kind pleases you, Pelican mustard," Lloyd said, motioning with his head for Jerome to leave the kitchen, saying when he didn't move, "Go on, they don't care." Then raised his voice to tell the three mutts deciding on who was going to kill the girl, "Me and Jerome gonna be in the den watching TV."

Mr. Paradise had liked to watch it in the living room saying the den was too small, crowded with the big brown leather chairs and the couch. There were three walls of Book-of-the-Month Club books in their jackets, fifty years of book selections in all colors from the counter to the ceiling. Against the fourth wall was where Lloyd put the TV, the guy who replaced the glass helping him.

Lloyd came in to see Jerome punching numbers in a cell phone, got to him and snatched the phone out of his hands.

"Who you calling?"

"A homicide detective, man. I'm his C.I."

"You mean his fink."

"You didn't hear them, they talking about killing some girl."

"I heard everything was said. It ain't your bidness."

"You don't care they gonna kill her?"

"I said it ain't your bidness," Lloyd said. "They got to pick her up first, bring her here."

"They gonna put a plastic bag over her head. Man, what's going on in this house?"

"You don't read the paper, watch the news? You running with those mutts, they haven't told you what they did here?"

Jerome looked like he was beginning to understand, nodding his head. He said, "I know they hit men. They whack somebody here and come here to hide *out*?"

"You want to read about it," Lloyd said, "I've saved the papers. They by the chair."

Jerome turned and Lloyd stopped him, taking hold of his arm.

"Lemme have your gun."

Jerome frowned at him. "Man, I need it."

"I told you this ain't your bidness," Lloyd said. "You won't need it, but I might."

HE COULDN'T SEE HER LIVING ON FARMBROOK IN a redbrick and white siding—what did you call it, postwar bungalow? With three small bedrooms, hardly any closet space for her clothes. She walked into the closet in her loft and was gone and would come out with pants and a blouse. On Farmbrook, a wood garage in back rotting in places, full of junk. Jesus, and the storm windows . . .

He thought about this standing in the entrance to the museum's Rivera Court, the artist Diego Rivera's giant murals of machinery and workers, a tight-mouthed boss, covering both walls of the court, left and right, chairs around the stage that came out of the far wall and was only a couple of feet off the floor, high enough to make the girls look seven feet tall coming down the runway with indifferent expressions but in command, striding to a heavy disco beat.

He knew Kelly the instant she appeared. He saw her looking for him without giving it away. She wore a slight smile, pleasant. He imagined that everyone in the audience, a few hundred in black tie and evening dress, knew she was fun and would like to know her. He raised his hand as high as he could reach, above the heads of those in front of him, when she came to the end of the stage and paused and made her turn. He didn't think she saw him. She was a knockout. She had his favorite girl look, her eyes, her nose. Jesus, looking at her and not noticing the outfits, none of them, he looked at their faces and wondered about them. But he did recognize Kelly's favorite, the suit she called a biker outfit with the chains, the chains the only thing about the suit he'd associate with bikers—but even then couldn't remember ever confronting bikers with chains. He thought of Maureen because Maureen didn't have his favorite look, but it didn't seem to have mattered. He lived on Farmbrook nine years with Maureen and the house was fine, it was their home. Maureen called the old storm windows that came with the house and you busted your ass to put up, those fuckers. He couldn't see Maureen in any of the clothes coming down the runway, Maureen shorter and heavier than these girls.

He had a program that described each look as it came along, like "No. 35, Black wool striped boucle jacket with lace inset, black lace chiffon skirt." They were up to cocktail dresses now, a different sound to the disco, and he felt his phone pulse against his chest. He said, Shit, because Harris had called earlier, as he arrived and was telling the valet guy to put his car right there, about thirty feet down the circular drive, Delsa showing the young guy his badge but low-key about it.

Then listened to Harris say, "There's been a tip on Orlando that's being checked out. I find out some more, I'll call you back."

Delsa, in a dark navy suit, introduced himself to the museum security man at the entrance, telling him nothing was up, his girlfriend was one of the models and he liked to watch her. Calling her his girlfriend for the first time, hearing what it sounded like. Getting it out in the open. He went up a wide staircase to the Great Hall crowded with dressy people standing in groups and at high cocktail tables drinking and dining on the "strolling supper," the tenderloin, the rack of lamb, pasta, the sushi. He didn't know anyone. He stood holding a glass of beer until it was time for the fashion show.

When his phone pulsed and he came out here again, the hall was set up with sweet tables and coffee urns.

Harris said, "Orlando's sitting in the squad room. You want to take his statement?"

Delsa said, "I'll be there when I get there. Let him chill."

He wrote a note on the back of his card and asked the security officer if he'd try to find Kelly Barr after the show and give this to her.

The note said, "*Had to leave. Don't know when I'll be free. If you want to make other plans go ahead. Will call you later.*" Delsa wanted to add something personal but felt time running out. He handed the note to the security guy and left.

The way it went down with Orlando:

Crime Stoppers got the tip from an informant telling them where to find him. They called ROPE, the Repeat Offenders Program, part of a federal fugitive task force with Detroit cops on it. ROPE had Orlando's homicide file and a flight warrant to pick him up wherever he might be. They thought he'd gone to Mississippi, but according to the informant he was in a house on Pingree between Second and Third. They watched the house until they saw someone who fit Orlando's description come out on the porch.

That "made" the house and it gave them probable cause to execute the flight warrant. They told the guy who opened the door, believed to be the suspect's brother, to keep his mouth shut and get out of the way. Orlando, taking a nap, was nudged with a shotgun and told it was "Time to get up, sleepyhead." He admitted who he was and they took him downtown.

On the way one of the ROPE guys called Violent Crimes and asked, "You guys still looking for Orlando Holmes?"

A senior Violent Crimes officer said, "Yeah, but we think he's in Mississippi."

The ROPE guy said, "No, he's in the back of my car."

Delsa arrived and Harris filled him in about the federal task force making the arrest. He said Orlando was waiting in the interview room.

"He confess?"

"Not yet."

"What's the problem?"

"Says he wasn't home at the time. Must've been somebody else did the Mexicans."

"I'll talk to him," Delsa said.

He thought of Jerome as Harris told him, "It was Orlando's brother's girlfriend's brother who called Crime Stoppers wanting the twenty thousand. They let him know the woman who'd put it up changed her mind, as she didn't have time to raise the money, but Crime Stoppers would give him a thousand for being a good citizen. Orlando's brother's girlfriend's brother said, 'I risk my ass to help you all out and that's all I get?' "

Delsa walked back to the interview room with a pad of Witness Statement forms and sat across the table from Orlando Holmes, who sat hunched over picking at a fingernail.

"What you're doing is fucking up my evening," Delsa said, and Orlando looked up. "Your girlfriend Tenisha, Tenisha's mother, and your neighbor Rosella Munson, have all signed statements that you were home the day you and Jo-Jo and another guy killed the three Cash Flow Mexicans. You can tell me a member of the Dorados posse made you do it. Two members of the Dorados have disappeared. If you stayed on the street much longer, you'd of disappeared too. We'll get to motive. I've got your prints on the chain saw Jo-Jo bought at the Home Depot that evening and a tape of Jo-Jo making the purchase from their security camera. So don't waste my time."

Delsa began filling in the top of the witness sheet, his name and Orlando's, time and date, where they were. He said, "I'm putting down that you willingly gave me this information. Now tell me what happened," Delsa said, writing it on the form, "at 2210 Vermont regarding the three men shot and burned, one dismembered, on or about April 15. What time did the three men arrive at your home?"

Orlando didn't answer, looking past Delsa now.

"I know later on at the motel you told Tenisha, 'My fuckin life is done.' " Delsa paused and said, "You think it is?"

Orlando was looking at him now.

"I'd like to hear your side of this," Delsa said. "Tell me why the three guys came to see you."

"It was about weed," Orlando said. "I told them I wasn't dealing with them no more and they become upset. They brought a hundred pounds and said I had to pay them for it."

"Where'd you take it, to your mom's house?"

Orlando straightened a little. "How'd you know?"

"So these Cash Flow guys tried to get tough, uh?"

"Thought they could make me pay 'em."

"They threaten you?"

"Say they be back."

"So what you did was like self-defense, shoot them first?"

"Exactly how I saw it. Shoot the motherfuck-ers before they come and shoot me. Wouldn't you do the same, you in my shoes?"

"Not exactly," Delsa said. "Why'd you try to burn your house down?"

"Was a Posse guy did it. He say get a chain saw, cut 'em up and burn 'em. You ever cut into a body full of blood?"

"No, I haven't," Delsa said.

"Man, I threw my clothes in with theirs. Those greasers, man, they spooks. I knew that house wouldn't burn."

"You know who put the stuff on you?"

"Somebody close to me, his girlfriend's punk-ass brother. Is how it goes. But listen, I'm on tell you something, I was scared."

"I would be, too," Delsa said.

"Thinking of 'em coming back with guns."

Delsa put it in.

In two hours or more he filled nine pages with Orlando's statement, each one signed. It was ten to eleven when he gave Orlando to Harris, going to the Seventh Precinct for the night, and had a chance to call Kelly.

Her voice said, "Leave a message."

He had told her in the note, if she wanted to make other plans, go ahead. And that's what she did. He had assumed she had a date last night, and she went to Alvin's to get the stock. Why didn't she tell him? Because he wouldn't understand why she wanted to get it and check out the value of what she had by herself—in case it was enough to commit fraud to get. His mind took him there, he was an investigator, he looked for motives. But he didn't believe that was the reason she made him think she had a date and went to Alvin's alone. No, she was honest with him. Except in the beginning.

Or she was tired and went to bed.

What he could do, drive over there and see if her car was in the lot.

MONTEZ SAID, "WE CAN'T TAKE MY CAR, SHE knows it, she's even been in it."

Carl thought about it before saying, "You don't want to go, do you?"

Art said, "It ain't even the smoke's car, it's that old man's."

Montez said, "She sees it coming she'll scream her lungs out."

"There's an all-points on the Tahoe by now. It stays in the garage." Carl said, "We'll take Lloyd's car," and asked him, "you want to drive us?"

"I don't drive at night," Lloyd said, "account of my vision ain't too good."

Montez said, "Who's staying here with Lloyd and the gangbanger, see they don't pull any shit on us?"

"I guess you are," Carl said, "since you don't like to put yourself out. Me and Art'll get her."

While it was still light they had checked out the loft, and where Kelly parked her VW in the lot across the street. Art drove. Carl sat in back. They waited on the south side of the lot toward the river. Art kept looking at his watch saying, "Well, she coming or not?"

Carl said, "Give her time."

Finally, when they saw the black VW coming from Jefferson and Art said, "This must be her," it was almost ten o'clock.

They watched the VW pull into the lot and find a spot and waited for Kelly to get out and lock the car. Now Art brought the Camry around the corner with the lights off, creeping up to where she would cross the street to her building, timing it. There she was, starting across, a leather bag hanging from her shoulder. She didn't see the Camry creeping up on her. Art braked and popped on the brights and saw her face and how scared she was as Carl appeared in the beams and grabbed her. They got her in the backseat with the bag, no problem, Carl's hand over her mouth. She tried to fight him but quieted down as he began to tell her, "I come across a gook sleeping in a tunnel one time. I didn't know was there others in there. Maybe this one sleeping was suppose to be on guard duty. I shun my light on him and put my hand over his mouth and he come alive on me like a wild animal. I hit him with the flashlight and broke it. I had to stick my forty-five under his chin and shoot him and got out of that fuckin tunnel as fast as I could."

He held Kelly in his arms patting her back.

Montez was waiting in the kitchen. He took her bag from Art and pushed her ahead of him through the swing door. She didn't know where she was until she saw the living room, the old man's chair and the TV set gone. Montez was feeling around in her bag now saying, "What you got in here?" He found her cell and put it in his pocket. Now he was bringing out the stock certificate, the papers and her printout. Montez said, "Gonna meet the cop and give him these, huh?"

She didn't answer. She hadn't made a sound since she was thrown in the car. They were in the foyer now and Kelly was looking at the two guys standing in the short hall from the living room. Like they didn't want to get too close to her. White guys. She realized they must be the ones from the other night. It surprised her and she said, "They're hiding out *here*?"

Montez said to them, "See? I told you she

could pick you out. This bitch is smart, man, she *knows*."

Delsa had told her their names, Carl Fontana and Art Krupa, but she didn't know which was which. They stared at her not saying anything. She wanted to run out the front door. She should've run out that night and not worried about leaving her bag. They kept staring at her.

She heard voices coming from the den, a TV commercial about acid reflux she recognized, looked over and saw Lloyd standing in the doorway. He nodded to her. Now a young black guy appeared next to him.

Montez said, "Come on," took her by the arm and they started up the stairway.

Lloyd said, "Miss, can I get you anything?"

She had stopped at the Rattlesnake with a girl from the show and they'd each had a couple of drinks. Now she said to Lloyd, "How about an alexander?"

Going back to the kitchen Art said to Carl, "The fuck's an alexander?"

"It's a drink, a cocktail."

"What's in it?"

"I don't know, it's kind of a tan drink."

They went in the kitchen to the table by the window, a lamp on, and sat down. Carl said, "We haven't been in any room in this whole fuckin house except the fuckin kitchen."

"I'm home, I always sit in the fuckin kitchen."

"Not when I stay with you."

" 'Cause Ginny's in there. We go out."

"You don't worry about her knowing what you do."

"I said to her, you tell anybody I'll shoot you, and I know I can do it."

Carl said, "Art, how do the cops know about us? This girl tells what we look like, they draw pictures of us and say, 'Shit, why that's Art and Carl'?"

"Unless," Art said, "where we got the guns— they'd been used before and that asshole told us they're cherry."

"That's been bothering me," Carl said. "Should we have trusted that kid? I can't even think of his name. But that could be it." Carl poured Club in his glass, ice melted in the bottom. He pushed the bottle to Art, saying to him, "You notice how much the two girls look alike?"

"Going by her picture in the paper. Otherwise you wouldn't know it was the same one in the chair. Yeah, they could almost be twins." He said, "I'm glad we didn't talk to her. You gonna talk to the one upstairs?"

"I'm not having nothing to do with her," Carl

said. "I'm not gonna talk to her and I'm sure as hell not gonna shoot her. How about you?"

"The smoke wants it done," Art said, "he's gonna have to do it."

"Would you let him?"

"What you're asking now," Art said, "would I shoot him before he puts a plastic bag over her head. I don't see any difference in whacking him or the fuckin dopers. See, but I don't know he has the nerve to do it."

"You don't worry about her saying it was us?"

"Did you see her the other night? I didn't. Where was she when she saw us, upstairs? She couldn't of seen us good."

"The thing is she's seen us now," Carl said. "She can tell herself yeah, those're the guys. You know what I mean? But I don't think the cops need her."

"You think it's the guns," Art said.

Carl was nodding. "I think we fucked ourselves buying those guns."

There was a silence as Art picked up the bottle of Canadian Club and then paused.

"How come Avern hasn't been on us to get rid of 'em?"

The bong was no longer on the dresser. "Confiscated," Montez said. He rolled a joint and lit and handed it to Kelly, saying, "For your pleasure."

She shrugged and took a hit. Like the other time.

Lloyd came with an alexander in a lowball glass, the crystal, he handed to Kelly in the chair and looked at Montez sitting on the other side of the bed, the lamp on, reading about Del Rio Power. Lloyd said to Kelly, "You need anything else?"

She said, "Tell me what I'm doing here."

"That's his bidness," Lloyd said, looking at Montez. "I jes work here."

"You have a cigarette?"

"I'll find you some," Lloyd said and walked out.

Montez came around to sit on the side of the bed facing Kelly, in the chair where she had tried to hide in her cinnamon coat that night. Today she wore dark Donna Karan head to toe, sweater, pants and heels.

"What I have here," Montez said, "is the paper that transfers the stock to Chloe, filled out, signed by Mr. Paradise. Where you sign it is down here."

"Even if the stock was good," Kelly said, "I'm not gonna commit fraud."

Montez said, "Those two white menaces downstairs, they brought you here while they de-

cide how to dispose of you. Understand? They
ain't letting you send them to prison."

Kelly said, "But if I sign this, what? You'll get
me out of here?"

"I didn't know you have this on you. Since you
do, I want you to cash it in for me."

"But before you found it," Kelly said, "you
agreed with the two guys, I had to be put away?"

"You lucky you brought it, huh?"

"And now I'm supposed to trust you?" Kelly
said. "Chloe's picture was in the paper. She's the
news, and she's dead."

"We wait a while, nobody remembers her
name. They look at you and the picture on
Chloe's license—you still have it, the driver's license?"

"In my bag. And by the time we get around to
doing it," Kelly said, "Del Rio is out of business
and there's no stock to sell."

Montez said, "Why couldn't the stock go up
instead of down? Del Rio Power, man, it's a giant
corporation."

Kelly sipped her drink.

She looked at Montez and for a moment or so
felt sorry for him. She said, "Why don't you go
hold up a liquor store? You do all this plotting . . .
for what? I'll bet you anything the best way to
make money in crime is armed robbery. You've

been fucking around with this idea, make a killing off the old man for how long, ten years? Don't you know those two—what did you call them, white menaces?—are going to name you to make a deal with the prosecutor? You know they'll be arrested. Frank Delsa said, 'Those two go around like they're wearing signs.' I think you ought to come to some agreement with the two guys that you won't tell on each other."

Kelly sipped her drink.

"Listen, and make sure they know I didn't see them the other night. I didn't, really. Not well enough to swear they're the same guys who were here."

She sipped her drink and again thought of sitting in this chair the other night in her coat, half in the bag, thinking, *Are you nuts?* Even considering what Montez wanted her to do, a houseful of cops on the scene? *Are you fucking nuts?* She was easing into that mood now, reminding herself she had to be smarter than these guys, and to keep her eyes open and watch for a way to get out of here. She thought of Delsa and tried to remember details he'd told her about the case. She thought of him and wondered if he'd made the show and where he was now and what he was doing. She did that whenever they were apart.

She said to Montez, "Is there anyone else involved in this besides the two guys? I mean who you ought to talk to?"

Montez laid the stock information on the bed, didn't say a word to her and walked out. Kelly finished her drink and set the glass on the floor. She looked up to see the young black guy standing in the doorway, the room dim with only the lamp on.

He said, "I have these cigarettes for you Lloyd give me."

Kelly said, "Thank Lloyd for me, okay?" and he came in the room to hand her the pack of Slims and a book of matches. She said, "You see the ashtray anywhere?"

Jerome pointed. "Right there, the end of the bed."

"Where I left it the other night," Kelly said. "I didn't see it. You can turn the light on if you want."

"Don't matter to me."

She opened the pack and popped out a cigarette.

"You're related to Lloyd?"

"I come with the two white dudes."

"You work for them?"

"We looking for a dude has twenty thousand

reward on him, but I don't work for them or ever would. I'm a C.I."

"What's a C.I.?"

"Confidential Informant."

Kelly struck a match.

"I work for a man with the Homicide police name of Frank Delsa."

Kelly was lighting the cigarette. She blew out the match and said to this guy in the dark red do-rag, "Why don't you hand me the ashtray and sit down for a minute? I know Frank."

Montez was at the round table now in the kitchen with Carl and Art. He said, "Y'all still drinking, huh?"

He saw Art look at Carl while Carl kept looking this way, staring at him.

"Bitch say to me upstairs she can't pick you out. Is she shittin' me? But then I wonder about it. I'm thinking, she's on the second floor as you run out. She look down from up there, she looking at the top of your heads. Understand what I'm saying? She can't see your faces, you got your Tiger hats on. What I'm saying, she can't put either one of you at the scene."

Carl turned to Art. "What he's saying is he don't want to shoot her, or put a bag over her head. He's changed his mind."

"There's no cause to mess with her," Montez said. "No, I think the one we ought to get over here and have a talk with is your agent, Avern Cohn."

AT ELEVEN-FIFTEEN LAST NIGHT DELSA DROVE TO the loft and saw Kelly's black Volkswagen in the lot and phoned her from outside the building. Her voice said to leave a message. Okay, she didn't drive. Someone picked her up, one of the other models, and they stopped off or ran into friends and went to a party after the show. He had to remind himself she had a life he didn't know much about.

This morning, Sunday, he phoned from the squad room, putting it off until ten in case she was sleeping in, and got no response. He drove to her place again, three miles from 1300, and saw her VW still in the lot. This time he got the manager to let him into the loft. The manager stood inside the door while he listened to phone messages, all from women in the fashion business, all related to the runway show last night. No calls from Montez.

But yesterday on the phone she told him the last thing Montez had said to her when he called the night before, "You think you done with me?" and she hung up on him.

It was time to see Montez.

Last night Kelly asked Jerome how he knew Frank Delsa. Jerome was self-conscious and didn't look at her directly telling about the shooting at Yakity Yak's he'd witnessed and how he became Delsa's C.I. and how he ran into the two hit men at the house Orlando tried to burn down account of the three bodies in the basement, one of 'em cut up into six pieces. Kelly said, "Six?" Jerome said the arms and the legs were four, the head five and body was six. He said people forgot to count the body.

Kelly said, "If you work for Frank Delsa and the two hit men are here, why don't you slip out? Tell Delsa the ones who killed Mr. Paradiso and my friend Chloe are here?" Jerome said Lloyd told him it wasn't none of his bidness. He said he had to go and left, closing the door. Kelly got up and locked it. She didn't know what she was supposed to do. After a while she stretched out on the bed in her Donna Karan sweater and pants, and a little later heard the faint sound of voices in the hall. Someone rattled the doorknob. At 2 A.M. she opened it and looked down the hall toward the staircase. She saw Jerome down there in an easy chair he'd got from one of the rooms. She walked toward him, got close enough to see he was asleep, but he woke up as she started down the stairs and told her she was supposed to stay in her room.

In the morning the chair was still there but Jerome was gone. This time she got to the bottom of the stairs and was startled to see Carl sitting in the foyer in one of the upholstered straight chairs. Carl said, "Go on in the kitchen you want some breakfast. Lloyd's in there." He said, "I'm gonna talk to you later on."

She said, "About what?"

He said, "The situation."

Montez was at the round table in the alcove with a cup of coffee. She said to him, "Would you mind telling me what's going on?"

Montez said, "We gonna have a sit-down here and get things straightened out."

"When?"

"We got to get somebody first. You want some coffee? Lloyd brewed a pot."

"Where's Jerome?"

"The gangbanger? I guess he's sleeping."

Lloyd came in and asked if she'd like a glass of fresh-squeezed orange juice. He could fix her eggs if she wanted.

"I've been kidnapped," Kelly said. "I'm being held against my will, and I get fresh-squeezed orange juice?"

"They do it at the market," Lloyd said. "Six-ninety-five a half gallon. It's nice and cold."

Kelly said okay, orange juice and coffee, and turned to the window. It looked like it would be a nice day.

Montez finished his coffee and left.

Nine o'clock Sunday morning Montez and Carl sat in Lloyd's car parked on 14 Mile Road at the south end of Bloomfield Hills. They watched the front yard of Avern Cohn's house, on the corner of Crosswick and 14, through a line of shrubbery, waiting for him to come out and pick up his newspapers, the *Detroit News and Free Press* in a plain plastic bag, the fat *New York Times* rolled up in a blue one.

Montez had wanted to stay home to keep an eye on Kelly. Carl was afraid she'd talk him into letting her go and he wanted to speak to her first, reach some kind of an understanding. Art wanted to come so he could walk in Avern's house, shoot him and walk out. He said what was there to talk about? Carl felt if they scared Avern enough he'd keep his mouth shut. This deal was now way out of hand; he wasn't shooting anybody 'less they got paid. Montez had asked, before, how he knew where Avern lived. "I said if he didn't tell me, we wouldn't make a deal with him to do contracts. He said, 'Why you want to know?' I told him so I'd come to the right house he ever fucked us over."

Carl said to Montez now, "We don't talk to him in the car. Don't say a fuckin word."

"How come?"

"He's gonna act surprised, want to know what's going on. You start in with him, the son of a bitch'll talk us out of what we're doing. He'll be scareder we don't say a fuckin word. He comes out to get the newspapers I'll quick pull into the drive. I'll grab Avern and throw him in the car, you pick up the fuckin newspapers."

That was how it worked. Avern came out in a pongee bathrobe, narrow blue and yellow stripes, showing bare legs and black velvet slippers with gold crests on them. Carl jumped out of the car and grabbed him, but had to yell at Montez to pick up the fuckin papers.

They brought Avern in the back way to the kitchen. Kelly looked at the guy in the striped pongee bathrobe, his skinny white legs, and said to Carl, "I bet this is your agent, Mr. Cohn."

Carl watched Avern raise his eyebrows and slide onto the bench next to her saying, "And you must be Kelly Barr."

Delsa pulled up behind a gold Mercedes convertible in the drive, a young couple getting out, going to the door. The girl in her twenties, nice-looking, turned to Delsa as he approached them.

"Hi, I'm Allegra, Tony's granddaughter, and this is my husband, John Tintinalli?"

The guy who sold bull semen. Delsa recognized the name and said, "Frank Delsa," as he shook their hands. Allegra rang the bell again. As they waited Delsa imagined Montez spotting him through a window and going out the back.

When the door finally opened there was Lloyd in a dress shirt but no tie smiling at Allegra, saying it was good to see her again.

She said, "Lloyd," hugging him, "do you know Mr. Delsa?"

Lloyd's smile faded and came back again and he said, "Yes, indeed, I know all about Mr. Delsa," looking at him now. "I bet you want Montez."

"I sure do," Delsa said.

"Lemme see can I find him."

Lloyd walked away and Allegra said, "I love Montez, he's so cool." Now she was looking at the paintings in the foyer, talking about them with her husband, Delsa listening, Allegra saying she loved them and asking her husband if he loved them—two paintings of dark woods with shafts of light coming through the trees; the third one an ocean at night, the same kind of shafts of light coming through dark clouds. Her husband said he liked them okay.

Lloyd was coming back now wearing his white butler coat and bow tie, looking at Delsa, serious, Lloyd's attention on him as he came through the hall from the living room. He said, "Montez be with you in a minute."

Now Allegra was asking Lloyd what he knew about the paintings. Lloyd said, "They always been hanging there's all I know. The man from DuMouchelle come and look at 'em but didn't tell me nothing."

"Well," Allegra said, "he told me they're the very early work of a Hungarian painter named Dizsi Korab. He used to live in Greektown and is hot right now in New York with his streaks of light. These early ones could be worth quite a bit. But that's not why I love the paintings and want to take them with us, to California. Lloyd, we're moving."

He said, "Well, yeah, it's your house, take what you want."

"No, it's your house," Allegra said, "we're giving it to you, *if* we can have the paintings."

Lloyd said, "You giving me this house?" Not sounding too sure of it.

"And everything in it except the paintings," Allegra said. "The other night you looked so at home, so cozy with your lady friend, Serita?"

"Yeah, she works over at Blue Cross."

"Are you serious about her?"

"I can't make up my mind," Lloyd said.

"The other night when we stopped in, you were so nice to us. I said to John, 'You have your new business—do we really need to sell the house?' He said, 'Not if you want to give it away.' John's anxious to get out of Detroit." She turned to him as he brought a deed out of his inside coat pocket and handed it to her, Allegra saying to Lloyd, "It's a Quit Claim Deed, dated and notarized, so all you have to do is sign it and have it recorded." Now she looked at the deed. " 'The grantor,' that's us, 'for and in consideration of one dollar, convey and quit claim to the grantee,' that's you, and we've added, 'and everything in it except the three Korab paintings in the foyer.' " Now she was hugging Lloyd, Lloyd looking over his shoulder at Delsa, his eyebrows raised.

John Tintinalli lit a cigarette and stood looking around for an ashtray. He walked into the den and Delsa followed him, saying with kind of a smile, "Your father-in-law tells me you deal in bull semen."

"I did," John said, turning to look Delsa over. "What's your opinion of Tony?"

"He's a defense lawyer," Delsa said, "and I'm a homicide detective. But we get along okay."

"You're working on the old man's murder, uh? You know who did it?"

Delsa nodded. "It won't be long now."

"To answer your question, I did broker bull semen, sold the company and bought a vineyard out in Sonoma. A bunch of 'em are going bankrupt and I made a pretty good deal."

"What I wondered," Delsa said, "was how you get the semen."

"Everybody wonders that. There're three ways, an artificial vagina, digital manipulation—"

Delsa stopped him. "That one. How do you do it?"

"You massage the bull's pecker."

"Who does?"

"The guy who does it, the pro. He strokes the ampullae, the seminal vesicles and prostate gland through the wall of the rectum, with a collection tube slipped over the penis."

Delsa said, "That's it, huh?"

"Nothing to it," John said.

He picked up an ashtray and Delsa followed him out to the foyer where Allegra was telling Lloyd the funeral mass would be tomorrow at St. Mary's, corner of Monroe and St. Antoine, the burial at Mt. Olivet.

"Yes, indeed I'll be there," Lloyd said.

Allegra and John left and Lloyd stood there holding the deed to his house, looking at it.

Delsa said, "You gonna live here?"

"Gonna sell it and move to Puerto Rico, where you know what the weather's gonna be every day you get out of bed." Looking past Delsa he said, "Here comes Montez."

Delsa turned.

Behind him now Lloyd said, "First thing I do, I'm gonna throw his ass out of my house."

Montez was looking at the sheet of paper Lloyd was holding. "What's that you got?"

"Your eviction notice," Lloyd said.

Montez frowned saying, "What?"

Delsa said, "Montez?" and got the man in black leather looking at him. "I'm gonna ask you about Kelly Barr, and I want a straight answer."

Montez said, "Man, she's out'n the kitchen. How'd you know?"

LLOYD FOLLOWED MONTEZ FOLLOWING FRANK
Delsa through the swing door and into the
kitchen. Delsa paused once he was in here, then
walked to the end of the worktable, pots and
pans hanging above him. Lloyd moved around to
the other side where Jerome stood against the
counter by the sink, dirty dishes in there he'd told
Jerome to clean up. Lloyd felt he should be near
Jerome, a street kid witness to big-time serious
business. Now Lloyd looked across the worktable at Delsa looking at the four seated at the
round table in the alcove of windows: Kelly and
Avern Cohn on the bench looking straight ahead
at Delsa, Carl Fontana and Art Krupa in chairs to
the right, their guns out on the table in front of
them.

No one said anything, all looking at Delsa.

Ten minutes ago, when Lloyd came in and told Montez the cop was here to see him, there weren't any guns on the table.

Montez, in this house where there'd been a double homicide five days ago, said, "A cop? What one?"

"The man in charge, Frank Delsa."

There was a silence then like the one now.

Lloyd thought the two guys and Montez might run out the back. He couldn't figure out what was in their heads. He thought Kelly would speak, try to get up, but she stubbed out her cigarette and sat there like she was afraid to move.

Montez said, "What'd you tell him?"

"I'd see if I could find you."

"Tell him I'm not here."

They had been talking about keeping quiet, Avern taking over, saying, "You don't say a word to them. They have to go with whatever they have, which can't be hard evidence. You three are the only witnesses."

Carl said, "You're staying out of it, huh?"

Then when Lloyd told them the cop was here, the man, they shut up until Avern said, "Bring him in, I'll handle it. This cop Delsa even came to my office to see if he could get you guys to testify against each other, the son of a bitch."

And here he was.

* * *

Art picked up his Sig Sauer, elbow on the table, and pointed the gun at Delsa. He said to Montez, "Take his piece."

Montez, behind him, lifted the skirt of Delsa's jacket and pulled his Glock 40 from the holster on his right hip.

Art put his Sig on Montez and waved him back to the table. "Come here and sit down."

Lloyd saw all three of the guys armed now: Carl with a Smith & Wesson nine, Art the Sig Sauer and now Montez with Delsa's Glock he was looking at before laying it on the table.

Avern spoke first, saying to Delsa, "Whatever is said here is off the record. Otherwise you can leave."

The lawyer telling the cop what to do.

Lloyd knew Delsa would say something good, he seemed like a cool cat. He didn't say yes or no to the "off the record," he said, "How can you represent these clowns and not have a conflict of interest?"

Lloyd nodded, watching Delsa. Good.

"At the moment," Avern said, "I'm not representing anyone. I thought we might look at what we're doing here as sort of an evidentiary hearing. Find out if you have reason to prosecute these boys. Are we off the record or not?"

Delsa said, "Okay," sounding like it wasn't important to him.

Then Montez said to him, "How you mean he'd have a conflict of interest?"

"He's part of the deal, isn't he? He got you, Carl and Art to do the old man."

"And Chloe," Kelly said.

"That's right, and Chloe," Delsa said, looking at the two mutts, Lloyd admiring the way Delsa got right to the point of all this, not seeming to care about the guns lying on the table.

Avern said to Montez, "Let me ask the questions, all right?"

Carl said, "Like you're not in this, huh?"

Art said, "He's up to his fuckin eyeballs in it."

Kelly said, "Somebody tell me what I'm doing here. I can't put these guys at the scene. I'm the only one at this table not involved."

Montez said, "The payoff comes up short, now you clean, huh?"

Kelly said, "I'm getting out of here," and tried to push up, looking at Delsa.

Montez made no move to let her out. He said, "You here with us, girl."

Lloyd noticed Delsa not doing anything to help her. Didn't say anything, either. Lloyd turned his head to check on Jerome by the counter, Jerome looking like he was loving it, fascinated by the ofays, how they went about it.

Avern said, "Will you all please let me handle this? I'm trying to find out if a warrant's been issued for anyone's arrest. And if so, what kind of evidence they think they have."

Montez said, "I know they got nothing on me. I explained I got the bitches mixed up and they let me go." He said to Delsa, "You here for these two dudes, huh? Come to ask me did I know where they are. They sitting right there, man, and that's all I'm saying."

Lloyd liked this talk, it was getting good, and knew Art wouldn't take that shit, no . . .

Art saying, "This fuckin smoke, I swear," Art shaking his head, pointing his finger like a gun at Montez, casual, elbow on the table. "You keep talking—"

"I told him," Montez said, "that's all I'm saying. You didn't hear me? Take the wax outta your ears."

Lloyd liked that, and the look on Art's face, the man rigid. But Montez wasn't through.

"You two have to work out where you stand. You so fucked up they must have something good on you. I bet your guns got traced to another gig. Y'all too cheap to throw 'em away."

Lloyd saw Avern looking at the two now like he wanted to ask 'em something.

Carl said, "Goddamn it, I knew this one was going to hell." He picked up his Smith and pointed it at Montez. But then he looked over at Delsa.

And Montez picked up Delsa's gun.

Carl saying, "Did he tell on us?"

Lloyd moved to the end of the table so he could see Delsa's face good, Delsa watching the two guys pointing guns at each other, Delsa taking his time.

Delsa saying, "I won't tell you what I have on them or on you. Or who told me."

Lloyd saw Montez shaking his head, aiming the gun, Lloyd believed, at Carl aiming his gun at Montez. He heard Montez say, "I never said one fuckin word about you two. Why would I? Ask him. They don't have nothing on me. You say I hired you? All right, answer me this. How much did I pay you?"

Lloyd saw Art pick up his gun.

But it was Carl who fired, *bam,* and shot Montez in the head, a pane of glass behind him shattering, sprayed red.

Lloyd unbuttoned his white butler jacket, reached back underneath and brought out the gun he got off Jerome he'd tucked in his waist, the Sig three-eighty racked and ready. He stepped over to the table, extended the gun at Carl, and shot him in the V of his open shirt, turned to Art bringing up his gun and *bam,* shot him in the throat, then watched to see if they might shoot back at him, but they both had strange looks on their faces, like they were drunk, and fell over on the table.

Lloyd turned to lay the gun on the worktable and look at Delsa.

Delsa said, "Nice going."

Lloyd said, "I had enough of this bidness, criminals using my house as a hideout."

Delsa said, "But where'd you get the gun?"

He told Wendell, sitting in the inspector's office, "I asked, but didn't care. The old guy stood up to armed felons and put them in Detroit Receiving, handcuffed to their beds. He shattered bones in Carl's chest and shot out Art's voice box. Lloyd said he took the three-eighty off Jerome, not wanting the boy to do something dumb. Jerome says Carl and Art picked it up with some other stuff from a house in Bloomfield Hills, while it was open for inspection, and Art made Jerome take the gun."

Wendell said, "You believe him?"

Delsa said, "No, but what difference does it

make? The home invasion was in Oakland County, but we've got Carl and Art for a double homicide. If they're never arraigned on the robbery, Jerome won't be either. I told him whoever put up the twenty grand changed their mind, reneged on it. Orlando's been picked up and the informant was getting a thousand from Crime Stoppers. Jerome wanted to know where they found Orlando. I told him a house on Pingree and he said, 'Shit, that's where Orlando's granddaddy said he was, but I didn't think he'd tell on him like that.' I said, 'A good investigator knows who to believe and who not to believe.' Jerome said, 'Keep it,' and left."

"He'll show up again," Wendell said. "What I want to know is why you went in there without backup."

"It wasn't a backup situation. I went to the scene of a homicide to talk to a witness. I don't know Carl and Art are there."

Wendell said, "One I never heard of, hiding out at the scene of the crime." He stared across his desk at Delsa. "Carl asked if Montez had told on them and you said . . . ?"

"I wasn't gonna tell what I had, or who told me."

"But nobody had told you anything."

"I threw that in."

"And Carl believed you meant Montez. You promoted the action, didn't you?"

"I gave it a nudge," Delsa said. "The one I keep thinking about is Avern Cohn, how we're gonna go about getting him arraigned."

He said to Kelly, "Avern's sitting in his pongee robe in the squad room with Jerome, both waiting to be interviewed. I hear him telling this street kid his offices are in the Penobscot Building if he needs a lawyer. He doesn't sound the least worried about his own situation. He says yeah, the Caucus Club is right there at the Congress Street entrance, where Barbra Streisand performed when she was eighteen, just starting out and sang 'Happy Days Are Here Again' but not upbeat, real slow, like she's being ironic, and you know what Jerome says to Avern?"

" 'Who's Barbra Streisand?' " Kelly said, propped up in her bed with a Slim, her other hand fooling with the hair on Delsa's chest.

He turned his head on the pillow. "How'd you know?"

"The way you set it up. Whatever he says has to be a surprise. A girl singer to Jerome is Lil' Kim. He doesn't know Barbra Streisand from Renée Fleming."

"Who's Renée Fleming?"

She leaned over and kissed him on the mouth and stayed there on her elbow looking at his face, so close. "You're a cool guy, Frank. You're getting those guys to go at each other and you'd look at me with those eyes and I kept quiet and watched you and waited for them to shoot each other. Did you know Lloyd had a gun?"

"Uh-unh. You hear him, 'I had enough of this bidness.' "

She said, "You want to move in?"

"As soon as we close the case. I get Carl to make a statement about Avern—"

"Their agent."

"And take it across the street, see if the prosecutor likes it . . . I don't know . . . I think he might slip through."

"Do you care?"

He said, "You're the only one on my mind."

Kelly reached around behind her to get rid of the Slim and came back to him saying, "You know I'm in love with you. You're my man, Frank, I'm hanging on to you." She said, "If you'll reciprocate."

Delsa said, "Watch me," and went at her, saying he was gonna eat her up and she loved it.

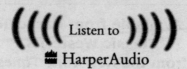